BOUGHT & Bound

LIZ HIGHLAND

Book Cover by RE Johnson Books

Interior Illustrations by RE Johnson Books

First edition April 2024

*To the kinky folk out there looking
to dive into a world of sin and sex.*

Content Considerations

This book is intended for mature adult audiences. This is not a how-to guide on kink or the kink community. Do not take the actions depicted in this work as a guide for proper enjoyment. For more information, visit www.kynk101.com. There may be triggering elements in the book, including graphic sex and violence. Please read with your mental health in mind and consider that it contains the following, if not additional elements not identified, that may be upsetting to some readers.

Heavy BDSM & Kinks

Losing Virginity

Dom/sub Dynamics

Breath Play

Cum Play (both male & female)

Bondage & Shibari

Praise/degradation Kinks

Multi-peniteration, including DVP

Sharing

Emotional Trauma related to parental neglect & abuse

Dubious consent & Consensual non-consent

Drama & Suspense, including kidnapping with forced
imprisonment and physical and mental assault

Playlist

Who doesn't love a good playlist right? Right. So here is the list of the first few tracks that you must have for your Bought & Bound listening experience. You can also check out the full mamma-mamma on YouTube by visiting https://youtu.be/HjV8qjZWtYc?si=BRW-J3cgi EMVh3Zm

Call Out My Name - The Weekend

Never Tear Us Apart - Bishop Briggs

Jokes On You - Charlotte Lawrence

Crazy in Love - Sofia Karlberg

Heartless - The Weekend

Not Afraid Anymore - Halsey

Sweat - ZAYN

Earned It (Fifty Shades of Grey) - The Weekend

I Feel Like I'm Drowning - Two Feet

Formula - Labrinth

Stranger - Keanu Silva

Craving' - Stileto

Chills (Dark Version) - Mickey Valen

Love is a Bitch - Two Feet

Take Me to Church - Sofia Karlberg

1

The Rules

Andi

C hrist almighty, what am I doing? This is fucking ridiculous. I can't possibly be this desperate.

Except I was.

Air rushed out of my lungs in an abrupt huff as I stepped out of the rideshare car and onto the curb. It was cold out, as per usual for upper east coast Harmstead winters, and this fucking leotard did nothing against the city wind that cut through me—even if I did have a coat. Turning the corner, I hoped for a break from the chill, but it somehow got worse, a wind tunnel kicking up right at the entrance to the building.

My stomach rumbled as I looked up at the unassuming exterior. *This is it- either this or you don't eat.*

After all, food didn't just pay for itself, and the funds were *not* pouring in from my aerial performances. I always did better when touring the local burlesque halls, but even those tips had started to run low. The customers had seen it all at this point, and once you'd seen a show enough times, usually one or two, you stopped going.

And O'Hara's wasn't drawing newbies like it used to.

I pulled out the folded piece of paper I'd been carrying around for a few weeks now, along with the letter from my landlord about the past-due rent. *Ugh.*

"Camming just had to get all corporate, huh?"

But damn if it wasn't true. It was way too hard to maintain. There were tons of hoops people in the biz didn't tell you about when you were trying to get viewers across multiple sites. The platforms didn't like that for some stupid reason, and I'd officially been bounced from too many to count because of it. *Assholes.*

"And you've decided you hate stripping, so..." I grumbled to myself.

It would be exponentially easier if I could just suck it up and work at the place nearby, but I just didn't move like those girls. I wasn't a grinder–and I especially wasn't one to clack my damn heels together because I hated that shit–and I didn't quite have the assets to fill out the costumes. *Yeah, not gonna happen.*

I still stood at the vestibule in front of the building–cold and nervous. The form I'd filled out said the entrance was around the back, not on the street side, so I shuffled to the rear side in search of some type of door. I'd been out there for only two minutes, and I could cut glass with how hard my nipples were.

"Please let this go well. Cuz..."

One upside of my ridiculous plan was that a single show here should take care of me for a long while. This place had even *requested* aerial performers like it was some kind of fetish or something. Hell, maybe it was.

And that didn't include what I could stand to make during tonight's...*event.*

When I found the glowing sign that said "S.O." in

red neon letters, I followed the concrete stairs down to the door. Walking up to the hidden entrance to The Scarlett Oleander, I gently rapped my knuckles against the steel. The sliding eye slit quickly pushed open, and a pair of browns glared at me.

"Business?"

"I'm here for the aerial position and the, um..." my heart hammered against my ribs, the frigid breeze suddenly refreshing, "auction."

"Andi?" the man questioned.

I nodded despite the fact that he probably couldn't see me well. "Yes. That's me."

The window slid closed, and I heard a loud mechanism adjust inside the door. My stomach clenched involuntarily. As it swung open toward me, I was gestured inside by a massive figure, my pulse louder in my ears than the final howl of the wind as I stepped forward.

It was hot compared to the chilly winter air outside, and I slipped off my black coat and hung it over my arm, standing nervously just inside the door. It was oppressively dark, the tight, shadowed hallway pressing in around me. I swallowed hard. There was so little light that I couldn't make out the details of the space, and whatever "entertainment" area awaited me was invisible from where I stood.

"This way." The man's voice stabbed through the darkness, making me jump ever so slightly.

Snapping into action, I was led down the hall to a sort of antechamber where a branch of three doors sat expectantly. The lighting here was a bit better. The bouncer gestured to the leftmost door. I shuffled past him as he reached for the doorknob.

"This is your reminder that once inside, you don't

leave unless there's an emergency or a guest accompanies you. You're aware of what you signed up for, yes?"

"I am." I couldn't help but swallow again, gulping like a little lamb. *Christ, I'm an idiot.*

"A quick rundown of the rules before I open this door," The bouncer's voice was deep, a good match for his thick build, "Here."

He handed me a black mask that matched the one he wore, hiding most of his features except the beard that framed the bottom of his face. I slipped it over my head, struggling to juggle my coat, and secured it at the back with a bow.

The weight of all the black surrounding me, even my requested attire, pressed down on me. The tight, thin outfit was the only aerial clothing I had in black and left little to the imagination between the fit and the deep v-cut that ran down my chest. Even the back was cut in that shape, and the crisscrossing laces that held it together ran up from my lower back to my shoulders.

"Good."

The man stood with his back to the door, facing me. The dim light made his form stand out in sharp contrast.

"One, you don't speak unless requested to do so by one of the staff or the guests. Two, your performance will come before the auction and take place on the main stage. The music requested has been prepared, and the silks have been hung. Once your act has been completed, the guests will be escorted to the auction room, where the bidding will take place. Have you looked at the menu?"

I nodded, my pulse too noticeable in my chest, and I traded my weight back and forth between the pads of my feet. This was all getting more intense as the seconds passed and the instructions were dolled out.

"Good. Three, purchasers will have control over their submissives for the duration of the contract. The club will retain a copy of that contract, and if anyone, the guest included, breaks the agreement, the arrangement will be null and void. Any submissive with a complaint against them will not be invited to return. The same goes for the guests. We have a zero-tolerance policy. Understood?"

"Yes."

"Yes?" He dragged out the word, his mask rising like he was cocking a brow at me.

"Yes, sir," I corrected, remembering the preliminary rules I'd already read back home.

I gripped the sleeve of my coat as I held it over my arm, twisting the fabric between my clammy hands.

When he spoke again, the bouncer's voice was softer but still matter-of-fact. "You're new, so there will be some leniency as you grow accustomed to the rules. Four, did you bring your disclosure form and waiver?"

I presented the documents from my purse to the bouncer, pulling them out and trying to smooth out the creases on the folded square. He looked over them, quickly but thoroughly reading the contents that made him aware of any physical issues or conditions of mine. He also held my agreement to press no charges against the club as a willing participant.

I had *entertained* myself with some BDSM stuff on the web, but I'd never actually encountered things like on the menu I had read. *You've never encountered shit, Andi. Your biggest experience is going to handy-town with a whopping two college guys. Oh, and let's not forget the string of shitty first dates, including the most recent crap-tastic asshole that creeped you the fuck out.*

I stifled my nervous fiddling with my coat and purse strap, feeling an odd buzz of excitement and fear crawling up my spine. As much as I didn't want to admit it to myself, the idea of this whole club thrilled me in ways being with those other guys never had.

The idea that I might, would very likely, lose my...I could barely think the thoughts without blushing and boiling with warmth. I was a filthy slut for wanting this so badly, but at this particular moment, I absolutely did not care.

But I also knew that the particular fantasy I'd been harboring most of my life was unlikely to be realized in this club. It wasn't like dashing Doms in shining armor actually existed or would even want someone like me. I'd be lucky if I got auctioned off at all.

The bouncer cleared his throat as he looked back up at me from the papers, and my pulse skittered as I realized he was assessing me again. *Get out of your head and listen, Andi!*

"Is this information up to date?" The guy's voice sounded tight, almost annoyed.

I furrowed my brow, "Yes, sir. Is something wrong?"

"No, apologies. I let my own experience color my thoughts. I didn't expect we'd have a blank slate so soon after posting the listing."

"Oh, yes. I am...inexperienced. I understand the choice, however." *And really broke.* "Umm, may I ask a question, sir?" I nodded to the man, hoping to show that I was ready to obey the club's rules.

He offered a tight nod. "Yes."

"Is the advertised..." I struggled to think of a good word, "compensation still accurate?"

"Yes. That is point five."

His tone continued to present that air of delivering a speech he'd done a million times before–like listening to the in-flight safety regulations.

"The club will receive a 20% commission for hosting the auction; the rest will go to you. The club's concierge will handle wire transfers and deposits to your provided banking information, and all charges will be verified."

"Okay, great." I nodded, needing something to do with the energy buzzing through me. "Thank you."

The bouncer held out his hand, "Six, I'll take your belongings and stow them in a locker through those doors."

I watched him point to the far-right wall before handing over the small purse that I'd been fiddling with.

"That is the after-hours area where you may use the facilities to shower, change, and refresh yourself. If you are leaving the premises with the guest, you can return here to retrieve your items," He looked at a small notepad that was far tidier than most I'd seen, "You'll receive locker 1200987. Your combination?"

He awaited my response, and I had to quickly think of something I could remember.

"115513. Is that all right, sir?"

"Yes, thank you. Your number and combination will be deposited with the facilities manager once you enter. You've left out all essential and identifying information from your purse, correct? No, credit cards or cash?"

"Correct, sir."

"Good. Seven, as our first aerial performer and a part of our newest act, you must let the stage hand know if anything needs to be adjusted. You may direct him as needed in this and only this case."

Oh, shit. I'm the first one! "Understood, sir."

"Eight, do not reveal any information about any guest, attendant, or staff member. As you can likely tell, anonymity is expected here to a certain degree."

I had to assume as much, considering the masks. According to the menu, not everyone wore them, but several guests apparently liked them.

"Again," I refocused on the man doling out the laundry list of regulations, "if a staff member or guest violates the code of conduct, the club will take care of it immediately. Safety is another of our chief priorities. Understood?"

"Yes, sir." *God, how much more is there?*

"Nine, have you read the entire code of conduct and sent the signed document to the club's email address?"

"Yes, sir. I think it should've arrived."

The bouncer took out a phone and scrolled through a few screens.

"It was received. Thank you. Ten, before entering, you will be required to physically sign the same code of conduct as well as a written account of the information I have just provided," he reached behind him somewhere impossible to see in the dark.

When he returned, he clicked on a small flashlight that illuminated the written agreement. Again, I swallowed down the apprehension that wouldn't go away. I was given a pen, oddly heavy in my fingers, and the document was on a black clipboard. As I leaned forward to sign, the bouncer's voice suddenly rang right in my ear.

"This is your last chance to walk away. Take this seriously. Do you want this?" He practically growled, and I shivered. It was clearly done because we were right here, on the precise, and if I couldn't handle this...

I wouldn't make it inside.

8

"Y-Yes." My voice quivered, but then I swallowed hard, putting more conviction behind it. "Yes, sir. I want this."

I quickly signed the agreement, my signature sloppier than normal.

"Good," he pulled away, and I almost missed the way he'd invaded my space like that. Apparently, I was in the right place–embracing the darkness within I'd tried to deny for so long.

"One of the servants inside will escort you to the main stage for your performance. Enjoy your time."

I could hear the smile in his voice as I stared at the opening door, my eyes shocked by the abrupt lighting change. I felt small in the disorientation it caused, knowing that it was a purposeful ploy to keep me off balance.

A tiny gasp escaped me as I saw inside The Scarlett Oleander–red and black and seemingly endless.

This was it.

2

The Scarlett Oleander

Andi

I was in awe. There was no other way to say it. The inside of The Scarlett Oleander was exquisite and not at all what I imagined. I couldn't see any exposed floorboards or rusty chains hanging from the ceiling. There were no stains on the rugs and no single light bulbs hanging from odd places, flickering.

It's not a back alley dungeon, Andi. Come on.

Everyone was dressed in formal wear, the epitome of black tie–men, women, enbys, lace, leather, and masks. It was all on full display in every direction I looked.

The space stretched impossibly far, with twists, turns, and tunnels leading to God knew where. All the furniture was sumptuous velvet and a striking crimson that stood in harsh contrast with the black floor and black outfits everyone wore. There were tufted couches piled high with pillows, "involved" guests scattered everywhere throughout the large, multi-level club.

Still raking my stare across the intriguing room, a tall, fit attendant greeted me as soon as I officially set foot inside. He wore another black mask and a simple, black suit. I couldn't tell much else about him, which was likely on purpose.

"This way to the stage." He gestured for me to follow, immediately turning and striding through the club with purpose.

I obeyed and had to maintain a quick pace to keep up with his longer steps. My performing slippers didn't offer much traction to keep my footing on the slick floor, either, and I nearly fell several times. As I walked, I could feel eyes turn in my direction from every corner of the room, raking down my skin hungrily. My short, asymmetrical bob left my neck exposed, and the sensation of hot breath skidding over me was someone dogging me as I slipped past the guests.

Even as I attempted to keep my eyes forward, I couldn't help but look over at the couches and chaise loungers. Many of the people, in varying displays of public affection, saw my curiosity and smiled, their fascination and interest lighting their own stares.

Passing through what I could only call the "living area," I noticed suspended curtains of black beads dripped down from the ceiling, encircling each seating area to create a vague notion of enclosure and privacy. That thought almost made me laugh out loud. *Nothing* was private here.

The lighting continued its bright red song as I followed the attendant in front of me, my eyes adjusting to the deep shadows it created. As we walked farther in, more of the space was revealed, and I counted a number of bars set into the walls.

Up ahead, the arrangement of chairs changed, assuming a semicircle around a medium-sized stage, which loomed over the plush chairs like a shiny idol. Scarlet aerial slings draped down from the ceiling in the center, and the stage's floor was a bright lacquered checkerboard of red and black squares.

The seats around the stage were currently empty. Still, many guests were seated nearby, clearly waiting for the entertainment to begin. As I passed, I noticed a taller man with dark hair and a beard, who was donning an impeccable tux, seated at the table closest to the raised platform. His eyes met mine as I walked in front of his table.

Shit.

Something zinged through me as we made eye contact. Mystery man seemed to sit up straighter, too, and the dark look he gave me beneath his mask was something I'd never seen before. It was predatory and hungry, and as I felt his stare rake across my body, wetness pooled between my legs.

Holy...fuck.

Despite the mask covering most of his features, I could pick out a few things as I took the opportunity to study him. Gentle white streaks touched his temples where the mask was sitting by his ears, and the green color of his stare as it devoured me was still bright even in the shadowed room. I was also very able to tell that that tailored suit wrapped around someone with a lean body, and I wondered about the physique hiding behind it.

"Right this way."

My attendant's voice cut through my distracted thoughts like a razor blade, and I snapped my attention back to him. He nodded, escorting me around the back of the stage, where a set of small stairs went up the platform.

"Is everything acceptable for a safe performance?"

The attendant held out his hand for me to inspect the rigging.

Nothing surrounded the stage, no curtains or enclosure, so I felt too out in the open as I climbed the stairs to check the setup. When I reached the slings, I chanced a look down at that man's table. He still stared at me, and a flush crawled through my skin.

Focus, Andi. Is it good to go?

I ran my fingers over the fabric that hung down. The hammock was the right size for me and hung far enough off the ground that I could safely perform my drops and skim the floor. I gripped the two halves of the sling and lifted myself up, allowing it to take my full weight. It held great. There was no wobbling or even an inch or two of dipping down. The fabric itself was incredibly well made, too, nicer than the stuff I usually brought.

It was perfect.

"Yes, sir. Thank you."

I looked to the attendant, hoping he would fill in the remaining information about my performance.

"Excellent. You'll begin in just a moment. We have the requested song queued up, and the team has created the proper lighting to suit your performance. The lights will be entirely shut off before you begin for a few seconds, and when they return, you'll begin. Do you understand?"

"Yes, sir. But, umm..."

The man cocked his head at me. "Yes?"

"I assume I'm performing just the one song?"

My attendant nodded.

"Okay, well, that's all I have scheduled. Will I be back to do this again based on the contract, or..."

"I have been instructed to keep you on time for this

singular performance. Perhaps," he glanced past the stage where that guy was still sitting, "it has been left unfilled for the sake of the auction."

Heat swarmed my cheeks, and I quickly nodded. "Right. Of course. Okay, umm, thank you, sir."

He nodded once and then left me alone on the platform. Tension radiated through my shoulder, and I clenched my thighs. I couldn't bear facing the chairs below, so I kept my back to the audience as I slid off my shoes and tossed them to the side. I didn't want to risk not being able to grip the floor since this was such a *crucial* performance.

Getting the silks ready in my grip, I felt that man's gaze cut through my leotard. Why did I love the idea of him watching me? Why did it make warmth pool in my core as I waited for the show to begin?

A voice came over an unseen intercom, and I jumped.

"Honored guests. Our performance for the evening is due to begin in just a few moments. Please make your way to the stage seating if you wish to watch from there. Of course, you're free to continue your current activities or view from your lounge seats. Thank you."

I shook so hard I thought I might fall over, and I was suddenly so cold even the warm breeze from the slow-moving fan in the center of the room made me shiver. Or maybe that was something else? Whatever was going on with my body didn't ring of normal stage fright, and I wasn't sure I wanted to examine that.

After only a couple of minutes, the seats near the stage were almost full, and the lights went dark. I quickly climbed up in the hammock, pulling it into a rope and hanging from it by my hips.

Just a performance. Focus on the silks. Gripping my legs, I waited for the music to start.

The seconds felt like an eternity.

But when the lights came back on in time with the song "Call Out My Name," all the nervous energy floated away.

This was what I did. It was my favorite routine, and I was *made* to twirl through this fabric. Tucked up in the sling felt like the safest place in the world. I was just me in here; the world was just blackness—out of focus and beyond what mattered. Sending myself into a spin, I slowly lifted up to balance on my hip bones, gripping the two sections of fabric on either side of me.

I breathed, just breathed.

My years of ballet class fueled the movements as I twirled in the air, stretching out long and pulling back into myself. Effortlessly, I positioned the bound-up sling at my thighs, creating a chair, and then opened up the fabric long, encasing my body. The beat of the music was loud, and I could sense the words in my bones as I lost myself to the song.

Continuing my rotation, I pulled a leg out. I hung from the hammock by the other leg, rolling the fabric down the inside of my thigh with my fingers. The music hummed in my veins as I swung my free leg back through the sling, situating it between my legs and resting on it.

From there, I began my favorite part of this opening. As the song crescendoed, I wound myself up in the hammock, wrapping the fabric tightly around my body as I traveled up its length. When the beat was close to striking, I worked my grip for the first drop.

Bam.

I let go and spun down the fabric, coming to hang

on one bent leg. Strike a pose, Andi. As the song continued, I took my other leg and pulled it back behind my head, creating a beautiful arch as I hung there.

I couldn't describe what exactly happened next. The power of the music, the energy, and the incredible wave of desire I felt coming from the audience were intoxicating. As I continued my routine, the sling and I were like one fluid thing. I twisted and dropped and spun through the silky fabric, utterly oblivious to the world around me—except for one set of emerald eyes I knew was watching closely.

Aerial had always been sensual to me, binding yourself up in the fabric, running it across your body, and trusting it to hold you as you tested your strength and skills.

This time was so much more.

Everything was electrically charged, and my movements became as sexual as ever. I ran my hands down my body, skimming them over my small breasts whenever my hands were free. The taut sling coming and going from between my legs was suddenly erotic as hell, and the squeeze of it all over me was akin to firm hands grasping me.

In the heat of the moment, I changed how I typically ended the performance, though no one would be able to tell. Instead of dismounting the hammock and walking across the stage to pose, I pulled the fabric around my hips for a final drop, landing just above the ground and sliding myself down the remaining fabric so that it tightened around my wrists as if I were restrained.

Bound.

The music ended, and the lights went dormant once more. Unsure where to go or what to do, I stood back up in front of the silks on the stage and awaited the attendant. Individual sections of the floor beneath the platform lit up as the stage darkened, and another announcement boomed.

"Honored guests. The auction will take place shortly. If you have chosen to participate, please make your way to the main stage. The Scarlett Oleander trusts that you've taken care of arrangements beforehand, as requested. We look forward to what is likely to be the most eventful auction we've seen in quite some time. Thank you."

Thanks to the booth lighting, I could see around me. Searching the stage for those stairs I'd seen, I padded across the cool floor, my skin heated. I found my way to my shoes just as another attendant walked up to me.

"Beautiful performance. Right, this way to the auction." He helped me up from sliding on the slippers and directed me down the stairs. I'd been nervous about the performance, but that was nothing to the full-on bats that soared through my stomach at the thought of the auction.

Someone is about to...buy you.

Swallowing hard, that nervous habit betraying me, I nodded at the employee. "Thank you, sir."

3
The Auction

Andi

Needing something to focus on, I inspected the new staff member showing me the way to the auction. He wasn't as tall as the last, but he was much more built. The tailored suit he wore barely contained his muscular arms, and I flushed when I realized I was staring. *But really, can you blame me? That's the entire point of this place.*

He guided me to another room further down the expansive space, scarlet walls continuing and decorated with doors alongside either side. The space at the far end looked precisely like a luxury auction house, except, of course, for the deep red and black colors that persisted as a Scarlett Oleander staple.

There was a large stage at one end and several rows of elegant, if space-saving, chairs in front of it. The air was still cool in her, and my skin prickled as the adrenaline from the performance backed off. Still, the way the audience looked at each of the people being brought it, the way they looked at me, made my thighs squeeze together and my pulse pound.

A gang of submissives–men, women, and non-binary individuals–was already waiting on the glossy black stage. Each one had at least one ribbon tied to their wrists if not more.

I was guided to my place at the end of the row and instructed to hold out my arms, no doubt for my own ribbons. With that, the attendant who'd brought me here left, disappearing behind a thick black curtain that led behind the stage.

"Name?"

Snapping my attention back around, I came face-to-face with another of the club's numerous employees, quickly responding with "Andi."

A more formally dressed member of the staff approached me, holding another clipboard. She was tall and thin, her long black ponytail hanging straight down her back. I snuck a glance at the paperwork she carried and saw similar information to what I had provided about my personal history.

I watched her perfectly manicured red nails lift up the first few sheets of paper, finding the one with my name printed at the top. The woman scanned it quickly, then reached into a structured apron of sorts and pulled out a wheel of ribbons in several colors.

She took care with the giant silver scissors as she tied ribbons around either of my wrists and cut the excess. By the time she was finished, I was decorated with six total, three on my left arm and three on my right. I struggled to remember the significance of each shade.

Red was approved for high-level bondage and submission.
Blue meant breath play was approved.
Green signaled that I was all right with leaving the premises.

Black meant I would be willing to try anything with a provided safe word.
Pink meant this was my first time with BDSM.
And white...white meant I was a virgin, and I was the only one wearing that *particular color.*

Not for the first time, I wondered what the fuck I'd gotten myself into. However, and again, not for the first time, I also felt a hot burning in my core as I looked at the expectant guests in the audience, their eyes scanning me from head to toe with obvious lust.

It was strange to be so openly gawked at like this, but I couldn't deny how a wanton thrill filled me because of being so exposed, so embarrassed by how they stared.

That's when I found myself looking for a familiar set of green eyes.

He was in the front row and seated dead center. He'd already spotted me and cocked a slight grin when I'd finally made eye contact with him. *Oh, fuck.*

I knew I had to be okay with *whoever* won the auction, but...

When the woman in charge of the ribbons stepped aside, my wrists were finally visible to the audience, a quiet hush coming over them. My gaze never left the man seated in the front row, and his eyes blew wide as he looked down to see what colors I sported.

I was almost touched by the shock on his face. Clearly, he didn't think any of what I wore was possible. Then, he met my eyes again, and once more, I was blown away by the look he gave me.

I nearly melted into a puddle when I saw the absolutely sinful glee he barely contained behind his mask. His lips never curled into an overt smile, but the way his eyes stayed wide and bored into me sent shivers down my spine.

I want him *to buy me.*

I was stunned by the thought, but it was true. I wanted his hands on me, his teeth in my neck, and his cock buried so deep I screamed.

The crack of a gavel snapped me out of my head, and I jumped, my stare flicking away from the mystery man to the presenter on stage. It signaled the start of the auction, and in just a few seconds, a submissive was ushered forward, and hands started going up to place bids.

Everything blew by in a flurry of activity. Several back-and-forth spats between a few buyers escalated the prices on some of the submissives to truly astounding levels, and my pulse ticked up higher as each one left the stage.

I was last on the docket, and as I watched from my corner of the stage, I saw many satisfied-looking grins. *Nothing like a happy customer, I guess.* I doubted I would draw the same attention except from Mr. Front Row. Still, a handful of guests eyed the white ribbon tied on my left wrist.

When my name was called, I proceeded to the front of the stage like the others. From there, I stood directly before my desired owner for the evening. I couldn't stop myself from looking down at him.

I'd completely forgotten about how I still wore my leotard until his eyes roamed down my body again, and my nipples hardened. It would be extremely noticeable in this outfit, and heat crept up my cheeks, that odd electric buzz zipping through my veins at the embarrassment.

"Last lot. Bidding starts at one thousand," the master of ceremonies announced.

I knew the money was good going in, but I was still in awe over the fact that I would really be looking at a couple thousand dollars soon.

"Ten," the man's voice cut through the room.

I nearly passed out. Between the silk of his deep voice and the incredible amount, I felt woozy on my feet and checked to be sure I wasn't locking my knees. No, they weren't locked but they were wobbly at just the prospect of finally getting to see under that mask, see under that suit.

"Eleven," came another voice, and I looked to the back of the room.

Seated as far back as you could get was a larger man who was likely in his fifties, putting him about ten years older than El Mystery Man. He was surrounded by his previous purchases, having won several of the over twenty of us. I had no reason to judge him. It was the purpose of the night, but Mr. Front Row had not bid on anyone else. His eyes had stayed locked on me, and the singly focused desire made my blood heat in the best way. I'd already wanted him to win, and it grew with each passing second he kept looking at me like that.

"Fifteen," his voice sang through my nerves.

"Twenty," came the other man's bid.

"Fifty."

My heart pounded so hard in my chest that I thought it might crack a rib.

"One hundred thousand."

"Three hundred." *Jesus, the man at the back must really be loaded.*

Wait, was I hearing this right? Three hundred thousand? For me? Were they high? *God, this is all because I'm a virgin, isn't it?*

"Five!" called out the man in the back.

"One million."

My eyes darted around the room, looking for the utter shock I was feeling to be reflected on other faces, but everyone seemed completely nonplussed. I was in fucking Wonderland. *I'm so not worth this. This is nuts. I should say something.*

"Two!" My heart sank.

I didn't know anything really about that other guy. He could be great, but something about the way he had the girls he'd bought crowded around him hit me funny. It was probably just because I wanted Mystery Guy, which was something I knew I shouldn't have gotten so worked up about.

The club was about anonymity, and I had to expect that *anyone* here had a right to me because of what I'd volunteered for.

"Sir," the master of ceremonies stepped forward from behind his podium, "I regret to inform you that your account's limit has been reached. Your standing credit line cannot support another purchase of that amount."

"Bah!" The older man quickly pushed out of his chair and snapped his fingers, indicating for his entourage to follow him out of the room.

The silence hung in the air like a knife over my head.

"Are there any more bids?" The speaker waited. "Going once. Twice. Sold. To Mr. R.O.B. Please proceed to the concierge, who will take care of your transaction and contract approval."

I did my best to stifle my sag of relief. Another attendant–how many were there?–collected me and walked me off the stage toward another back room, which seemed to be never-ending in this place. It was like an entire hotel sat beneath the empty glass factory above it.

Down a hall of even more doors, each which barely contained the sounds of pleasure coming from within them, was the concierge desk. Still clad in red and black, this area was more structured and professional-looking, with a long white marble counter at the far end that was the best-lit spot in the joint.

A hand at my back guided me toward the desk where Mr. Front Row was waiting. I took my place, standing near him and in front of the woman behind the counter. She smiled at us and procured a thick stack of papers from a hidden drawer beneath the desk.

"Good evening, Mr. R.O.B. and Ms. Andi. We're going to go over the contract, which has been pre-approved by the house, and upon agreement, we'll run your account for the bid total. Is that acceptable?"

"Of course, Ms. Evergreen."

Yup, if the rest of him was as hot as his voice, I was done for.

Strangely, there was also a part of me that was quite glad that the Scarlett Oleander staff appeared to take the safety of their clients and staff so seriously.

"Ms. Andi, you're to go over the contract and either agree or decline with an explanation so that Mr. R. O. B. may make an adjustment, or you can be returned to the auction floor with your limit understood. Do you understand?"

I kept my voice as even as possible, and still, a quiver echoed through it. "Yes, Ms. Evergreen."

She smiled and nodded at me, sliding the contract

across the smooth, cold marble. My fingers trembled slightly as I picked it up and started reading.

The expectations for a very intense time were not misplaced.

Nearly every type of act I could think of was on the table and some that I didn't even know. Everything was under the stipulation of a safe word that would be agreed upon at the final location, which I assumed was his place. The duration was set at a minimum of one week, which I'd thankfully prepared for, and a maximum time of-

"Excuse me, does this say permanent companion?"

My mystery man nodded slowly, a sinful grin appearing from behind his mask that made his green eyes sparkle, "Yes, it does."

He was a bit older than me, but in the moment, I couldn't do much more than admire his stare and that wicked smirk stretching his full lips.

"That's not required, though?"

"No. That is an option you may choose, which will, of course, come with an extended retainer and lodgings."

"You want..." I struggled to wrap my head around what was really being offered here, what was *desired*, "to keep me?"

For the first time since we'd made eye contact, I was speaking to this man, and I couldn't tell if I was terrified or aroused or both. He took one step closer, careful not to push it too far since the transaction wasn't completed yet. I could feel the heat radiate off his tall, muscular form. He bent at the waist so his mouth could hover just next to my ear. His breath fluttered across my neck, and goosebumps skittered across my skin.

"You're already mine, pet. I just need you to sign on the dotted line."

I breathed hard, all too aware of my pounding heart and the coiling desire building inside me that made my pussy positively weep. I didn't need to decide about a permanent contract now, and I could always fucking leave and just get out of town. It wasn't like any of this was actually legal.

It was a formality, an extension of the burden of trust that was being placed on the Dom. It gave the club something that they could defend themselves with, and it made any arrangement made here crystal clear.

You can walk away any time you want.

But that wasn't really the trouble, was it? No. The trouble was I couldn't believe I didn't want to walk away. Ludicrous as it seemed, I *did* feel like I was his already.

You have a damn problem, Andi.

He didn't move as I went to the counter, placed the contract on the desk, and signed it. His body remained inches from mine, and I could barely think, heated embarrassment and shock coating my nerves.

"Very well. Thank you for using The Scarlett Oleander. Should the contract be signed for permanency, please contact the club so that we may remove you from the roster of potential auction submissives." She turned to Mystery Man. "Should you wish to allow Andi engagements here, the club will also want a copy of that contract as well. We'll run your account now, Mr. R.O. B. It will be just a moment."

"Of course, Ms. Evergreen. Take your time."

This man's voice was sex, and I'd just signed up to let him do anything he wanted with me.

Okay.

I didn't know how long it was before Ms. Evergreen announced that his account had cleared, and we were permitted to leave with the club's contact information given to me directly in the event of any misconduct. I took the envelope from her as Mr. R.O.B.'s hand went to the small of my back—warm, strong, possessive—and he escorted me outside.

Holy fucking Christ. What did I just fucking do?

4
The Car Ride

Andi

A black car waited to pick us up at the curb just beyond the club. A driver swiftly exited and came around to open the door. I guess it was a limo, but it wasn't the giant, obnoxious type I was used to seeing with bridesmaids pouring out the top, hooting while they sloshed drinks and flashed strangers.

I followed behind Mr. R.O.B., his height dwarfing my miniscule five-two, and stopped short as he stepped to the side, gesturing inside the car.

"Ladies first." He grinned at me again, and I blushed, heat crawling across me, magnifying in my core.

"Thank you, sir."

I slid into the car, the black leather soft against the exposed skin of my legs. It was warm and low-lit, the only glow coming from a small bar built into the side where there should have been a door. There was a bottle of champagne on ice, two slim glasses, and...

Holy shit. It's a blindfold.

I sat down near the back, or I guess, the front of the

car. Christ, I was so flustered I couldn't even tell. All I knew was that I was seated when Mr. Front Row slid into the limo and sat across from me, that wicked grin still decorating his lips. The door closed firmly, and we were both shut in the near-darkness of the cab.

Up closer like this, I could see that there were indeed silver streaks dressing his temples, but he was built and, from what I could tell, wrinkle-free. I hazarded a guess that he was likely in his forties, and at my twenty-five, that put him about two decades my senior.

His beard was also expertly sculpted, and I wondered what it might be like if it rubbed against my skin.

The silence hung in the air for a moment as Mr. R.O.B. opened the bottle of champagne and poured some into the two glasses. His knuckles skimmed over the blindfold, and I shuddered.

"Ms. Andi, correct," His silky voice made my nerves sing as he handed me a glass.

"Yes, sir." I took a tentative sip, and damn, was it delicious.

I'd never had much of the "good stuff," but this was miles away from the usual bitter brut I was trying to slog back on New Year's.

"I imagine you'll have a few questions, and I'd like to address them now. If you're up for it." He sat back in his seat, adjusting his tie so it hung loosely around his neck. When he popped the button, a tiny bit of his chest was revealed. *Why was that so hot?*

"Oh, yes, sir. I do. Can I just ask them freely?"

"For now, yes. Go ahead." He sipped his champagne, his tongue sliding across his lips as he swallowed, and my pussy clamped down around nothing.

"Okay, well, I guess... What's your name? Or what

can I call you? Mr. R.O.B. takes forever to say." I shrugged.

He laughed, and the sound was like a promise from the devil. I wasn't sure what it said about me that I was so ready to sign that contract with him regardless. *A regular damn Faust, I guess.*

"You may call me Westley until I say otherwise. When things get going, you may address me as Sir or Master. We may play with other names later." He smirked. "You'll just have to follow my lead."

I swallowed another gulp of champagne, "all right. I mean, sorry. Yes, sir."

Westley chuckled again and began taking off his suit jacket and rolling up the sleeves of his white shirt. Jesus, I was living a smut reader fantasy.

"Next question."

There were so many swirling in my head, and as I looked around the plush interior of this incredible car, one stuck out slightly ahead of the others.

"Are you," I hesitated, but I just had to know, "Are you sure about this? You paid *so much*. I'm not, well, I'm not anything special, really. I just do some stupid stuff on a sling, and I'm not even that, you know, endowed." I gestured to my breasts.

Westley's eyes darkened, and he cocked his head, narrowing his gaze onJesusSetting his glass down in a cup holder, he moved over toward me, practically crawling across the ground because of the low ceiling. I instinctively pushed back, my mouth falling open and a fear trickling down my spine.

When he reached me, Westley's body was inches from mine. He looked me straight in the eye, and as much as I wanted to look away, I couldn't. I was frozen beneath the intensity of his stare.

"Do not question my desire. I understand this is new for you, and that's what I wanted, so I'll be forgiving—up to a point. I requested the aerial stage myself, had it built to my specifications, and I had helped to draft the wording for the advertisement that was circulated. I've been waiting for a performer—for you—and you're *so much* better than I even hoped."

Westley reached out and ran his hand across my cheek to the back of my neck, gripping my short hair and pulling me toward him. I slipped down onto the floor from the chair, my back landing against the seat as he trapped me beneath his towering form.

"We're not too far away from the club. Do you want me to turn around?" He leaned forward, hovering his lips over the shell of my ear to whisper, "Tell me what you want, sweet Andi. Do you want to leave, or have you been waiting for this as much as I have?"

The grip on my hair was iron, and the burn of his gaze was molten on my skin. I couldn't look away from the green glowing behind the depths of the mask. And damn, I wanted him to take it off so that I could look at him properly.

"Do you feel the electricity, the heat? Will you be my good, little pet?"

Westley let out a low growl, his breath slipping past the skin of my neck as he teased the skin with his mouth. I moaned, arching my head toward him.

"I..." my breath and heart thundered, embarrassment flooding me for how much I enjoyed this, "I want this more than I've wanted anything in my life, sir. I want *you*, Westley—desperately."

"Good girl," he purred as he slid his free hand up my leg to my ass, my bent legs giving him access.

Then I was face down on the floor of the cab, a flash

of movement that lifted me up onto my knees only to be shoved down to the rough surface, his firm grip on my hair pressing me into the carpet. Pain zapped through my nerves as he landed a hard smack down across my right ass cheek, my barely-there leotard doing nothing to dull the sensation.

I yelped, and the burn of his slap warmed my skin. I was shocked, mortified for being so exposed, so literally under his control, but it quickly melted away into an odd joy that made me quickly hungry for more. I hissed in a breath between my teeth, rolling my hips back and up into Westley's hand as he rubbed the tender skin.

You've lost your damn mind.

"Stay."

Westley practically growled, but I could hear the lilt of amusement behind it.

I obeyed and watched as he reached toward the small bar and took another sip of his glass. Then Westley retrieved the blindfold, and the tingle that ran through me this time wasn't fear or apprehension. It was pure, unadulterated lust.

Westley grabbed me by the hair again and pulled me up onto my knees. He knelt behind me and fastened the black blindfold around my head. The world plunged into darkness, and my senses swam as they overcompensated for my lack of vision. Forget the drink. This was intoxicating as hell.

I was directed back down to the ground, my ass high in the air, exposed and begging for Westley's touch. He ran his hands down my back, dragging his fingertips across my flesh until he reached my hips. My knees were shoved farther apart, and another slap came down across my unmarred cheek, evening out the burn I felt on my ass. I could sense his body inches away from mine, his cock no doubt inches from my pussy, and I clenched at the thought.

"Cross your arms behind your back."

I did as told, balancing on my shoulders and knees. Something soft and silky slid around my forearms, similar to the fabric of the aerial hammock. Westley bound my wrists together, winding the fabric down from my elbows and around my hands. He tied the remaining ends around my waist, completely trapping my arms against me.

It was a bit uncomfortable but not unbearable, and the smooth fabric reminded me of being suspended in the air during a performance. The pinch was reminiscent of dangling from a taught section of the aerial silks.

Then, one of Westley's fingers ran underneath the fabric of my leotard. He followed the seam as it curved across my ass and went between my legs. He pulled the black spandex away from my skin, and I felt cool air caress my pussy. *Holy, Jesus, fuck.*

"Hold still, pet."

I had little choice, but I did my best not to move at all. But I flinched slightly when something cold and distinctly metal ran across my thigh. I heard the sound of opening scissors, and then the crotch of my leotard was cut in half. Westley had sliced through the offending material and given himself full access to me.

My cheeks burned. I was naked where it mattered, exposed all the more to him, and I reeled at the thought. He could just see everything, and I knew I was wet. *Oh god, oh god, oh god.*

Westley's hands ran up my thighs, stopping on my ass and spreading me open ever so slightly as he squeezed. I moaned into the carpet, biting my lip so hard I worried I might taste blood. He'd barely touched me, and I was fucking dripping with desire, which he clearly noticed now.

"Such a good little pet and so very excited."

Humiliation roared through my veins as strong as any drug.

"Tell me what you want me to do, little kitty." He kept running his hands over my ass, squeezing and pinching.

I didn't know, not at the moment. Except I knew I didn't want him to stop. I wanted him to touch me, to explore me like this for as long as possible. Every time his hand even barely left my skin, I bit back on the whimper for the lack of contact.

"I...Whatever you want, sir. Of course." My voice was breathy and desperate.

"Such a good, little kitty. I think we're going to have to set that safe word now, though. It can't wait."

I shook my head as best I could, pinned to the floor as I was. "It's fine. I'm fine, sir."

His lips were suddenly at my ear, and I shivered as he spoke. "Trust me, love. You're going to need it."

I struggled to think but came up with something I thought I could remember if only to get him back behind me. "Unicorn."

He laughed as he slid behind me. "Very well."

"Please."

"Already begging?" That fiendish chuckle filled the interior of the car, which I'd completely forgotten about, thanks to the blindfold. "Oh, this *is* going to be so much fun."

Westley landed two hard smacks across either ass cheek, and I jumped, a short cry escaping me that melted into a moan.

"Can you be quiet, little pet? Can you hold in those delicious screams even for a moment? Hmm?"

"Yes, sir," I bit my lip again, shifting my knees as I felt my pussy throb.

"Good girl. I want to see my marks decorating this virgin ass for days." He punctuated his words with another smack across my skin. "Use your safe word if you need me to stop."

I clenched, adjusting my shoulders on the floor to better take what I knew was coming.

And that's when I realized Westley had been holding back. His firm palm landed on my ass with such force I shot forward, my head pushing into the ground. I didn't cry out, though. My breath being forced out of my lungs was the only sound in the cab.

He did it again on the other side, and I frowned into the carpet. But I still didn't make a noise. Another crack landed across my skin, and again, I was pushed forward hard onto my face.

Another and another and another.

Tears streamed down my cheeks as the burn in my ass fueled the throb deep in my core. I nearly cried out my safe word, but the desire to please him, to impress him, was suddenly a huge part of my personality. I could barely think of anything else.

Then he stopped, and Westley must have taken his glass from the bar because I could hear him swallow and exhale deeply. The blindfold made it impossible to tell what was going on beyond, and I cursed my inability to judge what was happening. I was also incredibly focused on the pain in my ass and my exposed flesh, which was, of course, the point.

Westley's fingertips grazed over my burning skin, and I arched as it overloaded my senses. Each tiny touch was a roaring fire that my nerves struggled to comprehend.

"So red. So raised. I can feel the heat in your skin. Such a good pet." I heard something move at the side of the bar. "Here."

I couldn't guess what he meant, but then a shock of cold shot through me as he trailed an ice cube across my sore ass. It felt incredible, and it quickly melted against my flesh, trickling water down my thighs and just past my pussy. I was vividly aware of every single drop that ran down my skin, and as one slid dangerously close to my already slick slit, I moaned.

"Such a sweet, dirty little pet." I could feel his breath on the wet trails as he spoke.

Then his tongue licked up a stray droplet that was centimeters from my core, and I squeezed my legs together slightly and whined out a moan. Westley shifted behind me again and spoke into my ear.

"This," his hand swiftly captured my pussy, cupping it and squeezing, "this tight virgin cunt is mine," Westley growled in my ear as he just gripped me, pain throbbing through my ass, and I came right then and there.

5
The Elevator

Andi

I shook in Westley's grip and dripped for more. I had no idea where I was or how to move. Hell, I could barely think. Westley's incredible voice cut through the daze of desire as he told me we were close to his penthouse.

"You're going to trust me to get you out of the car. Understood?"

"Yes, sir." My words barely made it out. I was completely overwhelmed.

Westley left my blindfold and binds in place as the car rolled to a stop. My heart picked up a nervous pace at the thought of him yanking me out of the cab and carrying me to his house, my goods out for all the world to see.

Even if I wanted to, which I had a hard time admitting that I didn't, I couldn't have done anything. I was helpless, all tied up like this. And it really shouldn't have been as hot as it was.

A cool breeze ghosted over my skin as the door

opened, reality along with it. *Oh god, the driver is going to see me like this. Oh fuck.*

"Thank you, Richard. That'll be all."

I heard footsteps move away from the car on what I guessed was concrete, but how much could I know without being able to see. My shoulders started to ache, and my kneecaps had been on fire for some time now.

"All right, little pet. Should we get you inside?"

Westley's hands helped me up to kneel, and I hissed at the increased pressure. He guided me out of the car, shutting the door behind me. The noise echoed, and everything smelled like wet asphalt. I turned my head like I might be able to see something, silently cursing the blindfold.

"We're in the parking garage under my penthouse. I'll walk you to the elevator, and we'll ride it up to the top floors."

"Floors? You have more than one?" I asked, my voice sounding almost drunk.

"Shh," he spanked my ass, and I cried out as pain flared through my irritated skin, "Yes, I do. Now, be a good girl, and you'll get a reward. Something *tasty*."

He said the last word right in my ear, and chills rippled through me.

From what I could tell of the trip, the elevator wasn't far. Westley expertly guided me to it, and I heard him push the button to call it. In the moments we waited, he ran his fingers across the raised welts on my butt, and I arched into his hand with a hiss, my nipples hardening. I couldn't tell if it hurt or felt terrific. The sensations were too tangled up in each other. Maybe that was why it *did* feel so damn good, if unbearable.

When the elevator dinged, Westley escorted me

inside and up against the back wall. The surface was cold against my back, and I instinctively pulled away.

"Turn around and face the wall."

I did as told, feeling that cool surface perfectly well through my thin leotard as it dusted over my hard nipples. Westley's hand went to the back of my head, pushing me into the wall. His other hand went to my hip, pulling them away from the flat surface so that my ass stuck out, completely revealing me to him.

Westley stepped back, and I suddenly felt even more naked without his hands on me. What was he doing? *I would kill to be able to see right now.*

"Look at that perfect little pussy weeping for me."

I clenched my thighs together, which did absolutely nothing to ease the ache between my legs or to hide the fact that I was so fucking aroused I thought I might drown in it.

"Your wet little cunt wants its master, doesn't it? Say it."

I moaned. I'd never used that word or heard it in this context, and I was suddenly obsessed with how it sounded flowing from between Westley's lips. My mind swirled, fantasies mingling with reality, and the desperate need for him—to *see* him—made my pulse pound in my ears.

"Yes, sir."

A slap traveled across both my cheeks, and I jerked slightly. I was getting used to the sting, but still, my nerves lit up when he cracked his palm down on me.

"Open your legs," Westley demanded. That low voice was going to be the death of me, and I'd die on fucking cloud nine.

I spread my legs as much as I could without losing my balance.

"Look at that wet sweetness all ready to be devoured. How would you like it if my hand smacked this?"

His finger barely grazed me, and I arched, hissing. God, he was fucking depraved, filthy for how out in the open and raw this was. I...I adored it.

"Oh, fuck, yes. Please, sir."

The needy sound of my voice verged on pathetic, but damn, did I love putting on this show for him. I wanted to please Westley, make him sing those praises about me again. Or maybe I wanted him to punish me again? That hard slap–the way he took, grasped, pulled–was too damn good. I desired that sting. Hell, I craved it, needed it.

I had never really understood what someone meant when they would utter "break me" in the things that I'd watched or read, but I did now. I *knew* it in my bones.

This older, confident man was going to take everything he wanted from my body, and I was so fucking hungry for it, even if a part of me was still a bit terrified.

"Don't move, pet."

The pain was abrupt and sharp, sending burning waves through my swollen flesh, followed by an exquisite tingling. I cried out, allowing the sound to bleed into a guttural grunt. Why was this so fucking fantastic? Why did I wish someone could see it?

"Sweet pet. Those sounds you make." he slid the very tips of his fingers up my body from my cunt to my neck, gripping my hair at the top and pulling my head back. "They're going to ruin me as I ruin you."

The ding of the elevator doors was obscenely loud in the private space we'd created. It was like they interrupted us. Westley used my hair to pull me up to standing and then threw me over his shoulder in a damn impressive bit of strength. I landed with a grunt, and he smacked my ass as I wiggled in his grip.

"Hold still, pet. Or no treats," he sucked in a deep breath, "Though having your delicious pussy this close to my mouth is going to make that promise difficult to keep."

I smiled where he couldn't see, still so infuriated that I couldn't see his face—take him in from head to toe—and I let myself slip a little further over his shoulder, angling my hips so that even more of me was exposed next to his face. As Westley walked us down the long hallway, he bounced me in his grip, laying a handful more slaps across my ass and pussy.

The repetitive burn was amping up the dull ache between my thighs, and I never wanted Westley to stop. Filthy, depraved, wet sounds echoed as his hand came down over my slick folds over and over. I was going to fall apart again right here on Westley's damn shoulder.

"Remember that safe word, love. We're home now, and I don't have to hold back."

6
The Penthouse

Andi

Westley quietly made his way through the penthouse. I could hear various doors opening and closing behind us. Still, I had no spatial awareness to navigate where I could possibly be. Plus, it wasn't like I knew the layout of the place. *Dammit, take this off, Westley. Just for a second.*

As we entered another room, I noticed the change in lighting beyond my blindfold. In brighter rooms, a bit of light managed to seep through, but here, it was much darker, and I could smell something fragrant in the air–vanilla sweet and spicy.

Westley set me down on some type of mat, which my knees were thrilled about, but I noticed it was elevated off the floor when my feet hung over the back edge. I didn't dare move as I listened to him walk around the room, still unspeaking and giving me nothing to go on. Westley was probably arranging things he planned to use based on what the contract had alluded to.

My mind whirled at the thought of what he might

be grabbing. I was completely new to this. I was a fucking virgin, for Christ's sake. Was he really going to go from zero to sixty? Did I mind?

I recognized the sound of his belt buckle, and new wetness flooded me. I desperately wanted to say something, to ask a million questions, but I held it in, waiting very *impatiently* for Westley's next round of delicious torture.

Then I felt his hands on my bound arms, working to unravel them. It took several moments, and each swish of Westley's fingers across my skin made me shiver. Even just touching him for a few seconds was enough to get me right on the edge again. As my arms finally swung free, my shoulders ached, and I exhaled hard.

"Down on your hands and knees."

The thought of holding my weight up by my arms and shoulders after the position I'd just been tied in sounded awful, and I hesitated. Then, a firm slap came down across my ass. I yelped and quickly fell forward onto my hands.

"Naughty pet. Do as you're told. Understood?"

There wasn't true anger in his voice but a stern expectation that I meet his rules, offering complete obedience.

"Yes, sir," I answered quickly.

"Good." A proud tone now, and my adrenaline flared higher at eliciting it. "Stay."

I felt Westley move around in front of me. The strong weight of his presence settled over me, holding me firmly in place despite how badly I wanted to touch him–the suit, the scruff of his beard, his *body*. His hands slid off the blindfold, and I gratefully blinked several times, trying to adjust my eyes.

The room was large and dark when it came into focus, with a few candles as the only light source. To my left, there was a huge bed covered in black silk sheets and a large table in front of me. I couldn't tell what exactly was on it, but I could guess. I could also see that I was kneeling on a raised surface. It was covered in a smooth, black material and sort of resembled a massage table from what I'd seen at the mall or backstage at the O'Hara, where some of the dancers offered them.

And then there was him.

My mysterious, alluring purchaser was still as handsome as I remembered, clearly not just my imagination taking over. And I found the green of his eyes beneath the mask he was wearing. Licking my bottom lip only to chew on it, I couldn't look away, silently screaming for him to take it off.

Let me see you.

He cocked a grin as if he knew exactly what was on my mind, and his strong hands went to the tie at the back of his head, loosening the ribbons and letting the mask fall away.

Oh.

I'd been right about him being in his forties, it appeared, but not even my vivid imagination could have prepared me for how damn striking he was. Westley was gorgeous, drop fucking dead gorgeous, and inadequacy crawled back through me as I wondered yet again why someone so incredible would want someone like me.

It was fading, though, because looking at him was too wondrous to dwell on that shit. His strong features cut a jawline that would make most men reel, wishing for such spectacular angles. His green eyes were framed by dark, thick brows, and of course, he had that manicured beard, trimmed to perfection–from length to how it gracefully surrounded his full lips.

But what really did me in was the expression on that handsome face–dark, hungry, calculating, as if he were running through all the various ways to unravel me for his pleasure.

Westley put a finger under my chin and lifted my face toward him. He'd unbuttoned his shirt to reveal his chest, his jacket and tie long gone. His sleeves were still rolled up, and he'd definitely taken off his belt. Somehow, he was even more handsome like this.

"Open up." His thumb pulled my jaw down, and I opened my mouth.

Westley dragged his thumb across my tongue, testing my limits, and I sucked in response. When he finally took his hand back, Westley smoothed it down the column of my neck, dipping inside my leotard to rub it across one of my nipples. He coated the hard bud in my saliva, and I whimpered as he pinched the sensitive flesh.

As he stood straighter, Westley returned his attention to my face, bending down to hover his lips over mine. I wanted to shift forward, close the distance between us, but I didn't dare. He absolutely knew, however, and chuckled lightly as he stroked the pad of his thumb over my bottom lip.

It was eons, ages, only seconds, I didn't know how long before he finally crashed his lips against mine. The first meeting of our mouths and tongues was earth-shattering, and I moaned into the kiss. I felt him grin against my lips, and he quickly took my throat in his firm grip and squeezed.

I hissed in air through my nose as Westley continued to kiss me and tighten his fingers around my neck. I struggled for breath as his dextrous tongue explored my mouth, getting wetter by the second. My head started to spin, and I was seconds from grabbing the hand at my throat when he finally released me even to draw in breath.

His grip remained on my neck, though, and he smiled at me, his other hand on his pants.

"Take a deep one," Westley said, his eyes lighting up with sadistic joy.

Breaths thundered through my lungs as he pulled his hard cock free. My eyes went wide at the size of him, and I shuddered. Just as he moved his hand to the back of my head and positioned himself, I took a large breath, very much assuming it would be my last one for a while.

Westley shoved his thick shaft past my lips and all the way to the back of my throat. My eyes immediately watered, and I gripped the table, steadying myself against the onslaught. He fucked my mouth hard and fast, the relentless rhythm making me cry as I tried to breathe through my nose. It was all too much, too hard, too fast, and I never wanted him to stop.

The sound of Westley's grunts grew louder, and he grabbed my head with both hands.

"Look at me."

I met his gaze, tears still streaming down my face, and he continued to piston his hips back and forth, his cock sliding past my tongue and threatening to choke me.

"Good girl. Look at that pretty mascara running," he gripped my throat again, "Swallow me down, pet. Take it like a good little slut, and you'll get your reward."

Westley fucked my mouth all the harder, grunting as he brought himself to orgasm. Hot cum flooded my mouth and throat, and I obeyed his command. I swallowed him up, every last drop, dying for his taste.

He slid himself free, getting his pants back in order, and stroked the side of my face.

"Oh, pet. I hope you enjoyed your treat. Would you like something more? Something just for you?"

I nodded.

"That's a good girl. Don't move. I'd like to dress up my sweet, little kitty."

I stayed unmoving on all fours as Westley cut through the remaining unmarred fabric of my leotard and threw it to the floor. He then went to the table and retrieved several unfamiliar items, along with a large bundle of rope. He grinned at me as he unwound it and folded it in half.

The feeling of it sliding over my skin was intoxicating, and Westley expertly created an incredible pattern, almost like clothing, that covered my entire body. He also secured my hands and ankles to the table. It all connected beautifully and squeezed just hard enough to leave me feeling trapped and exhilarated simultaneously.

Being completely bound before him, completely at his mercy, and completely naked was an exquisite torture that made my cunt drip and throb. But there were still the other items he'd grabbed. What more did this incredible man have in store?

"Let's address that needy cunt of yours."

Westley's fingers dragged across my pussy, parting my lips and dipping his fingers inside me. I moaned, quaking all around him and nearly coming. He pulled his fingers back, and the loss of them made me whine.

"Has anyone else touched this tight cunt, pet?"

My eyes flared at the inquiry, and I nervously nodded. I'd dated before; I just hadn't...

"But you never let those boys fuck you?" I could hear the demand for honesty behind his tone.

"No, sir," I answered quickly.

"Why?"

My mind reeled. I wasn't really sure why. I'd just never been comfortable with other guys. I wasn't... turned on–not really, not like now.

"I didn't want them. I wanted..."

"More?" Westley's dark voice was right by my ear.

I nodded. "Yes, sir."

A downright evil laugh sounded from the sadist I'd let buy me, and it should have terrified me. But this *was* what I wanted. I wanted fast and too much and rough. I wanted to be brought to the brink–a level anyone would have trouble with–right from the get-go.

"Oh, sweet, precious, Andi. I'm going to destroy you, pet. I'm going to make those pretty blue eyes well with tears as I mercilessly fuck your cunt."

He smacked my swollen flesh once more.

"There's no soft or gentle from me. You're mine, pet. Your first time and every time after belongs to me. I don't care what you think you can handle, you're taking everything I have to give, and you're taking it right the fuck now."

Then, something new was pressing into my entrance. A thin shaft that gently buzzed slid deep into my pussy, pulsing. I was reeling in seconds.

"Oh, I'm not done with you yet, kitten. And remember," Westley's lust-drunk voice sobered some, "you have a safe word."

Another hard round toy touched my asshole, and I instantly clenched.

Oh, holy fuck, really. Umm...

It was slippery, however, and Westley gradually

pressed it in. I'd messed around with this on my own, so I wasn't in immediate pain, but this toy was thicker than any I'd used.

With a final shove, it was thrust into my ass, making my back arch at the sudden but wonderful intrusion. I could feel its hook slide between my asscheeks to lay against my back, and the cold metal caused goosebumps to ripple across my flesh. The strange toy skewered me, and I could feel it rub against the smaller one in my pussy.

I was panting in seconds. I couldn't help but move back and forth, fucking the devices as I desperately sought a release.

"You are a hungry pet, aren't you? My good girl. Fuck them harder, love. Make yourself fall apart."

I excitedly obeyed, slamming myself against the toy in Westley's hand and rubbing my clit on his knuckles when I reached the hilt. I was so fucking close. The words came tumbling out, the only things I had control over, and I begged Westley to give me more.

"Please, please, sir. I want it so bad. I need it. Please fuck me."

He chuckled darkly behind me and slapped my ass as it bounced against his other hand.

"Do you need it that bad? What will you do if I say no? Hmm? What will you give me for a yes?"

"Anything! I'll give you anything, please! I can't stand it. Please fuck me! I want you to destroy me!"

His hand froze, holding the toy deep inside me. Something changed, and I was terrified he'd walk away. Another slap burned into my ass, and then his hand was gripping my hair. He pulled, forcing me to arch back, but I was unable to move from my bound position. I screamed as the toys pushed deeper, so close to orgasm.

Westley let go of my hair, and my head fell back down hard. The buzzing between my legs was suddenly gone, but then I felt his warm cock at my pussy.

"Scream, pet. Scream for me."

He shoved himself into me, and my cunt clamped down around him. Westley's thicker shaft stretched me, impossibly full. I did scream, ecstatic with the painful pleasure of him claiming my virginity in one clean stroke.

My pussy surged as he bottomed out inside me, new, intoxicating sensations overtaking me, and Westley fucked into me with a fury I could scarcely comprehend. I was nearly exploding when the sting of a whip sang across my back.

"Fuck!"

"Yes, pet. Scream. Beg me to let you come."

Westley rubbed my clit with his fingers and pummeled into me. It was too much and not enough. The round toy in my ass rubbed within me as his erection claimed every inch of my cunt. He sank deep, finding my cervix with the head of his cock, and I yelped.

It hurt. It lit up my nerves. It was amazing. And goddamn, was I close.

"Please! Please let me come, sir! I'm begging you!"

Everything ached, stretched, and burned. If I didn't come, I was almost certain I might die or at least pass out.

Westley swung down the whip again and again.

"Yes. Come for me."

Everything fell apart and came together at once. I came so hard my vision tunneled, and I saw stars. I screamed out, the pleasure overwhelming, and Westley growled behind me. I felt his cock thicken even more as he came inside me, ropes of cum jetting out of him in a nearly endless wave of ecstasy.

And then I was sobbing.

I couldn't stop myself. It was so much. I'd never felt that desired, that owned.

Time seemed to stretch out and warp. I couldn't track much through the crying that oddly racked my body and wouldn't stop. Suddenly, or maybe not so much, I was freed from the table and guided over to the large bed. Westley sat next to me, pulled me into his arms, and wrapped a blanket around me.

"Shh. You're okay. You did so well, pet. You're just coming down."

He must have had the conversation with others because he was saying exactly what my brain was word-lessly asking. The sobs slowed and eventually stopped as he rubbed my back. I was curled up into him, clinging to him like he was a life raft.

When I could gather my thoughts better, I looked up at his handsome face. I opened my mouth to speak, but my throat was raw.

"Here," Westley handed me a bottle of water from inside his nightstand.

I chugged down the cool liquid and sighed as it eased the ache in my throat. Westley smiled at me as he tucked my hair behind my ear, and it looked so different from his other smiles.

"Thanks. I'm...I'm sorry about that. I don't under-stand what happened." I couldn't hold his stare, turning my attention to the bed.

"It's all right. Like I said, it's a part of it. Are you warm enough? Coming down can make you cold." Westley rubbed my arms like I'd been out in a storm. It felt like I had.

"Yeah, I think I'm getting there. I'm...I'm *exhausted*, though. Can I... Can I-"

"Sleep here? Yes, of course. Do you want anything to eat before you rest?"

"No. I don't...I'm fine," I said, still staring at the black blanket that enveloped me.

His fingers came under my chin and lifted my face up, forcing me to look at him. "You're more than fine. You're perfect."

The tears started again, and I realized what it was. I didn't agree with him. I'd never thought that about myself, and the intimacy and raw lust of his possession made me face that fact head-on.

"Shh," he whispered as he pulled me close again.

Calm found me faster this time, and I yawned loudly.

"I'll let you rest." Westley moved toward the edge of the bed, and my hand shot out.

"No! Please...don't leave?"

A gentle smile found his lips again, and Westley scooted back toward me, opening his arms and laying down on the bed with me.

I slept hard, harder than I ever had, and it was the best night's sleep in years.

When I woke, Westley was lying next to me in the massive bed, and my stomach was growling. It was loud enough to get his attention, and he looked over at me, eyebrows raised at my hunger's very noticeable call.

"I guess breakfast is in order. Good thing it's my favorite." He sat up and stretched.

At some point, he'd taken off his shirt and pants, and I gazed longingly at his sculpted form. His body was taut–corded muscle and sex. His prowess last night made that much more sense. It was like he was created especially for fucking.

And it was even more impressive knowing that he was in his forties. Those silver streaks through his hair were the only thing that gave away he wasn't in his twenties.

"If you keep staring at me like that, I'm not going to feed you food any time soon."

The grin plastered on his face I recognized. I knew exactly what it meant, and my pussy throbbed at the memory. I echoed him with a mischievous smile of my own and let the blanket fall from my naked form as I sat up next to him.

"Fuck, pet. You're exquisite, and those lovely marks on your skin are driving me mad."

I looked down at my arms and legs. I had small bruises and welts from the whip and ropes. They covered me like an intricate map of our depravity.

Why did I...*love* them so much?

I felt an odd pride that my body had been able to handle it all for him, and I could wear these decorations as a reminder.

"Would you like to add more?" I asked quietly.

I startled as he pulled me into his lap, his erection pressing into my sore pussy.

"Yes. Yes, I would, but," Westley rolled his hips against me and then flung me down onto the bed as he towered over me, "I don't want to wait for that right now."

His briefs were off in a flash as he held me in place by my neck. I squirmed against his grip, fighting for air and seeking his hard cock simultaneously.

"You're a needy little thing first thing in the morning. Maybe I should make you wait."

"No, please," I whined. "I need to feel you again. Please, sir." I bit my lip as I pressed up into his hand.

He slammed into me up to the hilt. I shrieked, a huge smile spreading across my face. It burned, the pain so strong, and I melted into it.

Westley set a cruel pace, fucking me to the edge in just minutes. His fist squeezed down on my throat as his other hand took one of my nipples between his fingers and pinched hard. I gasped at the pain, rolling my hips into him and working myself on his erection. His cock found my G-spot, and I was thrusting and cursing as it assaulted my sensitive nerves.

Still gripping my neck so tight I could barely get any air, Westley dug his other hand into my mouth. He fisted it, making me tear up and struggle that much more for breath. It heightened the incredible pleasure boiling through my veins, and I met his hard thrusts with my own, wrapping my legs around his hips to push his cock as deep as it would go.

He grunted, and it lit me up from the inside. Hearing him lose himself to fucking me was officially my new favorite sound.

Sliding his fingers out of my mouth and down my body, Westley dragged my saliva across my skin. Everywhere it touched me, the air felt suddenly cool, and goosebumps spread across my body. It was positively filthy, but I reveled in it.

I looked up at Westley's face, and he grinned as I moaned louder and louder. My eyes rolled back as the orgasm crested like a wave at its peak. Everything burned, and my lungs begged for air. With my eyes still closed tight, I heard Westley spit and felt the warm liquid hit my breast. Blissfully shocked, my eyes shot open, and I watched as he licked it around my hard nipple, biting down on the thick nub till I screamed.

That was all it took to send me spiraling over the edge. I came hard, squeezing my legs around Westley's hips. He tightened his grip, cutting off the sound and choking me as the orgasm rocketed through me even harder.

When I thought I couldn't take anymore, Westley released my throat and took my hair in both hands. He pulled me into him as he lost what remaining control he had over his own release. He fucked me with wild abandon and filled me so full of hot cum that it dripped down my thighs.

As everything settled back into place, Westley looked down at me. I couldn't tell what emotion was playing through his head, not entirely, but part of it was shock.

"Did I do something wrong?" My heart pinched in my chest.

Westley quickly shook his head. "No, not at all. Um... Get cleaned up, pet," he crooned, soothing me, "I'll cook us breakfast."

He smiled at me and stroked a hand down the side of my face. I leaned into it.

"Okay."

The Dom

Westley

I directed Andi to a shower, knowing she would thoroughly enjoy every steaming minute of it. My entire place was immaculate, and the bathroom was no exception. I'd prided myself in creating a space here that was the ultimate lap of luxury. Hot water feels incredible on achy skin and muscles; at least, that's what I'd been told, and knowing that Andi had no choice but to use my shower gel lit me up even more. I loved the idea of coating her in my scent, my marks, my cum.

When she came down to find me in the kitchen, she wore one of the robes I hung on the back of the door. She swam in the fabric, her tiny frame doing nothing to fill out the shape like my own. I'd explain the basic layout of the penthouse so she could find me, and I was glad to see that she was navigating my house easily enough. Even I knew the penthouse was laid out a bit like an MC Escher drawing.

"Oh god, that smells amazing."

I piled up the bacon and eggs on two plates,

smirking as Andi practically ran to the small table to start eating. She adjusted slightly in her seat when she sat down, and I grinned. My effect on her would make sitting *interesting* for a while.

"Thank you. Can't go wrong with a classic, can you? How was the shower?" I sat across from Andi, picking up my fork and digging in.

I'd only bothered with a white T-shirt and sweatpants. There would be time for real clothes later. For now, I wanted to be comfortable–to show Andi that she could relax and be comfortable.

"Amazing." She rolled her eyes up to the ceiling. "That massaging head? Ugh. So good. It was just what my muscles needed, which, of course, is entirely your fault."

She smiled at me, and I couldn't help but chuckle. I'd thoroughly enjoyed myself with Andi, and taking that sweet virgin cunt of hers–hard and fast without waiting for some predestined moment–had been fucking divine. I took a bit of my bacon, ripping it off with my teeth.

"Yes, I should think so," I gazed across the table at her, unblinking, "and we still have *so much* time."

She hid her blush behind a sip of coffee, finishing her bacon with a large bite.

"About that, and no, I don't want to leave or anything. I just...I was just *curious...* did you always have that permanent part in the contract? Like for anyone that you took back here?"

I glanced down at the table as I swallowed, wiping my mouth with a napkin. I had a feeling this might come up, and I wasn't sure what I wanted to divulge yet. I was an extremely private person at the best of times, and even though I still very much wanted her to be my permanent submissive, I knew that people usually looked beyond that–to relationship status.

That's *not* what I did this for.

"I'm sorry. You don't have to... Shit."

When I looked up, her brows were knitted together, that innocent young face of hers screwed up into obvious regret.

"It's all right," I let out a short laugh, "It is. I just...I want to be clear with you, and I want to make sure I'm saying this the right way."

Downing the rest of my coffee, I set the cup down, placing my elbows on the table and resting my chin atop my tented fingers.

"I sent that contract to the club a few months ago. It's been in their files, waiting. I haven't bid on anyone or requested one of their staff submissives until now. I'd gone to auctions there but never found what I was looking for. The contract had been created, but there was only ever one thing that was going to set it in motion."

"What?" she asked quietly.

"You."

She visibly swallowed, and I sucked in a heavy breath through my nose. I hadn't planned on discussing this yet. Still...part of me couldn't just turn away from her inquiries.

"What?" Her shocked whisper barely made it across the table. "I mean, you've obviously, you know, done this before. I'm... Christ, and now I'm rambling."

"It's all right, Andi."

Just...just keep it simple, Westley. The facts, the conditions. Just like work. It's just a contract, a negotiation, a partnership.

"I've had submissives, yes. I've even had long-term submissives to a degree, but when I drafted the contract, I had something very specific in mind. I knew what I wanted. I wanted something longer-term and permanent. I don't like shopping. When I find someone I connect with, I'd prefer it to stay that way. I wanted the right person, and I never found them—not until you."

Andi's mouth fell open, and her eyes took up a glassy sheen.

"Westley," her voice was tight, her eyes tracking the contents of the table like she was trying to memorize them, "I..."

But whatever Andi was going to say fell away. She shook her head, sitting up straighter in her chair and smiling brightly again.

"You know, aside from the fact that you're very skilled with a number of fascinating items, including rope, I don't know much about you. What do you do? What do you like? How'd you end up with such a killer place?"

I chuckled low. She was so different from me. Andi was this very readable canvas–open and unsullied. Her natural extroversion was certainly at odds with my usual less-than-chatty demeanor.

"I guess I'll take those in order. I own a tech company that makes microchips for pacemakers and other things necessary for medical care. I like science and math. It's why I got involved in technology, to begin with."

This type of inquiry, however, I *could* handle. Talking about work–about what Cloudstone Technologies did for the world–was easy as pie.

"My company develops the critical components of medical devices, putting some good in the world. I don't really do much development anymore, but I'm proud of what my company does. The penthouse is a result of that success and the money my parents left me. They're gone now, but they were something of Harmstead royalty."

Andi cocked a brow, her eyes going to the table as she mulled over my response. At once, her stare shot back up, and she looked up at me with her mouth hanging open slightly.

"Whoa, I'm sorry, but your parents were Sebastian and Stella Pearce, weren't they?"

My own lips parted, and I laughed once through the surprise. I was frankly impressed she put two and two together.

"Wow, figured that out, did you? Well, yes. They were."

Andi nodded, and I could see the cogs turning in her mind. "So, you're Westley Pearce. You're the CEO and founder of Cloudstone Tech. They're like a Fortune 100 company. You must make billions. *Shit.* Just wow."

She sipped more of her coffee, and I could tell she was trying to digest all that better.

"The company does very well for itself, I'll admit. My parents were in finance before they passed, and they were able to set me up with quite a bit of the initial funding. Even if they would have preferred if I would've started my own investment firm."

When she looked back up at me, Andi still appeared especially bewildered, not that I blamed her.

"Why didn't you? I mean, you do you, of course. I'm just..." Her nose scrunched up as she considered.

"Curious?"

Andi nodded.

"Well, the financial world is full of a lot of searching for loopholes. Trying to find the best way to make a buck, and who cares about anything or anyone else. I didn't...I didn't want to be a part of that anymore."

"Anymore?" She raised her brows at me again that open, receptive expression doing something to my typical resolve to keep this all buttoned up.

I sighed, wishing it was later in the day so I had more of an excuse to crack open a bottle of scotch or wine.

"When I was younger, first developing my interest in coding and statistics, my parents...well, they had me using those skills to analyze market trends. They also learned I could skew data presentation to encourage competitors to sell or clients to buy. It was...unethical, to say the least."

"Oh, damn. Well, Westley, that sucks, but I assure you, I get it. Getting away from shitty parents is...well, it's a thing."

Looking over at her, there was something that hung behind Andi's blue stare. I could see the familiar haze of ghosts haunting the bright irises—she had been through something in her past. The memories clearly clung to her, draping her in a scratchy shroud of a similar make to my own. That protective ache in my chest when I'd first seen her flared brighter.

"What happened to you?"

My voice cut through the air, and Andi was yanked out of her thoughts by the sound. She swallowed, the bob in her throat noticeable from my seat, and then her gaze found the middle distance once more.

"Well, let's just say that it doesn't take too much money or some bullshit upper-class mentality to be neglectful to your child. I mean, hell, I'm a dancer. Sure, aerial silks, but I still hit the strip clubs and burlesque joints like the rest of them. Is there any performer out there that doesn't have daddy issues?"

Stereotyping wasn't something I tried to do. I knew too much about my own situation to thrust my judgment on anyone else. Still, I could see Andi's point.

"Did they..." My jaw clenched; sure, the past was the past, but if someone touched Andi, I was going to hunt them down and remove their hands. "Did they hurt you?"

Her eyes flicked up to mine, and she laughed nervously. "Not really. Just emotional stuff, words, not fists. And when I could, I got myself emancipated. Got out of there and didn't look back. I have no idea what they're up to now."

Subtle relief flooded through me, and still, the fact that I knew her asshole parents had emotionally abused her made me seriously consider looking them up so that I could have them charged or something. The law wasn't on our side, however, and dredging up the past could do a great deal of harm.

I should know.

"That's unfortunate, Andi. No one should have to deal with abusive parents, no matter what form it takes. It's damn impressive that you've been able to survive on your own as well. I can't say I'm familiar with 'roughing it,' but I'm also not an idiot. I know I've been privileged. It looks like we do share a similar parental experience, however. So...thank you. For saying you understand."

Andi smiled easily at me, and my chest constricted. I hadn't wanted to have this type of conversation. I still didn't. So, it was about time for a change of topic—and scenery.

"In any case," I smirked at her, going back to appreciating the look of her in her borrowed attire, "what would you like to do today? I don't have to go into the office since I planned for *this*. Anything you want, Andi. Sky's the limit."

8
The Outing

T he twinkle that lit up those baby blues was
positively charming. It seemed everything about
this fascinating specimen disarmed a person, leaving
them naked to face the utter impossibility of disliking
her. Andi was too damn good for me, despite what she
may have thought.

I, however, was intimately aware of how my nature
could only corrupt my sweet pet. I should have backed
off. I should have been the type of man to leave this
flower untouched, unscathed by the brutality that lived
in each of my cells. I *should* have backed right off when
I'd seen those white ribbons dangling from her wrists.

It hadn't been in my contract stipulations. A virgin
wasn't a necessity for me. Still, the moment I saw her up
there–exposed, innocent, pure–I had to have her. A
good man wouldn't have taken that status from her in
such a depraved manner. A *good* man wouldn't still be
keeping her, excited by the prospect of where he could
take her next.

But I wasn't a good man.

Andi was mine, and I was *far* too greedy to let her go. Corrupting her–crushing her petals in my fist–brought me to life in a way I'd never experienced.

"Really?" her brows raised to her hairline, and I watched the overwhelm grow in her expression. "Wow. Okay, umm..."

She chewed on her lip, and it took everything not to fling these fucking dishes to the floor and drag her across the table. I could give her something to occupy that mouth, and I knew for a fact that my pet was quite good at it. Andi didn't even know what she was doing to me, teasing her lip like that.

I smirked at her instead, smoothing my hand across my mouth and beard to distract myself.

"What would *you* do on your day off?" I asked.

If possible, her eyebrows rose even higher, and I stifled a chuckle. Andi's expressions were vivid, honest, and not toned down in any way. Watching them was... unnerving, if only because that level of genuineness was rare in my world.

"Me?" Andi put a hand to her chest, drawing my attention to the slice of skin I could see between the halves of her borrowed shirt. "Ha, well, it's probably not anything like you would do. I rarely get true days off. And I'm perpetually broke."

That comment landed hard. I didn't enjoy thinking about Andi struggling to get by, but I could certainly see it in her. She did struggle. She toiled, and I knew that money had been a significant reason for her to come to the Scarlett Oleander.

However, if my pet was honest with herself, it hadn't been her reason for joining me.

"You aren't today," I stood up from my chair,

holding out my hand toward her. "So, what'll it be, pet?"

Andi smiled from ear to ear and took my hand. As I pulled her to her feet, she flicked her glance down to the floor before meeting my stare again.

"Okay. I have an idea." She bounced a little in place, energy filling her. "But I *definitely* can't wear this. And I can't wear my shredded leotard either."

Another easy laugh left me, and I pulled her close before guiding us down a long hallway that led to the guest room, where Andi would *not* be sleeping, of course.

"I think I can help with that."

Looking up at me with a furrowed brow, Andi followed along as I walked us to that room and the attached closet. I could sense her intrigue and curiosity, so I moved quickly to show her what I had available.

Flinging the doors to the closet wide, I revealed the collection of women's clothing that I'd just refreshed the day before I went to the club. I, of course, had to guess the size, but I assumed smaller based on the usual body types of aerial performers. It appeared I had been pretty damn close to a perfect sizing.

Andi gasped, stepping forward into the closet and racing to drag her hands through the racks of garments. It was like something out of fucking Pretty Woman, for Christ's sake. But that wasn't far off from our situation, now was it. The warmth that flooded my chest as she eyed the clothes and started pulling out options, laying them on the long island-like table in the center of the room, was something I wasn't ready to examine.

"Seriously, this is nuts. You really just have a closet full of women's clothes? Should I be upset about that?"

Andi's voice wavered a bit, so I sidled up behind her,

gripping her biceps and pinning her back against my chest. Lowering my nose into the crook of her neck, I breathed deeply. She smelled so distinctly like her and, of course, like my personal body wash. God damn, I loved having my scent all over her. My cock thickened behind my sweatpants, and I knew she could feel every inch rubbing against her ass.

"No, you shouldn't." Andi whimpered as I squeezed her arms, stroking myself against her. "I knew what the contract entailed, so I made sure to have clothing at the ready."

Her head fell back against my chest, and I could see the smooth plane of her chest from over her shoulder.

"Okay, yeah." She squirmed against me, looking for more of the sensations. "That makes sense."

We stood there for a moment. I was so damn hungry to shove my erection up to the hilt in her tight asshole, but the idea of edging her, making her wait for the payoff, was extremely intriguing.

"Mmm," I hummed into her hair. How mean could I be? Could I work her right to the edge in seconds and then pull the plug? Yes. I damn well could.

Shoving Andi toward the center table without letting go of her arms, I bent her over the surface. It was covered in several of her choices, and I dragged my hand up her arm to her head to push Andi's face into the fabric. I kicked her legs farther apart with my foot, loving how the men's button-down she wore did nothing to hide her gleaming slit as she bent like this.

"Westley..." Andi's muffled words melted out around the shirts, and leggings scrunched up around her face.

"Ah ah."

Shaking my head, even though she couldn't see, I

cracked my palm against the deliciously fresh marks covering her ass cheek. Andi yelped, jumping as the pain roared through her, but as expected from my devious little slut, it quickly flowed into a hungry moan for more. Two more slaps, and her skin was a gorgeous shade of pink.

"It's Sir, right now, pet."

Just nodding against all that fabric, Andi began to moan low, and I glided my hand between her legs. *Fuuuck.* She was already so wet for me, and I almost didn't think I'd be able to edge her like I wanted—because, of course, it would certainly be edging us both. But...we had time. Toying just with the seam, dragging the pad of my finger up and down, I released her head.

"Keep it there, pet."

She nodded again, and I reached inside my sweat-pants to grip the base of my cock. Squeezing until I felt the lick of pain, I pulled myself free.

"I love how wet you are, pet. So needy for Master's cock." I dragged the head of my erection through her folds, coating me in her arousal. "But I'm not going to fuck you just yet. We have an outing planned after all."

She whimpered again, and the noise made my nerves sing. "Please, sir."

I smacked her pussy with my shaft. "No. But I want you to think about this. All. Fucking. Day."

Smoothing my shaft through her dripping cunt, I covered my skin in that delicious slick dripping from her. I was covered in it, and I was practically giddy at the knowledge that my sweet pet's juices would dress my erection while we were out in public.

Yanking Andi back up by the hair, I whispered low into her ear.

"I'm going to wear you, pet. This tasty evidence of

your arousal is going to cover my cock while I take you out. Do you like that? Knowing that your cum is coating my skin? That I'm carrying you with me?"

Andi's hips rocked as she tried to find my dick again with that pussy of hers. She nodded frantically, and her hand came up to the grip I had on her hair.

"Oh, fuck yes, Sir. So much."

"Good." I released her with a shove back down to the clothes. "Get dressed, pet. You said you have an idea, and I want to see what it is."

I'd left Andi in the closet alone to get dressed. I knew us both well enough to understand that if I stayed in there–if I got a peak at those hard nipples of hers–neither of us would hold up to our word of staying away from the other. And I had to admit to myself that I enjoyed the tease far more than I thought I would.

It had only been a few minutes downstairs, checking a few emails, before I heard Andi's gentle steps signal her appearance. I closed up my laptop once I hit reply on the memo from HR regarding the newest hires and fires. We'd had a good quarter, but there was one particular employee incident that they were being forced to keep an eye on without me as I took these days off.

Of course, if it was truly an issue, I would explain the problem to Andi, at least a bit, and then head to the office to help deal with it. But it was a single disgruntled employee, which was hardly news, and they'd assured me that everything was well at hand even though this particular employee had caused a number of scenes at the office over the past few months. I sent back a simple thank you, and that was that.

"Okay!" Andi's voice called out. "I'm ready. Do you want to know where we're going or keep it a surprise?"

As she descended the last few stairs, I completely missed everything that she'd just said. It flew right out of my mind as I took one look at her and what she'd chosen to wear. *Oh, little pet. You're going to be the death of me.*

It was hardly warm outside, right at the tail end of winter, but before spring had officially started, and I wondered if she remembered how grueling the wind could be. If that outfit was anything to go on, she either didn't care, ran hot, or was explicitly trying to drive me mad.

It was working.

Smooth, black jeans that hugged every inch of her legs were paired with a thick belt and had strategic rips across the knees. She'd also picked soft, flexible sneakers, probably because, as a dancer, she liked to be able to move her feet more. They sat low beneath her ankle bones, and a slip of skin appeared between her socks and the jeans.

Working my gaze up her body and really contemplating whether or not I was truly certain we should be going anywhere but the bedroom, I couldn't help but internally remark on the interesting combination Andi had created.

She certainly wasn't the girliest of girls, and she chose darker colors paired with more androgynous options. It made for a striking difference between her light, shoulder-length bob and the full curves of her ass.

"You're going to freeze, Andi." I cocked the side of my mouth in a subtle grin.

She jogged over unhurried, pulling up the over-the-shoulder sleeve of the black slouchy sweater she'd chosen with a smile. It split open down the middle, and I guess that's what made her consider the thing some sort of jacket.

Beneath it was a thin black tank. It was blousy at the bottom, with ultra-thin spaghetti straps on her shoulders. I recognized it because I'd actually approved that one. Mostly, I let my assistant, Melanie, deal with the shopping. She did an excellent job styling herself, and I knew she would do fine at this. Furthermore, she didn't ask questions.

So, it was because I knew this tank, that I knew it had a very low back where it was hidden beneath the sweater. There would be no way Andi was wearing a bra with it, and my cock twitched at the thought.

"I'll be fine. I run hot anyway." Andi's eyes sparkled as she grinned at me, that devious little smirk of hers making me want to wrap my fist around her throat and drag her down to her knees.

I stalked closer to her, pulling the tiny thing against my chest. Tucking her hair behind her ear, I noticed that Andi must've used some types of styling products from my bathroom to fix her hair. The tussled blonde waves were still a bit messy, but she'd smoothed them down a bit, arranging the shoulder-length bob so that it effortlessly flowed around her face.

"You do indeed, little pet."

Andi's eyes flicked down as she chewed on her lip, and damn, this woman for being so fucking beautiful.

"So, surprise, or should I tell you?" She looked up, still trying for that casual smile.

"I hate surprises. Tell me."

We held each other stares for a moment, and then

Andi hopped into motion, strutting casually to the door, with an actual spring in her step. She got to the entrance, taking my keys from the catchall dish where I'd stashed them last night after our *encounter*.

"All right, let's go. I'll tell you in the car."

She just smiled, fucking *smiled* at me. My blood boiled, the semi I'd been fighting turning to a full erection as I stared down my little pet who wanted to play at being a brat. *Oh, I'm going to fuck you senseless, little one.*

Walking over, the sound of my shoes was a crisp click on the floor as I crossed the room toward her. I snagged my light jacket off the back of a chair at the island. When I reached her, I took the keys, never breaking eye contact with her as I licked across my bottom lip.

"You, pet," I took her chin in a firm grip, "are going to have some serious punishment to look forward to."

Andi visibly shivered, and I opened the door for her.

"After you."

She ducked her head, quickly passing by me and going out into the hallway by a few steps. It was a single direction to the elevator, and I locked up as she headed that way. I let her lead on and push the elevator call button, walking up right behind her and leaving absolutely zero personal space.

I knew she could feel my erection rubbing against her ass, but I said nothing. When the elevator doors chimed and opened, I patted her ass to get her moving, and Andi hurried inside. As we rode down, I kept my stare pinned to her, and to say that I loved the way she squirmed under my gaze was a goddamn understatement.

"That was…interesting." I furrowed my brow even as I tried to nod at Andi.

"It was a movie, Westley." She laughed. "Don't take it so seriously. It's not like I was taking you to the Cannes Film Festival or something."

I couldn't stop the hard laugh that cut through me. "Clearly."

"You prude." She giggled again before pulling me along after her as we left the rundown, budget theater.

The truth was I adored the ambiance of it all. It was so *not* like the formal dinners and art shows I had to go to frequently because of work. There were just people milling about through it, laughing loud and joking. A few had even thrown popcorn at the screen. It was… charming. And I had to admit that the concessions were damn incredible.

Growing up rich had perks, privilege and esteem being two of them, but it didn't really have this. At least not as far as my own experience went. It didn't have shitty theaters where the person with you was the real entertainment. It didn't have crappy food delivered by the most vibrant people and eaten in such good company that you didn't care what it tasted like.

"Let's go get something to eat. Darco's is near here, and I'm hankering for a southwest veggie burger with sweet potato tots."

"None of that sounded like English." I smiled at her when Andi turned to glare at me, capturing her against my chest as we paused just outside the theater on the sidewalk. "But it does sound incredible. Lead the way."

She melted against me for a moment, leaning close as I held her chin. Andi went up on her tiptoes to kiss me, and I slid my tongue across the seam of her lips. It had turned out to be a gorgeous day for very early spring, and the sun shone down on her blonde hair, making it glimmer like gold.

I hadn't really planned for this part–for the outings and public displays, at least not here, or the way I was ready to let Andi drag me wherever she wanted to go.

My chest tightened at the realization, but I managed to push down the concern. It was still just some fun. Nothing...serious.

Because this was about a long-term *submissive*, not a romantic relationship.

As I released her chin, Andi lowered down to her heels, spinning around as she took my hand. She practically skipped forward, a massive smile on her face, and then promptly ran into someone who appeared around the corner of the theater out of nowhere.

"Oof." His low voice was quiet.

"Oh! I'm so sorry. My bad. I completely wasn't looking where I was going."

Andi had pulled up short, knocking back into me slightly, and I steadied her as she regained her balance.

"Obviously."

My attention immediately switched to the man she'd bumped into. His tone was especially short for such an innocent mistake, and something about it made my skin prickle with unease.

"She apologized. It was a clear accident. No harm meant."

I knew I sounded a bit rougher than perhaps the situation called for, but he was still glaring at us. Something about him seemed... vaguely familiar. But it was hard to get a true read on the man with his baseball cap pulled down decently low and a thick, unkempt beard covering his chin.

"No harm meant. Yeah. Your type always saying that kind of thing. Well," the man adjusted his jacket, ragged and unwashed, and then stepped to the side, "on your way."

Surging forward and ready to deliver a lesson in manners, I was held back by Andi, who just smiled graciously at the asshole and lowered her head, almost like she was bowing or something.

"I am truly sorry. I'm sure you were just looking to go about your day. We'll get out of your hair." Andi tugged me forward, practically shooing me away from him. "Have a good day, okay? There's a terrible movie playing inside, and popcorn is half off if you tell 'em Andi sent you."

The guy nodded, his mouth tight. "Yeah. Thanks."

As we walked away, I remembered that the vendor at the theater did seem to know Andi, and I wondered if she did this sort of thing for people a lot. Random acts of charitable kindness. She seemed like the type of person to give something even from her sparse offerings.

Walking down the street, the man grumbled to himself as he left us to our own devices. I could have sworn I heard him mumble something about Cloud-stone. My nerves prickled beneath my skin, my senses trying to tell me something that my brain couldn't process. He just felt *off*.

Andi looked back at me when I didn't follow imme-diately behind her. "You okay?"

I shook out of my head. I was being ridiculous, and I had much better things to be paying attention to than some bum we ran into on the street.

"Yes, sorry. Let's go. I would very much like to try these sweet potato tots."

She grinned, taking my hand and yanking me forward. "Oh, they're to die for. And it's just two blocks down."

"Should we grab the car?" I furrowed my brow at her.

"Nah. It's got a good spot in that parking garage. Besides," she looped her arm through mine, "it's good to walk. Good exercise."

Rolling my eyes slightly, I let Andi lead the way, as she'd been doing all day so far. I was used to exercising in a gym, maybe with a partner, but this...Still, it was a lovely day.

"Of course, pet." I looked down at her with devious intent in my mind. "Let's get you fed. Kitten's going to need it."

9
The Ropes

Back at my penthouse, I'd had enough teasing, and Andi had been silently begging me for a good fuck all through lunch. Licking that cherry juice off her fingers after popping the thing in her mouth fresh from her drink. *Oh, yes, little kitten. Master sees exactly what you're doing.*

The loud slamming of the door behind me echoed in the expansive, open layout, and Andi jumped slightly, spinning around to face me as she set her bag down on the island. The nervous, doe-eyed look she gave me was priceless, and my cock twitched in anticipation.

"West—"

I shook my head as she started to speak, stalking up to her, hungry and losing all the civility I'd shown during our outing.

"No, pet. It's Sir right now. Understood?"

Andi visibly trembled, swallowing hard, which made her throat bob deliciously. She nodded, unconsciously backing up until her ass hit the back of the couch.

"Yes, Sir," she breathed out on a whimper. "Umm, can I…"

Goddamn. The nervous trepidation, the way her cheeks pinked with embarrassment and arousal. Everything she did was fucking sublime, and I wanted to drink in that exquisite suffering of hers like a fine wine.

"What, pet?" I sidled up to her, nuzzling into her neck as I shoved the sweater she had worn down her arms.

"W-what are you…going to do? I just…" she moaned as I pressed my lips to the sensitive spot behind her ear, "wanted to be prepared."

Flinging the sweater away, I spun Andi around, reaching for her hips and unbuttoning the jeans that kept her from me.

"Do you remember your safe word?"

Andi nodded, her head falling back onto my shoulder as I downed her zipper. Yanking the denim off her legs, I shucked the damn contraptions clear across the room. As I looked up from kneeling, I was thrilled to see that Andi hadn't bothered with panties.

"Oh, such a filthy, little pet." I slowly stood, dragging my fingers across her skin before I reached her hair and fisted it hard in my grasp. "I'm going to do whatever the fuck I want. And I'm not going to stop for anything but that word. Understood?"

"Y-yes." Her voice quaked, but she nodded once, reassuring me.

With that, I slung her over my shoulder. Andi yelped as I walked us back to the more appropriate room for all the fun I had planned. Her already glistening slit was right near my face again, and I silently vowed to make it drip with cum.

When we reached the private chamber, I took Andi

to the bed, tossing her down. As she bounced, trying to collect herself, I tore the stupid fucking tank from those perfect, little breasts. She was completely bared, and as she gaped up at me, I rolled up the sleeves of my shirt to the elbow. Next, were the buttons at my neck, popping a few so I could breathe just a hair better.

Andi's eyes flared, and she chewed on her lip as I went for my belt. I unbuckled it, sliding it free and tossing it to the bed next to her. My cock jerked behind my zipper, desperate for some airtime and hardening ever more with each passing second.

Goddamn, she's gorgeous.

"Tell me, pet. How would you like to be wrapped up like a present for me? Bound up in my ropes."

Even in the dim light of my private space, I could see Andi's eyes dilate. Her lips gently parted as she sucked in a shaky breath, and she offered a slow nod.

"Yes, Sir. I'd...I'd adore that." Her voice was so airy, a soft hush against the stark black and red interior around her.

A low growl rumbled through me, the way she ached to please me lighting me up from within. I lowered my chin, staring beneath my brows at her, and smirked. As I held out my hand, Andi crawled forward, taking it as her fingers trembled. *Yes, yes. Tremble for me.*

I led her across the room to a large metal bar that dropped down from the ceiling. Rope hung from it, and I retrieved the soft yards of it before moving Andi to stand just beneath the anchor point. Reinforced and capable of holding a person's weight, it was one of my absolute favorite toys.

"Spread your legs, pet. I'm going to dress you up." A satisfied lilt touched my voice, and Andi did as told.

As I approached, I ran a hand down Andi's chest,

veering to the side to pinch either nipple–hard–before drifting downward and sliding my finger through the slick coating her slit. She was already so wet for me, and I groaned in approval.

"Such a naughty girl." I lowered my lips to her ear, whispering. "Do you want to be Daddy's little slut, Andi? My sweet, corrupted pet. Do you want me to ruin more of you?"

She whimpered, shuddering as I toyed with her clit, feather-light and slow.

"Yes, please," she wined. "Oh God, please."

I fisted her hair, yanking her head back and licking across her full bottom lip. "Say you're Daddy little whore then, pet. I want to hear the words."

A strangled cry left her, and Andi squeezed her eyes shut as she tried to maintain her balance.

"I'm Daddy's little whore."

"That's right, pet." I smacked her pussy, slick and smooth from her extensive personal care there. "Now, tremble, little slut, as I tie you up in ropes."

Releasing her with a hard shove, I began winding the considerably long length of rope around her tight, little body. Looping it around the back of her neck and then around her breasts to create a sort of top for her, one that squeezed her small breasts together and made her taut nipples punch out even harder.

I bound up her arms behind her back, dragging the rope through the top I'd created and this new section anchored to her arms. I'd be hoisting her up, and this would keep the weight evenly dispersed. Next were her legs, and I circled around the rope around either thigh just above the knee in two thick sections.

The ropes came around her hips to her back again, and I used a bit of the remaining length to anchor her foot back, creating the perfect bend of her knee so that it was raised high in the air exposing her luscious cunt.

Securing the final sections, I wound the rope around the metal bar above her, pulling Andi up into the air enough so that she could just touch the floor with her one extended leg. She wobbled and drifted as she tried to hold herself. It was futile, of course, and wasn't that just so damn lovely.

"Look at Daddy's pretty whore on display."

I secured the several feet of available rope so that I didn't have to hold it steady, but still allowed myself some slack to raise her higher off the ground if I so chose. Smoothing the pad of my pointer finger across the seam of her lips, I placed a gentle kiss there before gripping her chin and pulling her mouth open.

"I think we need this open, too, don't you?"

Andi stared at me with glassy, lidded eyes and nodded. I walked to the wall of supplies at the wall behind her and retrieved the spreader gag. Returning to her, I secured it around her head and between her lips, the metal ring keeping her mouth open for me.

"There. So damn pretty."

With a whimper, she looked up at me with a pained expression, her cheeks fiery red.

"Do you want more, kitten? Do you want to be so very good for Daddy?"

She nodded again—frantic and desperate. I chuckled darkly, enjoying the way the saliva was already dripping from her mouth and her little cunt was deep pink with arousal.

"Silly me. I didn't dress my sweet kitten properly."

Gone for just a moment, I retrieved the leather cat mask from the wall and quickly returned to secure it on Andi's face.

"Now, that's perfect. Daddy's needy little kitten all dressed up and ready to play." I smeared the dribble on her chin down her chest, smacking each breast. "Are you ready to play, precious?"

"Yes, please!" Her words were distorted around the gag but every trace of whiny begging was still there.

"So needy." I laid two more smacks across each breast before taking a nipple and squeezing down hard. "Very well."

Andi was a mewling mess already, and I'd barely begun. *My, how fun this is going to be.* I trailed my hand down the flat plane of her stomach to the glistening slit between her legs. I cracked my palm against the sensitive skin, making Andi scream out into the dark room. Continuing until her skin was hot beneath my fingers, I reached for my zipper, sliding it down to free my erection.

Whimpering as I stopped, I gripped the base of my cock, stroking as I slipped my fingers inside her cunt. Andi moaned low, arching in the ropes as she hung there, her body free rein. I pumped in and out in time with my strokes, changing it up every now and then to pinch her clit.

She cried out, and I focus even more on making that little pussy weep for me. Her hips were at the perfect level, and I maneuvered between her leg, thrusting my cock deep until I bottomed out, the blunt head hitting her cervix.

More of Andi's delicious screams filled the room. I fucked hard and furious, without mercy or restraint. Her cunt surged around me, her walls gripping my cock so damn tight. The orgasm was lightning-fast, but I was far from down with her.

Not relenting until her entire body quivered, I then

stepped back, reaching deep inside Andi with my fingers again and finding her G-spot. Hooking my fingers into it and working fast and hard, I fucked Andi's hot cunt, then I finally felt it.

Her sweet little pussy flooded with cum, and I upped my speed all the more. I milked her delicious release as Andi cried out, moaning and wailing. Slipping my fingers out to rub across her clit, I kept going as her body seized up into another climax. She squirted hard, covering my hand and arm with her cum. Better still were the pitter-patter sounds of her juices raining down onto the floor, as well as my shoe.

"Please! Sir!"

Those garbled words were music to my damn ears, and I shoved my cock back home, fucking several more releases out of her drenched cunt. She orgasmed again and again for me, screaming as tears trailed down her face.

My cock ached for release, seeing my little pet so destroyed for me so damn good. I stepped back from her and stoked across my length, covered in Andi's cum.

"Pet, look at the mess Daddy's tight, little cunt made all over the floor." I walked to her head, taking the rope and lowering her down onto her knees. "Be a good girl and lick it off my shoe."

Andi's breaths were ragged gaps as she struggled to catch her breath. She looked up at me from her knees, her eyes lidded and mascara smeared. I grinned, evil and sadistic, as she bent awkwardly, extending her tongue toward the shiny cum-soaked surface of my patent leather shoe. The tiny pink tip of her tongue dipped into the puddle at the toe, precarious and timid.

As the liquid touched her tongue, she melted into the fucking filthy goodness of licking her cum into her mouth. She lowered closer, dragging the flat of her tongue through the mess, moaning like the hungry little slut she was.

"Daddy's little whore likes her treats, hmm? Get your fucking mouth on my cock and prove it."

Andi was quick to listen, pulling herself up through the strain of the ropes. I grabbed a fistful of her hair, shoving my cock into her mouth through the large ring keeping it open for me. I fucked brutally, sinking myself down her throat as I pressed her face into my hips. She squirmed, still forced to take it until I let her pull back.

Gasping, a thick, sticky string of saliva connected her mouth to my cock, Andi stared up. Her eyes were red, but she just caught her breath, no utterance to stop or use of her safe word.

"That's Daddy's good fuck toy. Make me come, kitten. Milk Daddy's cream with your throat."

The barest hint of a nod shifted her head before I rammed my dick back between her lips. Setting up a punishing speed, Andi took every thrust and deep shove so well. She moaned and whimpered around my cock, the vibrations rumbling into my shaft. I was damn close.

That pattering sound trickled up from between her legs again, and I paused for just a moment.

"Fucking hell, kitten. Are you coming for me by just sucking Daddy's cock. You filthy fucking whore."

I went down to a knee quickly, reaching for that cunt and working her through another blistering orgasm, her cum soaking more of the ground. It was fantastic, so *damn* fantastic. My shaft throbbed, demanded release.

Pulling her mouth back onto me, I pumped into her mouth with abandon, thrusting until I felt the exquisite burn of release thunder up through my balls. I yanked myself free, climaxing hard and coating her pretty face in hot cum. It covered her tongue, decorating every available inch as the thick ropes spurted out nearly endlessly.

And then I sunk down onto the floor, easing the burning of my lungs with so many hard breaths before I would have the strength to pull Andi down.

10
The Afterglow

Andi

My body hummed, my head reeling. I couldn't really think or make heads or tails of what was going on around me. I was still so pinned down by the aftershocks of the experience. Salty, musky tastes danced on my tongue, though, and I managed to consider what I must look like. Goddamn, I was covered, *filthy* in every sense of the word.

I didn't hate it, however. God, if anything, I was falling right back into that sensory-overloaded darkness by just imagining how I looked, feeling that warm, sticky sweetness on my skin. I also still couldn't move.

"Such a good pet." Westley stroked my hair, and I nuzzled into his hand. "Fuck, you're pretty like this. I'm very tempted to leave you this way so I can come back and admire it later."

Holy hell. Being talked about like I was Westley's personal fuck toy was intoxicating. But the adrenaline was fading, and my body started to shake.

"Can't have that." Westley moved around me in a blur as my eyes refused to focus. "Bathtub."

Then, the ropes started to slide against my skin. I hissed as they dragged over too sensitive areas, but it seemed to go by quickly enough. I wasn't really sure. After however long, I was freed of the confines, but I almost...missed them. The constant pressure on my skin had been grounding. I whimpered softly as I curled into myself, and it occurred to me that I had been quiet this whole time.

"Cold."

"I know." Westley's arms scooped under my shoulders and legs, pulling me against him.

He stood up tall, walking somewhere as he carried me against his chest, and I pushed myself tight against him. The low clicks of his shoes on the floor ticked on in a pattern until we hit the house proper and were replaced by the shushing sounds against the carpet.

Suddenly, I was set down against a bed, and I burrowed into the soft pillow. The sound of water rushing somewhere filled the silence. More time dragged on, and then Westley was back at my side, pulling me up into his arms again. This time, I felt the comforting warmth of his skin against mine.

It was a short trip, and then, as Westley lowered himself into a seat, steaming water smoothed over my skin like a blanket, and I moaned.

Westley washed me up, thoroughly attending to each area in need, and I came more and more back to myself as the water cleaned and grounded me. When I was basically done, Westley held me against his chest, and I just breathed deep, remembering who we each were and admiring the soft lavender smell of the soap.

"Thank you." The words came out scratchy, and I had to clear my throat as the soreness seeped in.

"Of course. Are you hungry?"

I looked up at him, smiling as he gazed down at me, relaxed and unguarded. I liked seeing him like this.

"Yes. I think so." Nodding against his chest, I took one last squeeze and sat up in the tub on my own. "Oof, that was...I'm not sure there is much you can do to top that."

A wicked grin streaked across his face, and Westley's eyes darkened–penetrating and sadistic. "Oh, there is. Just wait."

My eyebrows shot up to my hairline, and I shivered despite the still-steaming bath. I truly could not think of what else he could mean. He'd done *so much* already. Still, the idea that there were still new heights to climb... intrigued me like nothing else. Westley chuckled, cradling my cheek with his hand and dragging hid thumb across my lip.

"Let's get you fed."

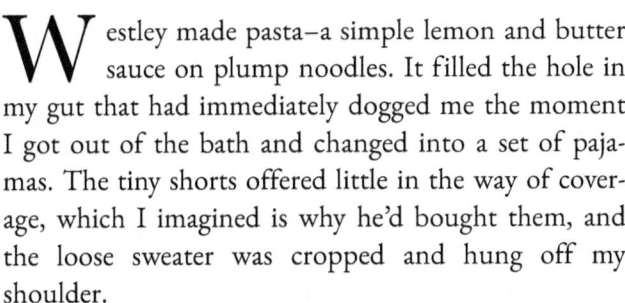

Westley made pasta–a simple lemon and butter sauce on plump noodles. It filled the hole in my gut that had immediately dogged me the moment I got out of the bath and changed into a set of pajamas. The tiny shorts offered little in the way of coverage, which I imagined is why he'd bought them, and the loose sweater was cropped and hung off my shoulder.

Still, the heat was blaring to keep me warm, and my body temperature was figuring out how to regulate itself again. As I took my last bite, sliding the fork between my lips to savor every last taste, I moaned happily. Setting the utensil down on my plate, I leaned back in my chair with a contented sigh.

"Fuck, that was good." I smiled as Westley grinned back from across the island. "And now I'm stuffed."

"Good. Just like you should be."

His eyes twinkled with mischievous glee, and I shook my head at him, rolling my head. "All right there, Mister. You can't possibly still be...*hungry.*"

I waggled my shoulders at him as I raised my brows. Westley stood up, collecting the plates. As he circled the island, he leaned close to my ear, his breath tickling the side of my neck.

"For you, pet?" His whisper made goosebumps bloom across my skin. "Always."

My entire body was immediately on fire. I wasn't even sure if I could handle more—physically and emotionally. But damn, my pussy still clenched, willing to give it a try even if my brain wasn't totally on board.

With a nervous chuckle, I watched him take the dishes to the sink. I couldn't bring myself to comment or make another sound. He just stared me down, rolling up the sleeves of his button-down and making my entire body shiver under his gaze. *Oh, God. Is he really going to...*

"Do you like music, Andi?"

He faced the sink, turning on the faucet to hot and beginning to rinse off the plates. I sagged, my held breath leaving me on a shaky moan.

"Yes. Of course. Who doesn't?" I leaned back in the chair. "Plus, I *am* a dancer. It's sort of a part of the gig, you know?"

A low, way too sexy chuckle left him, and Westley nodded. "Sure. Well..."

He hesitated while he squirted a bit of dish soap on the plates and grabbed a brush from the little caddy sitting next to the sink. Westley scrubbed away, washing the dishes like just some regular guy. And while I knew that, of course, he was a normal guy, Westley was far from typical. Seeing him like this, just going about an everyday annoyance, felt like getting a secret glimpse into someone's life.

He used lemon soap. He turned off the water while he was scrubbing, saving it. He liked a brush instead of a sponge. Just normal things about a person that you had to see for yourself to know.

"I play the piano. May I? Once I'm finished?" He looked over his shoulder briefly before turning the water on again and rinsing the plates.

"Wait, you're asking me if you can play piano for me?" My brows were up again as my mind reeled.

I didn't think I got to say yes or no to stuff. Not really. He'd *bought* my company, after all. A thought that was becoming less and less important if I was honest with myself.

Facing the sink again, he nodded. "Yes."

Scoffing lightly, too much giddy energy rushing through me. I nodded right back. "Umm, duh. Of course, you can. Who would turn that down?"

The laugh he let out was too damn good, and I smiled. I loved making him do that. Almost as much as being the reason he orgasmed.

"Wonderful."

The dishes were clean, and Westley turned around, grabbing a towel from where it hung on the oven, and dried his hands. He sauntered across the kitchen, pulling me off my stool at the island and dragging me to the living room. The piano I'd noticed before was in the far corner, and as he took a seat on the bench, I stood nearby, watching happily.

Gentle, almost sad music began to fill the large open space as Westley began to play. He was obviously talented, but I could also tell that he must've spent years practicing. He moved with an ease that only long-time performers could pull off. I should know.

My smile never faded as he continued playing. Westley's skilled fingers danced across the keys intimately, and a tiny bit more of him opened up. Not in any way that you'd be able to hear or do something with. But he lost himself to the music, his eyes closing as he focused on the story he was telling through treble clefs and quarter notes.

I was, too.

Hearing the mournful tune swept me away, making me think of all those days I'd spent alone. I'd been on my own for so long that I'd almost forgotten that it really was quite...lonely.

The song crescendoed, reaching its apex—that wonderful climb of notes that made your heart swell and your skin prickle. I could feel it in my bones, and I stared, mesmerized by the way Westley took command over the glossy white and black keys.

Like making love through the song, it climaxed and then naturally swelled downward into a cozy place of contentment, and Westley's playing eased to a stop. I smiled, the grin stretching my cheeks wide, and applauded gently.

"That was beautiful," I said softly. It felt odd to speak in the new quiet, my voice too harsh compared to the tune.

"That was yours."

Westley turned around after speaking, meeting my gaze with his stoic expression.

Cocking my head, I furrowed my brow at him. "What?"

I stepped closer, trying to keep my steps quiet against the smooth marble floor. But as I reached Westley, he just stood, pulling me close and then down to the piano bench. Staring up at him, I tilted my head back as I smoothed my hands up his chest.

"Lean back."

My touch hesitated, and I turned to nod at the keys just behind me, my heart rate steadily increasing.

"Will I...hurt the piano?"

He didn't flinch, eyeing me hard. "No."

A shiver ran down my spine, and I angled backward, the edges of the keys digging into my back. I eased down. The sound was discordant, but I'd managed to keep it from getting too loud.

Westley smirked, his gaze dark and hungry. He was fully in predator mode, and I knew without words that he was "Sir" now.

A tremble in my arms made the notes twitch, and I sucked in a shuddering breath. Westley sunk down to his knees, situating himself between my legs as he dragged his fingers up the inside of my thighs. All I could do was watch as he stared up at me until his fingers came to the tiny slip of fabric separating me from him.

Yanking it aside, Westley revealed my bruised, weeping pussy.

"No panties. Good girl."

I beamed, my entire being warmed through like I'd slipped into a warm bath. He didn't stop looking at me, and I was trapped beneath the intensity of his stare.

Hovering his mouth over my aching clit, Westley reached up and slowly pulled down the shoulder of my sweater, revealing my breast just to the nipple.

"Make those keys sing, pet."

Some stupid part of me wanted to protest. This couldn't be good for the beautiful instrument, but Westley's lips sealed around my clit, and everything else dropped away.

It ached. It was incredible. All I knew was that my mind was completely gone now. Gentle, maddening suction pulled the tender flesh into his mouth, and Westley just slowly pulsed his pulls to create an intoxicating rhythm. The overworked little bead was burning under the strong but methodical sucks, and liquid pooled in my core.

My eyes fluttered, wanting to shut, but Westley narrowed his stare on me, his machinations almost stopping when my eyes got too close to closing. He *wanted* me to look at him. A shiver ran down my spine as I just barely nodded, holding his stare as he sucked on my clit powerfully.

I could hardly stand it. Westley forced my thighs wide as he just sucked and sucked and sucked on the tip of my pussy, and I wanted to scream, to close everything up and hide away from the intensity.

But I didn't.

The only sound was the sporadic chime of the piano as I pushed backward in random jerks, bucking against the mind-numbing attention being paid to my destroyed pussy. And all the while, he just stared at me, lapping up my arousal as it dripped.

My entire body *ached* for how still I was trying to be, and the burning scream I trapped in my throat silently roared to break free. Westley's pulls hadn't stopped, and I was sure I was losing my mind. The tension increased, and my hands flew out to the side, gripping the piano for dear fucking life as he notched the pleasure higher.

Westley's tongue circled around my clit as he continued to suck on it, and I was desperate for him to penetrate me. His fingers, his cock, I'd take anything to relieve the horrible need to clamp down around something thick.

But he didn't.

He just kept fucking going, his eyes never leaving mine as I struggled to maintain that blistering connection.

At once, my stomach flexed hard as the edge of my orgasm crested. Westley worked faster, his grip on my thighs so damn tight that I knew I'd have bruises. *His* bruises. I couldn't hold in the moans anymore, and the soft, gentle whimpers rained from me in a never-ending tumble of needy pleas.

Holy fuck...I'm going to die...Oh, please. Fuck, fuck, fuck.

Westley adjusted again, the suction tightening down as he gently nipped at my clit. My eyes flared wide, my mouth gaping in a silent scream.

He smiled.

Just for a moment, and then it was gone, but my heart soared all the same. Unspeaking, I begged him with my broken expression. I *needed* to come.

Stillness, just that constant pressure biting at my sore clit. Westley's gorgeous green eyes were everything, consuming my entire existence as I hovered on that knife edge that slowly tore me open. A single tear slid down my cheek, and that smirk took over his features again.

He nodded, only a tiny twitch of movement, and then his tongue and lips and glorious pulls started up again at twice the speed.

I fell apart.

The entire room erupted into chaotic sound as I finally let the shriek leave me, the piano crying out in a smattering of sharps and non-existent chords as I bucked against it. Westley's fingers dug into my inner thighs, not stopping until I was raining down all over the bench and onto the floor—the filthy percussion for our little symphony.

Whatever was left of my coherent brain at that moment flew away into dust as Westley sat back and licked his lips.

"Good fucking girl."

11
The Door

Andi

Coffee was definitely invented by someone who knew the true power of exhaustion intimately—or at least perfected by one. My entire body was just...I actually couldn't settle on a mental descriptor. I was beyond tired, but I was also floating? Warmed through like a cup of hot soup on a cold day? Yeah, something like that.

Sitting at the tall island while Westley showered, I folded in around the toasty mug in my hands. The warmth from the ceramic bled into my palms and arms beyond that, easing the muscle tension that had greeted me–along with several bruises–when I woke up. The coffee was from a place downtown, a local roaster Westley frequented, I guess, and it tasted like heaven. And it was as addictive as crack at this rate.

It felt so ridiculous to be drinking a homemade latte from an espresso machine instead of just sipping away at the on-sale variety of Joe I usually snagged from the grocery store.

But, of course, the strangest thing about my situa-

111

tion right now was how I *smiled* every time I moved a part of my body. I was happy about my bruises, the marks decorating me thanks to Westley's hands. Hell, I was *proud* of them.

"You are a weirdo."

"Not exactly how I thought I'd be greeted, but I guess that's better than other names I've been called."

Westley's deep rumble startled me as he coasted down the stairs, jogging in his suit with the jacket unbuttoned. God, he was yummy like that. I could eat him right up. And at that, I reminded myself that he'd requested a few hours to deal with work stuff. I couldn't just expect him to completely give up his life just because I was here.

Yes, I very much wanted to spend every waking moment seeing what more he could do to me, but we both had lives we needed to check in on.

"Sorry," I offered, ducking my head to the side as he sidled up behind me. "I was actually talking about myself."

He cocked a brow. "Oh, and why's that?"

"It's nothing." I shook my head, my cheeks heating. "Really."

Westley's fingers came to my chin, gripping me so that I had to look up into his eyes as he spun me around in the chair. I don't know why it felt so odd talking to him about what I'd been thinking. I just...

"Andi," he lowered his gaze into my face, "I can see that pretty pink blush flooding your skin. What's making you so embarrassed? Tell me."

I fucking giggled—like a damn schoolgirl, hiding into Westley's chest. But then his lips were hovering over my ear, and when he whispered, goosebumps rippled across my entire body.

"Tell me, pet." His lips grazed my neck. "Tell me so I can do it again. I love seeing you so flustered. It goes straight to my cock."

My eyes flared, and I shuddered in a breath.

"The...the marks..."

He nuzzled into me, his fingers suddenly on my nipple, pinching as he held the back of my head with his other hand.

"What about them?"

"I..." A whine slipped free as Westley squeezed harder. "I like them."

With a final pinch that was hard enough to have me mewling on the chair, grinding myself against the seat as my eyes squeezed shut, Westley pulled back. I struggled to breathe as I looked up at him, gifted his classic smirk that had my panties wet in seconds.

"Of course you do. You're my good little pain whore."

My cheeks blazed, and I was sure I was twice as pink as before. Which apparently was exactly what Westley wanted.

"And I'll give you more when I get back home." He cocked his head down at me. "Can you be a good girl? No touching or playing without me?"

A part of me had definitely been planning on masturbating after that little tease, but I nodded. I could resist. For now.

"Good. I'll be back in a few hours. I just need to deal with some...well, some rather unpleasant matters. It'll be nice to have you here waiting."

I smiled–genuinely–and stood up off the chair to give him a hug. I wasn't sure why I suddenly had the desire to kiss him goodbye like he was my boyfriend or something. He was my Dom, that was for sure, and we'd...we'd certainly connected, but aside from the outing yesterday, we weren't really dating.

Still, he'd said he wanted me to be his permanent submissive. Just me. Was that dating? Was that anything beyond just an incredibly good time in the sack?

Shaking my head, I realized I was still wrapped around Westley, giving him a hug. I looked up with a smile. Dwelling on *that* wasn't going to do me any good right now. We'd just started this, and I knew we both needed time to figure it all out.

"I'll be good. I promise."

I lifted up onto my tiptoes and planted a kiss on his cheek. Westley smirked down on me, his eyebrows up to his hairline. There was a clear air of surprise behind his smirk, but then he leaned forward, sealing his lips to mine.

Hanging there in the moment for as long as he'd let me, I let out a tiny sigh—equal parts moan and whimper.

Westley stood back, buttoning his jacket. He smoothed a hand down my cheek before walking to the table near the door where he kept his keys, and my chest tightened as I watched him gather his stuff. He swiped up his briefcase and slung it over his shoulder.

"I'll see you soon, pet."

"Okay." I chewed on my lip, waving awkwardly with my baggy sweater sleeves covering my hand. "Bye."

With one more smile, Westley turned and left, locking the door behind him. I sagged into myself, feeling suddenly small and stupid in the giant sweater I'd borrowed from Westley. *MIT, yeah. You'd fit in real well there, Andi.*

I had that closet full of options, and I'd snagged a pair of leggings from there, but it was this sweater I'd seen dangling in the back of Westley's closet that I wanted to wear. He'd been totally fine with it, and as I stood alone in the open floor plan, I put the sleeves to my nose and breathed in his smell, still clinging to the fabric.

"Ugh. Okay, that's enough, Andi. Come on. You're an adult." I sighed, shaking my head until I felt a little bit more like myself.

I wasn't sure what I wanted to do now that I had the place to myself. Westley had said I could go anywhere. He wasn't keeping anything secret from me. He'd only asked that I didn't leave, wanting me to be here whenever he got back. A boring stipulation, to be sure, but it was only for a few hours. I could find a way to entertain myself.

Walking to the couch, I took my phone from the coffee table and flicked through social media for a moment before it got tedious. I was glad that the club had delivered my stuff, but not even good old doom scrolling was cutting it right now. I tossed the cell down on the couch next to me and laid back, staring up at the ceiling.

"You don't miss him. It's been fifteen minutes. Come on."

I didn't know who I thought I was kidding because clearly, I *did* miss the guy a little. Westley was damn intriguing, and boredom was not something that existed when he was around. I liked that. Way more than I probably should after just a few days of being with him. It's not like you could actually fall for someone that fast, though. It was just the "horny" talking–and apparently, I was insatiable now that I'd tried the good shit.

Lying there did not help, so I got up with the pure intention of roaming around and checking out the penthouse. Westley's home was spectacular, with massive windows, a gleaming kitchen, and an exceedingly tall stairwell that boasted an entirely glass surround. Everything was sleek and modern, not usually my taste, but it dripped class. I could also tell it all must have cost a fortune.

Still, it wasn't exactly...homey. The colors were cool and dark. The furnishings were too clean, too structured. Not like the comfy couches you'd find at your mom's. Not that I knew what that would be like. He had art of all types on the walls but no family photos or mementos.

Gorgeous black and white nude photos from a J&J Studio were by far some of my favorites. Striking, high-contrast bodyscapes and lavish sets where the female models reclined like lovers whom you'd interrupted during an intimate moment, the work was all incredible.

He also had prints of Dali, Van Gogh, and Monet. There were even some pieces in an Asian style that I'd never seen before, vaguely surreal but beautiful, with pops of red against muted colors. There were dozens and dozens. It was wonderful to be able to study them like this. It wasn't like I'd had the time before.

I chuckled to myself at the thought, strolling casually through Westley's halls and enjoying the varying styles and levels of popularity of the artists. He had tons that were from people I'd never heard of but were stunning all the same.

The closer I got to his bedroom and the "playroom," as I'd come to call it, the more sexual the art became. There were pieces that directly evoked the BDSM lifestyle that I was familiarizing myself with and some that even depicted fantastical settings and characters—a snake woman fucking a human woman was particularly intriguing.

I wandered into the playroom, dragging my fingers along the wall as I walked aimlessly through the near darkness. The bed was refreshed from the last time we'd used it, and I had a sneaking feeling that Westley was the "clean freak" type. The walls were decorated in posts and racks where too many floggers and whips to count dangled innocently.

"God, some of these look vicious."

Toying with a long-handled paddle, I noted the smooth bumps that covered one side. They were essentially studs but rounded and soft. Still, I imagined they would leave quite the interesting pattern. To my right was the wall of masks I'd seen previously, the cat one I'd worn hanging delicately on a set of two thin bars that slotted through the eye holes.

"Hello, there."

I walked over, reaching out and stroking it. I loved the way the leather felt against my fingers, smooth and cool. Picking it up, I held it to my face, moaning to no one as memories and desire flooded my veins. The weight of the mask both stilled and excited my blood. I wished I could purr in that moment. It would feel so right to roam around the filthy suite like a cat in heat.

Fucking hell, Andi. Where is your brain?

But I hesitated to put it back. As long as I didn't... take matters into my own hands, surely Westley would like seeing me in it when he got home. Right? The thought made my pussy clench, pooling with arousal.

Ding dong.

Jumping, I dropped the mask, and it landed on my foot. Pain jolted through me as I scrambled to pick it back up and hang it on the wall again. Someone was at the door? Really? Why now?

I hurried out of the room, closing it up and rushing

for the stairs in the living room. But then I stopped. I didn't want to answer Westley's door. I didn't know who it was. It could be anybody, and I wasn't even sure if people knew I was supposed to be here. It felt like an intrusion to answer the door for him, so I just stood there on the last step, squeezing the sweatshirt sleeve in my grip.

The bell rang again and again I jumped a little.

Maybe it's a delivery? Westley said he sometimes gets packages...

I took the last step down and padded closer to the door. When I was just a few feet away, I holding my hands in front of my face like they might protect me, I shouted out.

"Just leave whatever you have there. Thank you!"

There was no response, but after several seconds, the bell didn't ring again. I was still hovering just in front of the door, unwilling to step forward or backward. After a good handful of minutes, I cautiously approached the door. Reaching out, I unlocked it, the heavy click making my nerves go haywire.

"Oh my God, you're being ridiculous, Andi. Come on."

I turned the knob and gently pulled the door open. The hallway beyond was empty. No one there and nothing to see. I peered down the hall in either direction, sticking my head out the door. *Nada.*

"Okaaay."

Even checking the floor to see if something had been left, I pulled up a whopping zero results. From my right, I thought I heard a clicking sound, but when I whipped my head in that direction. I didn't see anything.

"Hello?"

No response. With nothing else to do, I just ducked back inside. Shutting the door, sure to lock things up again, I realized there was a peep hole I could have used. But it was a little late for that now, wasn't it.

As I walked further into the penthouse, I noticed the clock hanging on the wall to my left. It had only been about forty minutes since Westley left. I needed to find a way to entertain myself if I was going to avoid going stir-crazy. Since masturbating was out of the question, I decided to check that closet for any other amenities it might have.

Maybe I could paint my nails or something. At the very least, I could go back to the playroom and mess around on those bars he had. My muscles would appreciate the good stretch after everything. Plan in hand, I wandered off back through the house again, silently hoping Westley would be home soon.

Because you are a pathetic sap, apparently.

12
The VIP Room

Westley

S low. The one thing no one in the tech industry, least of all the medical tech industry, could afford. And it was all over my fucking project with the new chip. The team was working their ass off, and I didn't blame them at all. It was a hard needle to thread. The thing had to be more than just efficient, it needed to be powerful, small, and it needed to be cost-effective.

That was taking far too fucking long, though.

I rubbed the bridge of my nose for the umpteenth time, so very ready to be home and back with the one person who seemed to always put me in a good mood. At least for the few days, I'd spent with her thus far.

Andi.

Damn, I needed to be home–like now. But, of course, rush hour traffic had other plans. As I passed through the familiar loops of the Harmstead spaghetti bowl, I switched on the radio. Using driving in silence gave me a chance to "have a conversation with myself," but right now, that sounded less than appealing. There was an event coming up in town, a convention for the tech sector at the large convention center, and I was due to present there about the chip.

The local station was blaring its advertisement for it, and my stomach clenched. I squeezed my fists on the steering wheel, unable to change the station while I was going through this large curve. *Dammit, that chip has to be ready.*

But you're going to fail again, aren't you? Just a fucking useless little baby. Go cry to your mommy.

My father's voice wormed through my mind, and I clenched my jaw. The pain of gripping the wheel so tight bloomed through my hands, slow and steady, but it did nothing to distract me from the familiar tirade of thoughts.

Dumb, pathetic, good-for-nothing excuse for a son. What the hell did I raise you to do? Fail? Work on some bullshit charity case instead of going for real success? You should be ashamed of yourself.

Bile rose up the back of my throat, and I just squeezed harder. My jaw actually cracked as the tension built, and shaking my head was doing nothing to dislodge the thoughts. The memories.

My father had been a piece of fucking shit, and even dead, he was haunting me with his verbal abuse. At least he couldn't hit me anymore. That was a plus.

A phantom pain seared through my back as the last of the loop straightened out and the ad on the radio finished. I could *feel* the hard slash across my skin like it was happening all over again.

"I want to go into the medical sector, Dad. I did a bunch of research. I know this major could be perfect for me. I'll be successful. I swear."

He raised the bottle higher, finishing it off. Why had

I gone and talked to him now? It was never smart to catch him when he'd been drinking.

Reality swirled then as my father beat me within an inch of my life. He smashed the empty bottle on his table, creating a jagged weapon.

"Ha, fucking whiny little brat pissing his pants because what? Because you're fucking scared of me? Good. I wanted a son, a man to carry on my legacy, and I got this waste of space. Don't ever come to me about this bullshit again, you hear me? You'll do what I fucking tell you."

"Please, Dad. Don't," I cried, begged. It was no use.

Consciousness flickered. I was fifteen. I was fifteen, and I was very likely going to die. My father pulled his hand back, and I faced away, trying to drag myself across the floor.

The broken glass tore through the flesh of my back, ripping me open and leaving me bleeding. So much pain. Just pain...forever.

A car honked at me as I nearly swerved into their lane, and I cursed. *Dammit.* My exit was just up ahead, and I managed to refocus, pushing down the past into the dark well where I kept it. But a darkness crawled through my veins, nasty and edged. I recognized this mood, and I knew there was only one way it was going to level out.

It was wrong of me–to want to use Andi like that, but I was going to do it all the same.

Because I had to.

As soon as the door opened, I was greeted with the excited call of my name. It was certainly a change from the usual. And I liked it–a lot.

"Westley!"

Andi ran up to me, wrapping her arms around my waist and squeezing hard. I hadn't been gone long. There was no way she missed me already. I'd only been gone for like four hours. Still, it was way too pleasant to have someone here to greet me, to welcome me home.

"Hey. Hmm," I squeezed her back, lowering my head to her hair and breathing deeply, "if this is the type of hello I get, maybe I'll go away more often."

She looked up at me, playfully scowling, and I couldn't help the laugh that slipped free. Stepping back, Andi cocked her head as she grinned.

"How was work?"

The question was so normal, and our relationship– or whatever it was–was anything but. My chuckle continued, carrying me through slipping off my jacket and walking to the couch. As I sat down, exhaustion pulled at the corners. I knew sleep would be a night-mare-infested wasteland right now, though. I needed a release.

I had a feeling we both might if Andi had been a good girl for me.

"Awful. I don't really want to talk about it."

Andi frowned, sitting next to me on the couch and taking my hand. "I'm sorry. Is there anything I can do?"

My cock immediately roared to life, stiffening behind my zipper. I narrowed my gaze on her, and Andi squirmed as she took in the intense change in my expression.

"As a matter of fact..." I pulled her into my lap,

kissing and nipping at her neck, "Yes. But I'd like to do something a bit special. If you're up for it."

Moaning low, Andi's thighs clenched around my own, and I lit up as she squeaked for me when I grazed my thumb over her nipple.

"Umm," she lightly giggled through the word, "okay. What did you have in mind?"

I pulled back just enough to look up at her, continuing to tease the hardened bud at the tip of her breast.

"Hmm, I want it to be a surprise. But I'll say one thing."

She squirmed against me, her pelvis seeking out attention as she straddled me. Fucking hell, I adored this woman. *My sweet, little pet.*

"Okaaay," Andi whispered. "What?"

Bucking against her in a sharp jab, I bounced Andi in my lap, making her clit smack against the firm length I was keeping from her.

"I think you've been a good girl. Based on the way that hungry pussy of yours is trying to grind against my cock."

Her cheeks flared bright red, and I surged; embarrassing her was so damn delicious.

"I was. I swear. No touching. I did go through the entire playroom, though. I was curious."

Laughing, I wound my fingers through her shoulder-length bob, gripping the roots and angling her head back. I nibbled at her neck, reaching between us with my free hand and flicking her clit. She yelped, and I damn near came right there. I was so wound up for her.

"That doesn't surprise me in the slightest. You're as curious as a cat, aren't you, my little kitten."

She struggled to nod against the hold I had on her hair.

"Hmm," I hummed against her neck, "then how about Daddy takes you out to the club again? Hmm? I want to parade my little pet around. I want to see how you handle VIP service."

She stilled slightly, her body continuing to tremble ever so slightly against me. "R-really? What...what does that entail?"

"Ah ah," I chastised, "It's a surprise. Understood?"

Andi nodded as much as she could against my grip. "I...I want to make you happy, sir. Whatever you want."

"Unf," I ground her down on my cock, "you are my good little girl, aren't you? I want you to get changed. I'll let you pick, but I need easy access to all of you. Got it?"

"Yes, sir."

"All right," I shifted to stand, planting Andi on her feet in front of me. "Off you go."

She whimpered gently, and I patted her ass. As I did, I felt just a hint of extra warmth, and I cocked a brow. Andi's blush deepened, and I spun her around, bending her over. On her light gray leggings was a visible wet spot, and my cock jerked inside my pants.

"Oh, precious." I rubbed my fingers against the area, and it just got wetter. "Did you make a pretty little mess in your pants? Are you *that* wet for Daddy?"

The delightful whine that left Andi was positively perfection, and she nodded as she whimpered in my grasp.

"Naughty, little pet. Go get changed."

Smacking against her pussy hard, I pulled Andi back up to stand and shoved her forward. She stumbled a bit before righting herself and practically sprinted up the stairs. I gripped my cock as I watched her run, squeezing so hard it hurt.

Plenty of time, Westley. You have all fucking night.

The Scarlett Oleander was packed as we entered, but the slave in service at the front door this evening knew exactly who I was. When he'd pulled my card and settled everything for the evening ahead, he nodded politely and led Andi and me back to the VIP booth that I'd used a few times before.

She was positively sinful in the outfit she'd chosen. Andi had clearly read the assignment, and I was damn impressed by her initiative.

The black leather cat mask she'd worn previously hid her face, and she'd paired it with the latex bra and panties I'd snuck into the wardrobe. The panties had a zippered crotch that wrapped all the way around to the very back, and Andi had put on a set of garters with them. The back-seemed stockings made her legs look miles long and stopped right at the middle of her thighs.

Best of all, my pet had found the thick collar I'd bought most recently and secured it around her neck, offering me the long chain that dangled from it like a leash.

Glowing red light seeped through every corner, and the comfortable deep black and maroon loungers in the cordoned-off area looked as decadent as ever. There was a circle of red beams, carved to look like gems, hanging around the round VIP booth, and the illusion of privacy it offered was enough that Andi relaxed more against my side as I pulled her next to me.

"Here you are, sir. I'll have the attendants you

requested delivered to your booth shortly. There is champagne just there for your enjoyment. Should you need anything, please don't hesitate to demand it from one of the slaves at your disposal."

I nodded, and the man left. When I looked over at Andi, the shocked expression she'd been holding back finally broke free.

"Slave? Demand? Holy shit, Westley, this is..."

Pulling her down to the comfortable booth, I smirked at her, running my hand up and down her arm.

"Sir."

Andi's eyes flared, and her lips parted. She quickly gave a tight nod and ducked her eyes to the floor.

"Of course. Sir." She was picking up on the rules quicker than I expected, and I adored it, honestly. She was a natural, the submission a part of her soul already, and I smiled, lifting her chin up.

"Good girl."

When she smiled, something in my chest tightened. But it wasn't the usual ache. I wasn't sure what it was, and right now wasn't the time to study it.

"I'm going to ask for several things from you, pet. I need you to use the safe word if necessary, but I'd like to see how far we can take this." I regarded her, doing my best to impart my meaning through just my expression. "Understood?"

Andi cocked her head, but then her brow furrowed, and she nodded.

"We haven't had as much time to discuss vocalizations before now. So, I'm going to ask even though it was technically in the contract."

That document felt like eons ago, and a refresher was always a good idea.

Chewing on her lip, Andi offered another nod. "All right. Do you want me to be...honest, sir?"

It was understandable that she needed clarification; in fact, it was a good sign that she was asking, and I echoed her nod.

"Yes. Now," I met her eyes, steady and unwavering, "I want to, well, there's no better way to say it than bluntly, so. I want to be mean to you, Andi. I want the *others* who are coming to be mean to you. Do you understand?"

She visibly swallowed, and that trickle of uncertainty–of fear–had my cock dying to be let out of its fabric cage. Andi wobbled her head, a tiny smirk touching the corner of her mouth.

"You've been pretty...fond of the degradation so far. Is that what you're referring to?"

I was impressed she remembered the word and happily confirmed. "Yes. I'd like to lean hard on that tonight. Yes?"

There was a pause, and as Andi chewed on her lip, I noticed her squirm ever so slightly in her seat.

"I...Yes. Can I...can I request something?" She had trouble meeting my eyes, and I lifted her chin again.

"Tell me. I'll see."

"Umm..." She sucked in a breath of air, hard and slow. "Can you just not use the word bitch? My, umm, my mother–"

"Understood. Bitch is a hard line. I won't cross that, and I'll inform the others."

Andi sagged into the seat, relaxing. "Okay, thank you. Sir."

Almost as if on cue, the crew of submissives I'd requested filtered into the private booth, and the last one to enter pulled the cord that shrouded the area with a black curtain. We would still be heard, of course, but the thick veil between us and the rest of the club offered a deeper sense of privacy, which I knew Andi would appreciate.

"Excellent."

I looked around. The attendants were dressed in the attire I favored—the female presenting in a variety of lace masks and leather harnesses, the male presenting in thick leather pants with structured black masks, and the nonbinary individuals secured in the option that suited them best in this case, one in pants with tape secured over their nipples and the other in a harness and a lace mask.

When I looked over at Andi, she shivered, and I clocked the wide dilation of her pupils as she roamed her stare over the people there. God, I loved her innocent naivete. I loved *taking* it from her.

The submissives knelt down on the floor in front of us, unspeaking and simply waiting for a command. Exactly the way I liked it. I scooted closer to Andi on the luxurious velvet booth. Her entire body shook, but she couldn't tear her eyes away from the people gathered in front of her. I grinned, pulling her neck to my mouth and nibbling greedily.

Sucking in a breath against her skin, I reached for her hand, moving it to my cock. "Goddamn, pet. I can't wait to see you break for them."

She moaned low, turning to face me as she rolled her hand up and down my erection through my pants. But I could feel the tremble in her limbs.

"What?"

Andi chuckled nervously. "I just...I didn't think *this* was what you had planned. I'm honestly surprised."

"Oh, sweet pet. This is just the beginning."

13
The Share

Andi

My pulse fluttered hummingbird fast, and I was spinning from the desperate need clawing through my body. My pussy pulsed, hungry for something to ease the ache of emptiness, and I fucking *dripped*.

"Cuff her."

The slave closest to me pulled out a set of leather handcuffs, the inside cushioned with faux fur, and moved closer. He took my hands, guiding them behind my back and locking them together behind me.

Everything felt suddenly small, and that pound in my chest doubled down. I was terrified, but that was only serving to ramp up the arousal pooling between my legs. When the slave stepped back, I felt so exposed again, and I longed for that presence near me again—all of their presence even.

I was just in underwear essentially, and I could *sense* the weight of each person in the oversized "booth" intimately. When Westley had used the word, I had to fight back a scoff. This was far more than just a booth; it was basically a room. Plenty big enough for everyone there and then some.

More like a pool cabana. A filthy, filthy pool cabana.

Westley got up from the seat, standing before me and reaching for something on the low coffee table that sat in the middle of the circular layout. As he held it out in front of me, I realized it was a lace mask. As I looked up at him, I settled into the cuffs holding my wrists behind my back.

It was strange how badly I wanted the people there to do whatever Westley had in mind, and not only because I knew it would get him off. I wanted that attention.

Being a performer, I enjoyed being in the spotlight to a degree, and the idea of combining sex with that level of intense focus, well, damn. Sign me right the fuck up. What was strange was that Westley wanted to share. Possessive was an understatement when it came to the usual vibes he gave off.

I stared into those gorgeous green eyes of his.

"Are...are you sure, Sir?"

Westley secured the lace over my eyes. I couldn't truly see, just flashes of changing light as they all hovered around me.

"Yes, pet. I want to watch them make you fall apart."

The comfort of his hands on my head disappeared, and I searched in vain for him. There was definitely something about a blindfold. I was already helpless to move, but cutting off my vision? That kicked things right up to the stratosphere.

Suddenly, Westley's lips were at my ear, whispering. "Not one of them is going to touch that pretty pussy of yours. They're going to use every other part of you, and only when you're begging for release am I going to fuck Daddy's cunt."

I clenched around nothing, at once ravenous and petrified in the best possible way.

"Go on then. Make my date lose her damn mind."

And then they were on me. With my limited vision, I had no way of telling who was doing what, and the thought that I was being completely used, taken from every angle by every type of person, was exhilarating and sinful. I'd never been much concerned about gender. Hot was hot, right, and this, *this* was a fucking inferno.

The zipper at my crotch slid all the way back, exposing me, and a hand yanked my leg up and out of the way. A hard slap detonated on my ass, and I shrieked. There was no warm-up or restraint, and the pain zinged through me until it settled in my core, making my pussy flutter.

As soon as my mouth was open, a cock was shoved inside. It wasn't Westley. I knew his size and shape, but whoever this was could boast nearly as much as my Dom could. He picked up a furious pace in seconds, and I drooled everywhere as he fucked my mouth mercilessly.

More sets of hands shoved the latex fabric away from my breasts, pinching my nipples. I cried out around the cock in my mouth as the squeezed me terribly hard. My pussy clenched, and still nothing touched it. The person at my backside laid down another slap before I heard the sound of spit, and warmth was spread across my asshole.

Oh, holy shit. Oh, God. I'll come in seconds.

A finger drove into me, fucking my ass, and I moaned, the erection testing my jaw sinking deep. I thrust back against the wonderful sensations, feeling the phantom pleasure worming through my pussy as whoever was there stroked me. I was right there, right on the edge. I just needed a little–

"Don't you dare come. Daddy's filthy little slut will not come until I say so." A hand gripped my hair, yanking my head back and sending the dick popping out. I immediately knew it was Westley. "Understood, pet?"

I nodded against his grip. "Yes, sir."

My voice was scratchy and harsh even as my mouth was dripping with saliva.

"That's right. Such a fucking whore. You're such a sinful little slut, loving how they use you."

All I could do was nod again. My brain had completely left the building.

"Get her on her back. I want to see you *all* ride her."

I had no idea how that was supposed to work, but then suddenly, I was flipped over and a pillow was shoved under my hips and at my back. They forced me to arch, but it took the pressure off my hands. *Clever.*

Before I could be too grateful, however, a different body part was shoved in my face. Warmth enveloped my mouth as wet pussy was glided across my lips. The taste exploded on my tongue, and I eagerly began to lap up everything that was offered.

Sensation got hard to map at that point. My own cunt throbbed, begging for attention as a cock found my asshole and probed in just a few inches. I whimpered and moaned against the slick riding my face, delving my tongue as deep as I could reach. The moans coming from the owner lit up my center, and then a hard length smacked against my breast, sliding back and forth across my nipple.

God, that's fucking...Oh, shit....

Whoever was doing that alternated with flicking and pinching the pebbled flesh, and I screamed against the clit I was sucking when the pain ticked up another notch. At my other breast, and I could not understand how, I felt slick warmth gliding across my nipple. Slippery juices coated my skin, and I could picture whoever this person was rubbing their cunt over my breast.

The seconds dragged on like that, every bit of my body used–except for my pussy. Holy God, did it *ache*.

Clenching, the woman at my mouth came against my tongue as I enjoyed the feeling of sucking her clit into my mouth and making her legs quiver. It tasted divine, but was quickly pulled away.

A hard slap cracked down over my cunt and then my cheek. It had to be Westley, and then he was whispering in my ear again.

"Filthy fucking whore. You're a goddamn slut, eating up that pussy like your life depended on it." His fist went around my throat, squeezing, and my eyes flared behind the lace. "You're just a cum slut, aren't you. A set of holes to be used like the fuck toy, you are. Say it. Say you're Daddy's little fuck toy."

Desperate tears fell from my eyes as my pussy throbbed. "I'm Daddy's little fuck toy."

"Yes, you are." He smacked my cunt again, the dick in my ass pulsing as I clamped down. "You're covered in all their juices like a fucking dildo."

Time blurred, and I didn't know how much more I could take. I was truly covered in writhing bodies that milked mine for all it was worth. If I didn't come I was going to fucking *die* at this rate. My clit *ached*, every tiny sensation from my ass, from everywhere, going straight to the oversensitive bud, and driving me further into madness.

"Cover her in your cum."

My mind reeled behind the intoxicating lust that swirled through me. It was by far one of the most depraved things I could think of, being coated in these slaves' spend, and I was *dying* for it–like the good little slut I was.

The panting and moaning picked up, slippery body parts used me to get off. It started with the woman who'd ridden my tongue. She came back for a brief few sucks before she pulled away, only to grunt low as she made herself come all over my face. The cock on my breast was next, coating me in sticky ropes of cum that reached from my neck to my ribs.

"That's right, little whore. You'll take everything they give you. Fucking disgusting goddamn slut." Westley's cock shoved in my mouth, and he gritted out a low groan as he rammed into me. "Daddy's abused fucking toy."

Part of my brain wanted me to feel guilty about enjoying myself so much, but I quickly dismissed it. Because you know what? Fuck that noise. I was living for this depravity. I was a fucking whore, and goddamn, it felt amazing.

Warmth splattered over my breast as the other person there squirted across me, and before it even finished, my lower belly and slit was covered in cum as the cock slipped free of my ass. The incredible array of sensations, Westley battering my throat, was too damn much.

I was going to come.

Moaning against him, I cried out all the harder as I tried to fight back the orgasm clawing forward. Westley pulled back, smacking my face twice more.

"Are you crying? Does Daddy's whore need to come so bad that she's fucking crying."

I sobbed harded, my clit burning. "Yes! Please, sir!"

His voice was right at my ear, the quietest whisper. "Beg me."

"Please, sir," I heaved in a breath, my pussy slowly weeping onto the floor, "I beg you. Please, I need to come."

He didn't say anything, and for several moments I worried that he was going to leave me like that–nearly destroyed for the horrible urge to orgasm.

But then his cock shoved so far into my cunt that he hit my cervix, and I screamed, soaring off into the most intense climax yet. My entire body jerked and thrashed at is shattered apart, my pussy clamping down on Westley's thick cock in rhythmic pulls that demanded his cum along with all the others.

He barreled into me, fucking without mercy. Grabbing my throat, Westley pistoned with everything he had. My brain fogged, spinning as the oxygen-depleted in my blood.

"Dirty little whore." He thrust up into me, bottoming out and grinding upward against my G-spot until warmth surged forward. "That's it, little slut. Squirt all over Daddy's cock."

And I did. I damn well gushed all over. So fucking much that it puddled beneath me despite the pillow trying to soak it all up. A furious growl rumbled through Westley, and then he pulled back, yanking my head up by the hair.

"Open your fucking mouth."

I did as told, and Westley grunted before spraying his thick, hot cum over my face and mouth.

"That's right. Eat up, whore."

Ropes of it covered me, spreading over the mask and coating my tongue in its bitter, salty goodness.

The world slowed down, and after several *long* moments, I realized that Westley and I were alone in the VIP room. Something warm and fragrant smoothed across my skin as the lace mask was removed. I blinked against the suddenly brighter light.

"Don't rush. You'll be lightheaded."

I nodded. My vision was crap, but it was a wash-cloth. A heated, lavender-scented washcloth was being dragged over my skin, cleaning me up. I smiled.

"Ugh, that was...Mmm." I hummed like I'd eaten something yummy. "I did good."

A stupid chuckle trickled out of me, and then my wrists were freed from the cuffs.

"You did excellent, pet. Now," Westley kissed my cheek, "let's get you home."

Home. The thought reverberated through my skull. But it was true. I was going home.

14
The Watch

Him

They'd gone inside that wretched club. Filthy, depraved nonsense. Fucking rich people bullshit, with their private club and swanky sex clothes. *Horrendous*. And I couldn't follow them in there. Security was too tight, and I most certainly did not have an invitation.

Bunch of bullshit.

My ass bones ached from sitting in the beat-up sedan. Two hundred dollars on Craigslist. Barely ran, but it was clean. No plates, no previous owner to come looking because I stole it. As good a choice as any when I'd been forced to stoop this low.

Because of *him*.

Coffee had gone cold hours ago. I was fucking tired. I hadn't been sleeping. Too busy. I had to watch. I had to *see*.

See too much of that fucking prick bastard and his whore.

Andi. That's what he'd called her. I wanted to break her. *Hurt* her. She belonged to him. I wanted to take

143

what belonged to him. I *needed* to. He'd fucked me over too damn hard, tossed me aside like some lousy rat. A neck to step on his way up to the top.

"I don't fucking think so, Westley. No fucking chance."

People came out of the club, lust-drunk and disgusting. The tips of my fingers itched, hungry to tear their stupid eyes out. Rich pieces of self-entitled shit. They all deserved to get wiped off the earth. Damn them *all* to hell. But a yawn dragged through me. *Can't have that.*

I reached for the coffee anyway. Cold was better than nothing. *Where are they? Taking his sweet time fucking that whore. All they do is* fuck.

Turning to the seat beside me, I fingered through the stack of photos. Shitty, newfangled versions of Polaroids. They were fast and easy. Stores didn't sell the good shit anymore. *Had to settle for some hipster bullshit. Works, I guess.*

Westley fucking his whore, this Andi lying back against the piano—her cunt up in his face; it was all there. Even the image of her sticking that useless pretty face out in the hall. I'd snapped a good one then.

Useless hipster bullshit came in handy. The store had even sold a zoom lense for the tiny camera. It was powder blue, like a leisure suit. Christ, these kids these days. Not a lick of sense in their empty heads.

I smoothed my thumb across the picture of her face. Pretty skin and deep blue eyes. She was a looker. A looker that looked real young. Youngest I'd seen around him. Yeah, it'd only been a few months, six or seven, but she'd been pure, unprivileged. Not anymore. He'd tainted her, taken away her safety net when he'd pulled her into his stupid fucking penthouse.

Can't have it all and still be clean. No fucking way.

My nail curved into the image, scratching through her face in a thin, jagged line. I liked it–cracking her.

Going to tear you apart, pretty. Going to hurt you real good, so your Westley suffers. I turned down the corners of my mouth, considering. *Maybe have some fun too.*

I liked little tits, after all. A horrid fact that the piece of rich shit and I had something in common. Thick nipples, though. I could see a knife taking them clean off, a little snack for later.

The door to the club opened again. I looked up–to see *them*. Westley was wrapped around his precious slut. A car pulled up quickly, the driver stepping out and letting them inside. He'd let her go first. The Andi girl's legs were wobbly. Stupid cunt. She'd let herself get fucked silly.

I fired up the car, gripping the shifter and yanking it down into drive. It could be his fucking neck. I'd break it real nice.

But they took off fast, and I needed to keep up. I followed them back to Westley's penthouse. I wanted to throw a brick through every damn window. Penthouse-living bastards all deserved a brick to the face. Dead and done with.

Stepping out of the car, I walked up to the security gate to slip inside and take the elevator. They weren't switching shifts, though, so I couldn't get in now. I had to wait. *I hate waiting.*

Moving to the back of the building, I caught a glimpse of my reflection in a window pane–dirty, tired, thin. Had I always been like that? Like...this? So... broken? No. Yes? I'd had money, enough anyway. Westley took that away. And I...

But this had been there beneath the surface. That's what everyone would have said. I got along well with people–knew when they were scamming me. I don't like to be scammed.

Or fired.

Normal guy loses his mind after losing his job. Easy enough. And true. To an extent, anyway.

There was a smaller building next to this one. I could get up on top of the roof through the staff access elevator. I'd set up up there. Binoculars, camera, bedroll, I had everything I needed to watch and stay comfy.

They got inside the penthouse. Andi girl was still wobbly. Westley carried her to the bedroom. They went to bed quickly. Tomorrow, I would call. I'd say hello. Or not. Plans change, after all.

15

The Spa Service

Andi

Soft, silky sheets were warm beneath me as I stretched and came back to consciousness. My wrists ached. I had new sore spots on my ass too, and damn, if that didn't make me beam inside. Westley was in the bed next to me, and as I looked at him, sleeping peacefully with his dark hair, a wonderful mess around him, my chest *ached*.

God, what had happened was...I couldn't put it into words. There was no way I hadn't enjoyed it, but...Did Westley? Did he really?

Part of me still felt so torn up in knots that I'd enjoyed other sex partners, even if it was at his instructions. Not that I had a problem with non-monogamy, it was just unfamiliar. And hell, I had been brought up in the States. Sex-positive was not the way of things here.

Westley stirred, and I smiled as he rolled over to face me, his gorgeous green eyes opening as he moaned happily.

"Hi." My voice was tiny.

"Good morning, pet. Sleep well?"

I couldn't help the chuckle. "Ha, umm, yeah. Like the dead. I was damn exhausted, after all. You completely spent me up."

He maneuvered across the bed, pulling me into his arms and kissing me. "Good. I like you that way."

With a hard swallow, I blinked, tracking my stare down and then back up at him. "Did you?"

"Did I what?" Westley's brow was furrowed, tangled up in wrinkles of confusion.

My mouth felt like it was lined with sandpaper, and I had to sit up in the bed. Lying there next to him didn't feel right, and as I moved up into a seat, I hissed. Westley's smirk nearly stopped me from vocalizing my inner struggle, but I knew he'd get it out of me eventually.

"Did you like last night? Was it...okay?"

His brows shot up to his hairline, and Westley chuckled. "Are you serious, pet?"

Westley's tone was light, but I still frowned, slumping into myself.

"Hey, hey, now." He quickly followed me up to sit and wrapped his arms around me. "None of that. I adored last night. I asked for it, didn't I?"

Nodding slowly, I leaned more into him. The feeling of Westley's strong body around me helped me find myself in my bones again, and I sighed.

"You did, yes. I...I know I'm being silly. It's just..." I struggled to find some tactful way of saying what was on my mind, so instead, I went with the Andi special–blurting it out completely bluntly. "I cannot believe anyone was okay with watching me get fucked by a gaggle of slaves at a sex club. I enjoyed it *way* more than I ever thought I would, and I didn't even tell you that I was okay with other genders, so I don't know how you knew that would be kosher. I'm really glad it was, but man, years of purity culture and a monogamous-central upbringing are not making this easy for me to admit I like."

The was a tiny pause where I considered just running away despite being naked, and the firm belief I had that Westley would just hunt me down and find me. And didn't that just bring up another host of wild emotions over how much of a BDSM slut I was turning out to be?

And then Westley laughed, pulling me against his chest and kissing the top of my head.

"Oh, pet. I really love how blunt you can be. *And*, more importantly, I get it. This world largely has just one way it wants you to be. When you don't fit into that mold, it can be extremely debilitating. Living as someone who isn't you is torture. I hope...I hope that going to the club with me, experiencing all this with me..."

He gestured around us.

"Has made you feel seen. Your desires recognized." Westley tipped my chin up so he could gaze down into my eyes, and like always, I lost myself to those deep emerald irises. "And *tended* to."

I didn't think it was possible for a human to actually melt into a puddle, and yet, there I was, boneless and made of liquid as Westley's words sunk into me–into my damn soul.

I smiled–from ear to damn ear. "Thank you, Westley. I l–"

But I stopped myself. Now was not the time for that. He quirked a brow, and I went with the only other thing that was demanding my attention right now.

"Ha, well, I'm fucking starving. Do you think..." I shrugged. "Food?"

His warm chuckle bled into me, and Westley gave a quick nod. "Of course. Breakfast it is."

As Westley took away the plates of french toast, which I'd cleaned every inch of just shy of licking the damn thing, I leaned back in my chain. I was stuffed, my belly content now that it was full of sweet, cinnamony goodness. My fingers were still a bit sticky from scooping up a bit of the syrup, and I grabbed a napkin from the island to wipe them off. It wasn't exactly working.

"Ugh, I need a shower."

Westley hummed. "Oh, that actually reminds me."

He set the dishes down in the sink and rinsed them off a bit before joining me at the island again. As he wrapped his arms around me, leaning down to nuzzle into my neck, I squirmed happily in my chair. His beard tickled against the side of my neck, and I had a feeling that we'd both get a bit too distracted if I didn't pump the breaks.

"Reminds you of what?" I leaned back, making him look at me.

Westley narrowed his eyes, obviously a little displeased, but he sighed and nodded.

"I've set up a spa day for you. They'll be here in about an hour if you'd like to get into something comfortable and freshen up a bit."

My mouth fell open. "I'm sorry, what?"

"A spa service. They're coming to the penthouse

soon. You should probably get moving if you're thinking of showering."

I was completely flabbergasted, just sitting there with my mouth hanging open. Catch a fly in there. I think that's what the old folks would say, and I had to physically remind myself with a headshake to close the thing back up.

"You arrange for me," I pointed to my chest, "me, to get a spa service in your penthouse? W-why?"

The smile that spread over Westley's face was maddening. He was so damn handsome, with those deep green eyes and silver streaks in his hair. I could die right now and just be thrilled I was looking at him when I kicked the bucket.

I could also tell that he was very much up to something.

That smirk wasn't just a bit of teasing pride. There was something sadistic and lustful about it, and I shivered, my pussy clenching.

"I want to do something nice for you. And," If possible, the smirk lit up even more. "I want you to get good and pampered, really relax and enjoy everything they can do for you because afterward..."

Lightning fast, Westley slipped his fingers up my neck, fisting my hair and yanking my head back into a deep bend.

"You're going to be my good little whore and take everything I give you. Last night was round one, Andi dearest," His gaze darkened, and he crawled the other hand beneath my shirt, finding my breast and pinching my nipple brutally, "and round two is going to be so much worse."

Oh, how I reeled. My entire body went haywire at just

this little tease. I was already so gone for this man, this incredible, brutal, sadistic man, and I was looking forward to this evening more than I could put into words.

I nodded against his grip, whimpering and mewling as he tweaked my nipple harder. When he abruptly let go, I actually crumpled, and it was his reflexes that kept me from falling to the ground.

"Oh, pet. You're staining your panties again. Go get changed. Your pampering will begin soon."

Dizzying arousal bore through me like a hot knife. I forced myself to stand and nod again. Westley looked positively tickled that I was such a puddle again, and I really didn't care how pathetic I looked. As I cleared my throat and started toward the stairs, I could *feel* the wetness between my legs, and my cheeks burned.

But I hesitated on the bottom step for just a moment. "What are you going to do?"

"Unfortunately, I have to deal with some work nonsense. Don't worry about it. I'll meet you in the playroom, as you call it, when it's time."

He wouldn't be around at all? For the entire day? Oh, hell, I wasn't going to make it. But I just offered another nod and turned to head up to the shower. Still, Westley had looked...concerned when he said he had to work. There was definitely something there, but I didn't want to pry. I'd ask him about it later.

For now, it was apparently time to get ready for a spa service, which was a first for me.

P ampered had not cut it when it came to the sheer amount of treatments that Westley had arranged for me. I'd had my nails done–both sets, mind you–the fire-engine red polish glossy and shining, I'd had an IV to ensure I was hydrated, and two massages. Yes, two. One was traditional, with incredible lavender-smelling oils, and the other had been with smooth, hot stones that glided across my body like silk. That one had also been paired with an exfoliation treatment for my entire body.

Oh, and I was freshly waxed–everywhere.

There had been two facials, a gentle chemical peel and a hydrating mask, which went along with a massage for my actual face. Special fucking air had been brought in. This strange device that I got to inhale as my legs were waxed, which did help to dull the sting.

I'd worried about how my bruises and marks would come across to these people, but a strange part of me felt that they were Scarlett Oleander employees of some sort.

A mask for my entire body, light therapy, and even a trim and style for my hair. There was certainly more than had gone on, too many products and treatments to name, but after the first hour or so, my brain had gone fuzzy, and I was just blissed out through the entire experience.

I felt like a new person, and damn, I looked incredible, my skin glowing.

It was a bit of a shame about the hair and light makeup because I knew they were going to ruin it short, but looking at myself in the mirror was so nice that I didn't care for a minute.

It was nearly time to meet Westley in the playroom,

and one of my attendants for the day helped me to slip on a robe.

"Ms. Andi. We do hope you've enjoyed your day." I nodded as she took my arm gently. "Now, if you wouldn't mind coming with me. I'll help you into the attire Mr. R.O.B. has chosen for you."

My eyebrows raised, and I nodded. She'd confirmed my suspicions. Not only had she used his name from the club, but she was actually going to help me get outfitted for the fun he had planned. With an easy smile, the woman gestured for the door, and I laughed a little as I walked out of the bedroom with her to the playroom.

"Is something funny, Ms. Andi?" She didn't say it rudely, but there was a hair of coldness to her voice.

"No, I'm sorry. It's just, umm, Mr. R.O.B. I should have known he'd do something like this, but he's always surprising me."

She grinned, and I noticed a hint of sadistic joy in her eyes, like Westley's.

"You like it," she said.

It wasn't a question, and I nodded. "I do. Umm, what's your name. If I can ask."

The woman's eyes were a very pale blue and paired with her black hair, it was a striking combination. I'd be lying if I said I wasn't interested in spending time with her if Westley decided to bring me to the club like that again. She was a bit taller than me as well, probably five-eight, and her curvy body was like something out of a naught cartoon, very Jessica Rabbit.

"I'm Elle. I work as a Domme at the Scarlett Olean-der. I have a history in management as well. Makes me a good fit to wrangle the girls."

She cocked her head toward the bedroom, and I giggled, smiling easily around her.

"Well, it's a pleasure to meet you. I...I appreciate what you've done today. They did great."

Elle ran her eyes over my body, the appreciation there unmistakable, and I shivered. "They did, didn't they. I guess I won't be too hard on them then. Unless they're naughty on the way back."

My pussy clenched as I met her eyes, and damn, I was ready for Westley now. Of course, I was already ready for him, but this woman, this Domme, was incredible.

"After you, Andi."

She held her hand out toward the playroom door, and I swallowed, nerves suddenly getting the better of me.

Her voice was suddenly right at my ear, her hand at the small of my back—firm and warm. "Let's get you dressed for your Master, hmm?"

16
The Calls

Westley

The office was quiet except for the sound of my fingers rattling away over the keyboard. I had three more emails to send before this meeting with the new investor for the microchip, and I'd been delaying sending them for too long. Still, I was a perfectionist when it came to the design releases, and even if these were just upgrades to the existing tech, I wanted them to be spotless and utterly free of error.

I'd checked out the design schematics for the last one that came through and noted in the document when I saw some useful updates. The team was doing great, however. I knew they'd been working hard on each of the improvement blueprints, and I couldn't avoid being impressed by their work.

Not that I was looking to. I hired the best and the bright for a reason. I knew well enough that no man is an island. You can't achieve greatness without a team— or have great sex, sometimes.

I laughed to myself. Fuck, last night had been damn incredible, and my cock thickened in my pants just thinking of how wonderfully filthy Andi had wound up. Moreover, that intriguing part of me that swelled to life at just the thought of her beamed in my chest.

She's all fucking mine, and I couldn't be happier about that.

My fingers stilled on the keyboard. It wasn't necessarily new to be feeling possessive over a submissive like I was, but this...this was stronger than any bond I'd had with one of my slaves yet. Andi was...

"Okay, you need to focus. You have a meeting in five minutes."

I logged into my account and opened the video chat program, then opened the meeting room provided for me and Mr. Brunswick, the latest investor from Germany interested in supporting the new chip's development.

I hated the sound on my home computer, so I opted to dial in through the phone line with the video there on most occasions. As I reached to press the speaker button to call the unique number on-screen for the meeting, the phone rang.

Jumping a little, I followed through with motion, opening up the line and answering. Maybe it was the club needing one of the girls back.

"Mr. Stanton."

I waited for a response. I waited a good ten seconds for a response and got nothing. The line was connected. I could see as much on the phone display, but it was just dead air.

"If you can hear me, I'm hanging up. Try back to see if the call goes through."

Clicking the phone off of speaker, I waited a moment but it didn't ring again, so I started to dial the number for the meeting. The other line rang when I was halfway through the number. The second line was rarely ever called, but some investors had the number, so I answered. *Just in case.*

"Hello, this is Mr. Stanton. Can you hear me this time?"

The line was open, and still, I was getting dead air. However, this time, I could actually hear something in the background. Breathing? Wind? There was something there, which meant the call had definitely gone through.

"Hello? Do you plan on talking?"

Nothing.

"All right. I'm done."

I hung up again, immediately going to dial the number for the meeting. The line rang—again. I didn't bother answering this time. If it was an investor with maybe a shitty connection or something, they could call back. As it was, I was damn sure this was just a stupid kid, and I didn't have time for that shit.

"Fucking pranksters."

The line connected to the video chat service, and in less than a minute, Mr. Brunswick was on the screen, smiling professionally as he nodded his hello.

"Mr. Stanton. Good of you to meet with me like this. It's difficult for me to leave the country right now with a newborn."

"Congratulations, Mr. Brunswick. Is this your first child?" I smiled, acting very much the part of being interested even though I was ready to get this meeting moving already.

"It is. And it's been a long journey. My wife has been through a lot, which is actually why I'm looking to broaden my horizons into medical technologies."

The man was about thirty-five. Good skin and a

thick head of light brown hair provided solid assets, and he faced the screen head-on without flinching. I could tell he was a shrew businessman, and hearing him mention that he was diversifying his portfolio gave me the idea that this new child had opened his eyes to the unfairness of life.

He wanted to be better for his kid. Not a bad motivation as far as business went, and I nodded back at him as he turned the floor over to me. *Not everyone gets all moral when they have a kid. Probably didn't start off too rough.*

"I see. Well, I admire that compunction of yours. The world needs our tech to make its citizens happier and healthier. I aim to provide research that will be invaluable throughout the coming decades, starting with this new microchip processor for cardiac medical devices."

Brunswick smiled, and I leaned back more comfortably in his chair. I was damn good at reading people, my poker opponents would attest to that, and it was a good sign that the guy felt ready to get more comfortable in his chair.

"Excellent. Well, I understand that funds are obviously required, especially for this significant undertaking. When are we looking for the release date of the initial prototype?"

My least favorite part of weeding out potential investors was getting through this section of the discussion. Fast did not produce results. You want fast, you get crap; that's always been my motto, but bigwigs the world over don't seem to understand that the development of anything can't be rushed to meet their deadlines.

"We're working on moving into phase two of the

project by the end of the month. That will consist of actually drafting up a lifesize model and seeing to basic security and performance checks. Overheating, shortage, malfunction, the words. A true beta test prototype won't be ready until likely the end of the year."

There was a pause, and I worried this was where I'd lost him. I preferred being honest upfront, however. I wasn't here for leading the investors on, promising too much and then having to bail my ass out when the unachievable plans were, in fact, not achieved.

"That looks like a fair timeline. I know you don't want to rush development with something so crucial."

That was the best response I could have hoped for.

"Exactly. Thank you."

Brunswick held up a pen, looking over his desk for a piece of paper, and then skribbled something down.

"Perfect. Well, okay, so I'm making a note here to get with your finance department on Monday so that we can go over the specifics of what looking for the most support right now. I know your company is still private at this time, and I'd like you to maintain that for as long as we can as your investor. Public share gouging can push the chip to a place where it's speed over results. You know this."

I nodded, impressed by the guy's know-how. "I do. And that sounds wonderful. My CFO is Isaac Jackson. His team can help to take care of all the details, and I'm always available whenever you need me."

"Excellent. Thank you so much, Mr. Stanton."

Smiling genuinely, I nodded. "Please, Westley is fine. Mr. Stanton reminds me too much of my father."

I offered a tension-breaking laugh, and Mr. Brunswick was quick to join in. "Oh, man. It's that just the thing. That older generation. Well, excellent, Westley.

You can certainly call me Conrad in the future. I look forward to working with you."

At that, a newborn cry sounded in the background, and we both laughed. "Well, at least she has good timing. Talk soon, Westley."

"Talk soon. Send my regards to your wife, Conrad."

"Thank you."

With that, the call ended, and what I'd worried would be another letdown had turned into one of the best damn investor calls I'd had all year. *Thank God. I needed that win.*

When I closed out the window for the meeting, I saw that a new email had come in while I was chatting with Conrad. I clicked open the message. It was from Marnie, the head of HR.

Mr. Stanton,

Hello, I just wanted to inform you that the company's restraining order against Mr. Owen Adkins has been granted by the police department. Captain Geofferies has faxed a copy of the report and standing order to the HR department, and I have filed it with Mr. Adkins's employment information.

Additionally, Captain Geofferies included in his fax a note made for you to let you know that the theft of company property, which we are also filing charges against Mr. Adkins for, is currently under investigation with his lead detective, Mr. Calloway.

Please let me know if there's anything else that you need.

Marnie Hopkins
Director of Human Resources
Stanton Technologies, Inc.

. . .

I shot off a quick response, thanking Marnie for her email, but the email had nearly soured the good mood I was in. Adkins had been a thorn in my side for some time now, and as far as disgruntled employees went, he took the cake.

As I closed up the laptop and stood up from my desk, I jotted down a note to send Captain Geofferies a thank you for everything he was doing. He'd been there for me a number of times over the years, thanks to my situation with my father, and knowing I could count on him even now was a relief.

The sun was setting outside my office window, and the oranges and reds of the late sunlight were gorgeous. Red was by far a favorite color of mine, I noted absently, and I imagined the playroom where Andi was waiting. Black and red with pops of chrome. What a sweet way to end the evening.

I packed the laptop into my briefcase, grabbing the bit of other paperwork I needed to take back to the office with me tomorrow. Leaving my things at the ready for me come morning, I walked to the door, shutting off the lights as I reached the threshold.

That setting sun spilled otherworldly light into the room, and I glanced out at the cityscape. My office view was incredible for certain, but that familiar pang ricocheted through my chest as my mind kicked up the same bullshit thoughts that it always did when I tried to let myself just be...me.

Useless, good for nothing son. You'll never live up to your father's name, and you'll carry those scars with you forever.

Swallowing hard, pressure from every angle threatened to drown me. I needed out of my head. I needed something good, something mine, something that I could watch *break* all for me.

As far as coping mechanisms went, mine were shitty. But I wasn't looking to change them anytime soon, and unlike others, I knew how to reel it in. I'd never truly hurt Andi. I couldn't.

But regardless of how strong that emotion flared in my chest, I still wasn't ready to consider why that was, why she was the only sub I'd ever had in the penthouse–living with me. The only one I wanted to keep.

Forever.

17
The Degradation

Westley

As I left the office, I turned down the hall toward the far end where my playroom sat. Yes, even I was calling it that now. My mind was still itchy, unwanted thoughts invisibly simmering at the back of my head. I could never be rid of them, not truly.

But this helped push them so far down that I could breathe again.

My shoes clicked against the wood floors, and I scanned over the photography and art prints that lined the walls leading up to my destination. They stoked that low burn in my gut that was hungry for this kind of release so very often—and for Andi always.

The women from the club who'd come to work their magic were instructed to leave through the front as soon as they were finished. I checked the security feed, seeing them leave out the other side of the door and turned the remote lock on my door to engaged. *Ah, there we are.*

A comforting chime sounded from the app as the security system armed once more, and I stopped outside the playroom to deposit my phone on the small table just outside the door. That's what it was for, of course. Entry into the playroom meant that everyone involved, including myself, would be checking their worldly responsibilities at the door.

Relinquishing my hold on the cell, I reached for the knob, sucking in a deep breath before I finally opened the door. Anticipation was half the fun, and I was dying to see how Andi had turned out.

The first thing I saw as I entered was my sweet pet down on her knees, facing the door with her palms facing up and awaiting my instruction.

Goddamn. Absolutely beautiful.

Next to pique my interest was, unsurprisingly, the splendid cat mask that I'd first chosen for Andi. It fit her so perfectly, my naughty kitten, and I adored seeing her in it. Now, it was paired with a full-body leather harness that hugged Andi's slim dancer's body brilliantly. The harness evoked similar vibes as the leotard that she'd worn to the club to perform, and I picked it out specially for today, having it rush delivered.

I ran my eyes across her body, marveling at the way the outfit accentuated her tiny waist. There were shoulder straps that wrapped around her arms, of course, but they uniquely connected to three crucial sections of the design. One, the straps that crossed diagonally over her breasts. Two, the underbust section that had a large metal o-ring secured to the center. And third, to the thick collar that encircled her neck, which also had an o-ring and a leather strip that ran between Andi's breasts, connecting the entire piece.

She also wore a matching leather garter that nipped in her waist and supplied two o-rings on either side that secured to Andi's wrists on the cuffs she wore. She still had a good degree of motion available to her, but she was still quite stuck with her hands, only able to go about six inches from her waist.

The garter did connect to leg pieces, but not the traditional stockings. No, that wasn't nearly good enough for my precious little slut. Instead, the two straps that ran down her thighs on the front and back connected to leather cuffs similar to the collar with o-rings in the middle.

"Oh, pet." I stalked forward, circling around her and inspecting every visible inch of her. "Look at my good kitty, all ready to play."

Her tits were framed so beautifully by the harness, and I had access to that tight pussy and asshole however I wanted them. Andi's fair skin was glowing as well. I could tell the ladies had truly gone above and beyond for her, and it warmed me through to my core as my cock throbbed.

I dragged my thumb across her lips as I came to stand in front of her, cocking my head as I peered hungrily down at the lovely creature waiting so patiently for my punishment.

Andi moaned subtly, keeping her head lowered. "You're doing well, listening to what the Domme said to do. I'm glad."

I could hear the slight intake of breath as Andi basked in the praise. I was happy to give it to her because there was little more coming after this moment.

"Andi," I slipped around behind her again, forcing Andi's neck to crane back as I held her chin, "I need something special right now. You have your safe word. You'll always have that. But..."

Letting the tension hang for a moment as I rolled

up my sleeves and discarded my tie, I watched Andi's skin prickle with goosebumps as I towered behind her.

"But I want this to be similar to the club. Your no's, your pleas for mercy, will mean nothing. Unless I hear that one safe word, I will not stop. In fact, I want them. I want you to scream and cry and thrash as much as you want, knowing that it will continue. That *I* will continue. Understood?"

She nodded. "Yes, sir. Unless unicorn is used, you'll do whatever you want."

Her voice was mostly even, but a thread of a tremble shook it as she said, "want." I smirked down at her, spearing my fingers through her hair and gripping to hold her head in place.

"And you want that, don't you, pet? You want me to abuse you."

She whimpered, trying to breathe around the strain in her throat.

"Yes, sir."

"That's my good girl." I released her with a hard shove. "Let's get started."

Moving to the supplies, I retrieve a few choice items–an ankle spreader, the Hitachi, a flogger, a set of nipple clamps, and the clear glass anal plug. As I walked back over to Andi, setting my tools on the bed just behind us, I yanked her up to stand by her hair.

"Spread."

Andi obeyed quickly, and I smiled, pleased. Securing the ankle spreader in place, I smoothed my fingers across the supple skin of her legs, gliding them up until I was hovering just centimeters away from her pussy. She was warm and wet already, and my cock twitched behind my suit pants.

"Already so wet. Such a dirty, dirty whore." I

stepped to the side. "Turn around. Face the bed and bend down. I want that ass up high for me."

She hesitated only slightly, unsure how to move with her ankles secured so far apart. But that was very much a part of the fun for me. I loved watching her struggle to do as I asked. Still, she'd be punished for even taking a moment to consider my order.

It took her a good thirty seconds to get around, and she flopped forward onto her shoulders as she reached the bed, a bit out of breath.

"You took far too long to listen to me, pet."

Reaching for the flogger that was right below her face, I slid it free, stepping behind her and rubbing my hands across her waiting ass. She was already decorated so beautifully with my marks, and I surged at the thought of adding more.

"Do not make a sound." I patted her right cheek gently and then got harder until her skin was warm. "We'll start with this one."

I lifted the flogger up nice and high, and after only a second of making her wait for it, I cracked the leather down across her skin. She jerked forward but didn't let out so much as a whimper, and I smirked down at the reddening flesh.

"Count to five. That was one."

Another blow landed across her right cheek, and Andi jumped forward, a breath of air rushing from her lungs.

"Two."

I changed angles, coming straight down instead of from the side, and unleashed another smack of the flogger.

"Three."

The same thing again but much, much harder.

Andi hissed, her legs quivering, and I could see a sinful trail of cum sliding down the inside of her thighs. Stepping a bit closer, I ran my fingers up through her slick and then rammed them inside her pussy–three in a hard thrust. And then I landed another blow.

"Four." Andi's voice was shaky now, and she clenched around my fingers as I held them deep inside her, unmoving.

"One more on this side."

Raining down the last blow, I didn't hold back, using the leverage of the handle to smack against Andi's bright pink skin with great force. She bit back a yelp, swallowing it before it could break free as she clenched around my fingers again.

When she spoke, it was breathy and almost a whisper. "Five."

I pulled my fingers free, moving to Andi's left side. Reaching for her mouth, I shoved my fingers between her lips, and Andi gagged as she tried to steady herself against the intrusion.

"Suck them clean, pet."

She lapped hungrily at me, paying attention to each digit as she licked her cum off me. I raised the flogger up near her left cheek now.

"Count to five."

I smacked it down hard, starting at a six out of ten now that her adrenaline was pumping. She tensed up just after the strike, fighting against the urge to bite on the fingers in her mouth.

"One," she garbled around them before quickly getting back to work.

It was bliss, using her so completely, and I let her finish her duty before yanking my hand free and wiping the mess across her face. Lowering my fist to her throat,

I spread my hand across it and gripped hard enough to cut off her air.

Andi's eyes fluttered closed, and she did her best to sip in steady streams of air through her nose.

"I'm going to watch those pretty fingers. You're going to count for me on them. Hold up one."

Looking down, I feasted on the sight of watching Andi getting a finger out from where her fist was pressed against the bed. She was still relying on those tiny sips of air, so I would make these next blows fast.

In quick succession, I launched my attack, cracking the flogger across Andi's left ass cheek. As I did, I checked her fingers as she counted. *Two, three, four, five.*

"Good girl."

I met her eyes now, hauling her up to stand by the grip I had on her neck. I squeezed just a bit tighter for a moment and then let go. Andi sagged forward, steadying her breathing against the sudden need to gasp. She was still doing so good at staying quiet.

Dropping the flogger to the bed, I reached for the nipple clamps. When I faced her again, I gazed into those tear-filled blue eyes and smiled.

"You may make quiet sounds, pet. No words."

She nodded, and with that, I fastened the first clamp to the hard bud at the tip of Andi's slim breast. She squeaked, whining as I tightened it until the dusky pink of her nipple was paled ever so slightly. The second one went on, and Andi whimpered all the same.

As I finished, I grabbed Andi around the waist and spun her around. With her back to the mattress, I shoved her to the bed. A slight gasp escaped her, and I reached for the cordless vibrating Hitachi. Switching it to the highest setting, I crawled next to Andi on the bed.

I stared down at her glistening pussy, sliding a finger

lazily through her seam. "Look at what a filthy whore you are? You're dripping. Desperate to be used and fucked and punished."

Another whimper left her as I took my hand back, raising it to her lips and smearing her juices across her lips.

"Do you want to cum, little slut? Does Daddy's pain whore want her needy pussy fucked?"

She nodded.

"Hmm. You say that now."

I gripped her throat again as I shoved the wand to her pussy. The buzzing racked through her, making Andi arch up off the mattress. Filthy, wonderfully depraved sounds rumbled as the vibrator hummed against her wet skin. Holding it there, as firmly against her skin as I could, I nuzzled it deeper between her labia, making sure it was directly on her clit.

She was very close.

"Now, little fucktoy. Now, I want you to scream."

Releasing her throat, I went for her cunt, spreading her lips wide for the toy just as Andi let out a pained wail. She bucked against the toy, her legs trying and failing to close around the too-intense sensations. I could see when she reached the apex just before her orgasm. Andi's eyes lulled back, and her hips squeezed up toward buzzing.

This time, I counted. "One, two, three, four, five."

And then I pulled the toy away, leaving Andi to scream her pretty little lungs out as her climax was snatched away.

"You make such pretty sounds, pet. Let's hear them again."

18
The Relief

Andi

My entire being hollered as the vibrator pulled away, my chest heaving as my scream eventually died. It had been far too much at first, the buzzing right smack dab on my clit was so damned strong, and I'd wanted Westley to back it off. But it just stayed there. It cut through to the center of me, and I'd ramped right up to the precipice of a climax.

Which he'd stolen away. *Fucker*.

"Nooo," I whimpered. Tears prickled at the corners of my eyes, and I wanted to close my fucking legs so badly.

I wanted to claw for that damn wand too, but with my wrists secured to my waist, thanks to this admittedly hot outfit, I couldn't do much more than grip the sheets. As my clit throbbed, pulsing like it was trying to get itself off at this point, I could sense each pinpoint place on my body that was supplying intense sensory information.

Burning consumed my ass cheeks, a dull ache throbbing there. My throat was scratchy from the grip

Westley had used, choking me. Every flinch and jerk made the clamps on my nipples move, and it revamped the pain every time, stealing away the numbness that had slowly claimed them because of the constant pressure.

And my pussy, my pussy was so fucking hungry for Westley that it was maddening.

"Oh, little pet. I love that frustrated pout. Such as needy little whore, desperate to come."

I looked up at Westley, squirming against my predicament. I didn't dare speak more, though the idea of being flogged or spanked again was actually appealing because I was sure it would either completely distract me from the need to come or send me over the edge with one stroke.

"You're such a slut. You at how you're pleading with your eyes. Tell me, Andi, are you Daddy's whore? Are you just so damn dirty?"

The tears fell, and the sting of being humiliated, forced to confess just how much I like this, sparked harder than ever. I nodded, mumbling out, "Yes. Yes, I'm Daddy whore."

Westley slapped my face, and I yelped, my pussy clenching around nothing, edged that much closer to coming without permission. His fingers stabbed into my mouth again, and he fucked me with his hand, making me gag around him like I was blowing him. It felt *so* filthy, and I could feel my cunt weep. As he kept it up, his other hand went to my right nipple, patting the clamp and making new pain light up with each stroke.

I was screaming against it in seconds.

Worse, or maybe better, I was getting closer to coming again. The pain was flaring, swirling together with the lust pumping through my veins like venom.

He switched to the other nipple, and it doubled every-thing down. I could hardly stand it, whimpering and crying as he pummeled me like just some fucking toy.

Then his hand disappeared from my mouth, and I gasped for air. It didn't take him long to return, however, and he held another of his little devices in his grip.

"Open up."

I hesitated. I knew I did, and I knew I'd be punished. As soon as I snapped into action, I opened as far as I could, but Westley just looked down at me with that sinister expression. He secured a metal ring between my jaw, a spreader that kept me open for him. My jaw immediately ached, and drool pooled. I had no choice but to let it spill from the corners of my lips when I couldn't swallow properly.

"Naughty kitten. You didn't obey right away, did you?"

He narrowed his eyes at me, and I nodded with a sob.

"Punishment."

With that, the toy was back at my clit, his fingers spreading me as wide as possible so that every inch was assaulted by the aggressive vibrations. I surged, bucking up as it sent me reeling toward another orgasm too fast to process. I writhed against it, fucking humping the damn thing to try and find that release I needed so badly.

"You're not coming, whore." He smacked my tit, and I yelped. "And just look how desperate you are for it. Can you feel how much your pussy is leaking all over the bed? Laying in a puddle of your own cum."

My cheeks flared even as my attention was consumed by the aching need for an orgasm. I was so fucking close, but I tried to hide it. I tried to trick Westley into letting me come. It did *not* work.

"I can see you fighting your reactions, little slut. I can see you trying to get an orgasm."

He pulled the toy away, and I fucking lost it. I screamed around the gag, whining as best I could. *I'm going to fucking die!*

I was so gone that I didn't notice when Westley changed positions, getting up on his knees near my head. It was only when he yanked my head toward him by the hair, downing his zipper and pulling his cock through, that I realized what he was about to do.

Westley shoved between my spread lips, sinking in up to the hilt without warning. I choked, trying to breathe around the thick erection that rocked me. Westley's grip manipulated my head so that it bobbed up and down over his shaft as he fucked mercilessly. I was dribbling all over him, shiny strands of saliva coating him and dripping down all over my chest.

He yanked himself out of my mouth, and I gasped for air as I gagged slightly. His cock smacked my cheek, smearing my spit over my skin. I'd been wearing makeup, and I could just imagine the mascara running down my face as my eyes teared all the harder.

Rubbing his dick over my face, Westley glared down at me. There was such fire and intensity behind his eyes, but also something else. Need. Powerful need for this, to be here and nowhere else. I only knew it because I... recognized it.

Shifting forward, Westley stroked up his cock as he laid his sack against my mouth. I instinctively licked, knowing that's what he wanted. Seeing his grip rock up and down his shaft was hot as hell, and my pussy surged again. God, could I come by just watching him jerk himself off?

Yes. Yes, I fucking could.

Then he was back down my throat, testing my limits even more, and he thrust hard and fast, using me for his pleasure. Wetness seeped out of me, and I wiggled as I tried for any sensation that might tip me over the edge. But his brutal pace was too much, and I couldn't focus on anything besides the need for air as he rammed into me.

When he sat back, smearing himself on my face once more, Westley smiled. The glistening length that strained in his grip looked just as needy for release as I felt.

"Good fucking whore." He sneered down at me, stroking idly as he roamed his stare over my exposed slit. "But you look so empty, don't you?"

I nodded frantically, sobbing as I begged, praying that he was finally going to fuck me. Before I could refocus and open my eyes, Westley grabbed me by the hair again, forcing me to sit up. He pulled me off the bed to stand, then spun me around and bent me over the mattress again.

Suddenly, something cool and smooth slid through my labia, and I jerked, nearly coming right then. It rubbed all along the outside of me, and then I felt Westley grab my ass cheek and spread me. The sound of him spitting hit me only moments before the warm slippery liquid hit my asshole, and I moaned.

Oh, hells yes. Please, fucking...Goddamn it, please.

The round toy playing through my folds moved up toward my ass, and I fought against the needy whine trying to break free. I couldn't have Westley stopping. I was sure it would kill me. The smooth head pressed against me, and I felt that stinging strain as my asshole stretched around it. It was bigger than the first toy Westley had used, and I arched as he inched it inside me.

"That's right, whore. Take it. Take it in your filthy fucking ass like a good little slut."

It slipped in, and I closed around the neck of the plug. The fullness stimulated my hungry nerves, and I clenched everywhere as it ghosted against my G-spot. I was so close, and I couldn't stop the whimper this time.

Westley smacked my ass, and I cried out, clamping around the toy. The chain that was connected to the neck of this outfit slipped forward over my shoulder, and then I felt it slide back as Westley took control of the leash.

"Well, are you just going to lay there dripping all over those thighs?" He pulled, and the tension on my neck made me arch backward. "Or are you going to fuck Daddy's cock?"

My face flared, fire hot, and I whined as I struggled to breathe against the strain. I wanted him inside me, though. I needed it, and I needed to please him just as much.

I shuffled backward, searching out his erection and trying to slip down around him. My pussy bumped into his blunt head, and I moaned. I had to get him inside me. Circling my hips and squirming down around his erection, I rocked my hips back, trying to get him fully seated. Instead of this shallow penetration, which was fucking torture.

He absolutely wasn't helping, though. I practically hopped, working so hard to get Westley there, and his sadistic chuckle made everything burn so much harder.

"Come on, little kitten. Earn Daddy's cock."

Screaming from the frustration, hot tears streamed

down my face as my pussy wept, clenching around the head of his cock. I sucked in a breath against the strain in my throat, thanks to that damned leash, and then shoved myself back hard. His cock rammed into me as I let go of the comfort of laying against the mattress and gave myself over to being hauled up and arched back for him.

Westley groaned low, and I damn near passed out from the heavenly feeling of his thick shaft shoving inside me with such force. He bottomed out, reaching up to jab into my cervix, and I screamed all the harder. With everything I had, I fucked him, rode his fucking cock like the wanton harlot I was, and I absolutely lost my damn mind.

"Oh, there's my little whore. Yes, baby girl. Fuck Daddy's cock. I want you squirting all over this damn floor."

I had no problem obeying that order with all my being. I rutted on Westley's dick like a wild animal, grunting and howling as my swollen, abused pussy surged. His hand came to my hip, gripping me and yanking me down harder on his erection as the other hauled back on the leash.

Incredibly full, my ass and pussy stretching for Westley's assault, I approached that cliff again. My clit burned, and my entire body seized up. *Oh, God, don't take this one. Please.*

He didn't.

And with that, I launched over that cliff into the most intense orgasm of my life, and that was saying something. I fucking fell apart at the seams, though, trembling as I came and squirted gushes of cum down my legs and all over the floor–just as told.

"Daddy's little slut, obeying so good. I want more.

Everything you have belongs to me. Don't fucking disappoint me."

Both his hands came to my hips, and I felt the bite of the chain as it dug into my flesh. He barreled into me with everything he had, his thumb pressing down on the plug as he brutally fucked me. And I came again easily. More cum flooded as I screamed out. The orgasm was the best pleasure of my life, all while filling me with a searing pain that dragged a jagged blade through my soul.

His words had made me feel filthy and depraved, humiliated and degraded. But his actions, the way he gripped me, made me feel seen, desired. *Worshiped*.

When my legs were as good as jello, Westley tore himself free, and I screamed again as the abrupt change sent my nerves reeling. I was shoved down to the floor and spun around to kneel at his feet. I stared with lust-lidded eyes as he stroked his shaft, slick with my cum, hard and fast. He gripped my head, lining up with my forced-open mouth and face.

My pussy clenched, a smaller but blissful orgasm making me drip onto the floor as I knelt in the puddle I'd created.

Westley grunted low, and Goddamn, the fucking sight of his flexed arm and his fist wrapped around his cock so tight that his knuckles whited was...everything.

We held each other's eyes, and then he came, a warm jet of cum soaring out and landing right across my tongue. I melted into the salty, bitter taste of him as Westley continued to cover me in his cum. He went on for ages, the thick, sticky ropes fucking frosting me like a damned cake. It filled my mouth, raining over me onto my cheeks and eyes and lips. And all over the cat mask as well.

It was so indescribably filthy, so maddeningly, wonderfully depraved, that I didn't think I'd ever get enough of seeing the beautiful cum spurt out of his delicious cock. I could see his shaft twitch with each release, and he paused just once before he stroked again, and more of that amazing treat spilled out of him.

I'd never seen a guy actually come more than once, but I knew it was technically possible. This wasn't just possible for Westley; it looked necessary, his huge erection red and strained as he loaded up my face and tongue all the more. A thick stream gushed out of him as he released himself and let the sensations back down. The way it poured from him forced another burst to rock through me, and I let myself feel the humiliation as I trickled onto the floor again.

Stillness slowly settled in, our exhausted breaths filling the quiet room. Westley stared down at me, reaching for the buckle of the gag and freeing me of it. My jaw throbbed, but before I could think anything more, Westley pulled my mouth open with his thumb.

"Look at that filthy mouth." He smeared more of his cum past my lips. "Drink up all your cream, pet."

When he released my chin, I swallowed for the first time in so long, and it made my jaw pinch. Still, I ate up every drop he'd given me, opening wide again to show him as much.

"Good girl." He smiled, satisfied and almost sleepy. "Let's get you cleaned up."

19
The Come Down

Westley

Andi was as good as a cooked noodle, and I had zero trouble lifting her up and taking her to the attached bathroom. She hummed low as she nuzzled into my chest, and where normally I would have minded mussing up this shirt too much, I couldn't care less now. She was just...too much.

"All right, pet. Can you stand right here?"

She nodded sleepily, and I helped to unbuckle the mask and leather harness. I opened the Velcro at her wrists first, then went to the closure at each thigh so that I could slide the down her legs. They trembled as I did, and as soon as I could, I directed her to the edge of the tub to sit down.

Andi seemed grateful for it, smiling up at me with her eyes closed. *Ugh, you have no right being so fucking adorable, pet.*

My chest pinched, and I grinned down at her as I reached around her head to undo the buckle at the back of her neck. Looking down to get a view past her blonde bob, I noticed the shake in my fingers. At once, my gut clamped down, and I had to clear my throat.

This how a real man fucks? You're going to waste all this time cleaning her up? Dumb bitch can do it herself.

It was my father's voice searing in my skull, and I tried to physically shake the thoughts out. He was dead and gone. Wrong and dead and gone, and he couldn't ruin this for me. Ruin her.

Shoving it down, I took the mask to the sink using a damp cloth to wipe it clean and allowed it to dry on the counter. The harness was mostly untouched by our mess, so I just ran the cloth over it briefly and left the pile of pieces to dry in the tub behind Andi.

The adrenaline rush was coming down for her, and she shook where she sat. I smoothed a hand down her arm, which made her flinch slightly. As much as I knew she was just out of it right now, the action stung for some reason. And I hated myself for that.

"Shower. Okay, pet. I'm going to get it going."

Turning for it, Andi's thin fingers wrapped around my wrist. "You too?"

She looked up at me, her eyes tired but pleading. I nodded, laying a kiss on the top of her head. "Yes, I'll come in with you."

I was gone for the moment it took to start the shower, and then I started unbuttoning my shirt to get undressed. I was still clothed, tussled for sure, but a bit of straightening, and I could have gone somewhere if absolutely necessary. A jacket over the shirt would hide anything too obscene, after all.

Andi was completely naked now. And even with the harness, everything had been exposed. I liked that about the power dynamic that I created between my submissives and me. I liked having the control, the composure, when they were forced to bare everything.

I still did, of course, but standing in front of Andi now, glancing down at her as my hands hovered over the halves of my shirt ready to pull it away. I realized that I didn't do *this part* with other women.

Clothed was always my modus operandi, and right now, I didn't enjoy the feelings swirling behind this move to be naked in front of Andi. I knew it had everything to do with my scar, my past, and that disgusting feeling of inadequacy churned in my gut.

My hands shook as I went for my belt, and nausea flared.

"I'm cold," Andi whispered, and the shiver as she pulled her arms around herself served to knock me far enough out of my head that I could get moving again.

I finished stripping and lifted Andi into my arms, carrying her to the shower. I set her down on the long bench inside the glass box and moved to pull down the sprayer to run the water over her goosebump-laden skin.

As I faced away from her to get it down and check the temperature, the sudden touch of her small fingers on my back made me spin around, snatching her wrist–too hard.

She froze, and I immediately dropped her hand. "Apologies, pet. You...you startled me."

"Sorry," she said, her brows knitted together as she wobbled on her feet. "Saw that scar. What happened?"

I had to force myself to swallow, to remain in the shower and not bolt out. It was unconscious how I looked up at the ceiling, however, eyeing the rainfall water spout mounted there and the expanse of tile that curved down from above me down into the shower wall.

This "box" was big enough to be a closet in most houses, and it wasn't even the master shower. That was even more impressive. I didn't like to be wanting for things. For as much money as my parents had had, they didn't share–particularly not with me.

That pinch in my gut worsened, and I had to suck in a deep breath of the steamy air. With a practiced smile, I shook my head, retrieving the handheld shower head and directing Andi back to the bench.

"Nothing, pet. Stupid accident when I was young. Get comfortable."

She nodded, scooting herself back onto the bench. I ran the hot water over her toes first, working my way up her body so that she could get used to the temperature. Sighing, Andi let her head fall back, and I stepped forward, switching to the massaging spray and focusing it on her shoulders.

I knew the strain there had to be significant, but I had to admit that I was impressed she wasn't more noticeably sore on her ass. However, the bench had been cool when she sat down. Tomorrow, though? That's when the real ache would start.

Getting the soap was tricky because Andi whined when I moved the sprayer away, and I didn't have the heart to deny her the massage she was so clearly enjoying. Which was surprising, to say the least.

"Here, love. Can you hold on while I soap you up?"

She nodded, smiling easily. As the minutes tacked on, filled with me caressing her abused skin with the body wash, Andi seemed to perk up a little. And my mind circled over the mantra that I'd come to need myself after our sessions.

She's just your sub. That's it. Just your sub. Just your sub.

"Westley. Can I call you Westley now?" Her voice was small.

"Yes, pet. What is it?" I stroked her cheek with my thumb.

"You seem..." She held my eyes, the sparkling blue flooded with concern that bit into me as good as fangs, "upset? Off? I don't know. Quieter, I guess. Are you... okay?"

I didn't want her drawing attention to the fact that I was apparently screaming my bullshit to the stars like a damned neon sign. And yet, it was obvious that I wasn't doing as good a job feigning my composure as normal. *Irritating*.

"Yes, pet. That was just...it was intense for me too. Does that make sense?"

Andi paused before chuckling lightly, her smile still weighed down by exhaustion. "Yeah, actually. My brain...I kept thinking about stuff that I haven't in... ages."

Curiosity peaked, and I sat down next to her on the bench, taking the sprayer and putting it to her hair.

"What things?"

I want to know, even as I realized how hypocritical I was being, asking for details about her life when I was willing to give up so little. But the idea that she'd been mistreated or neglected–by anyone or anything–well, I had to know.

"Oh, I guess...my parents, life before emancipation." She hummed as the water trickled through her shorter blonde locks. "I've been poor all my life too. All...all this? It's...sometimes I don't feel deserving of it. I'm just some chick who grew up in Harmstead and likes to swing around on silks. I'm...a no-one."

Unfamiliar rage pooled in my gut, a strange urge to

yank Andi around to face me and demand she take back those words. She was someone. She was *my* someone, and that was all that should matter. Of course, then, my rational mind reminded me of the gnawing feelings of self-loathing and insecurity that lingered in my own head. *Yeah, you're one to talk, Wes.*

"You're not a no-one, Andi. Don't say that." My voice still came out harsher than intended, and I cleared my throat. "Let's...are you hungry? Before bed?"

She nodded, resting back against me. "Yeah, but... can we stay here? Just a little longer?"

My heart felt like it might crack in two. "Yes, pet. As long as you want."

20
The Gym

Andi

F ed, cleaned, and tucked in bed, I was as warm as
could be. I struggled against Westley's side, and I
was so grateful for his seemingly endless body heat. I
was still chilled from the come-down, but I was feeling
better—more like myself.

Myself, who happened to have a delicious sting radi-
ating through her ass like a sunburn.

Still, something lingered in the back of my mind
that I didn't want to dwell on anymore. But my brain
wasn't listening. And furthermore, I had no real proof. I
didn't know for sure that Westley had...lied.

I sighed against him, my sweet Dom already asleep
while I lay there ruminating. I'd only been with him for
a handful of days, but I could tell something was up. He
was always so calm and collected or ruthlessly fucking
me, but tonight...after the session...it had been very, very
different.

And somehow, I knew that scar hadn't come from
an "accident."

I didn't want to pry, though. Westley would come around when he was ready–if he ever was. I would not be the girl to hurt him through my pestering. No, thank you. I understood privacy and fucked up pasts. They went hand in hand together, and it was a lot more than just probing someone to get them to open up.

So, instead, it was sleep, and maybe tomorrow would bring something even more incredible. Though, based on that last session...

I wiggled happily as every inch of me felt sore. I didn't care what it said about me; I fucking loved that shit, and I was very excited to see just how Westley was going to step it up after that.

"**D**o you think that would be okay? I can bring my cell with me, and you can text?"

Westley smiled skeptically, and I put my hands in front of my chest, making my best puppy dog face. "Please."

"Oh, all right." He rolled his eyes, finishing buttoning his shirt as we stood in his closet. "But my driver will take you. I don't want you going out unescorted."

"You're such a worry wort. I'll be fine."

He glared, and I rolled my entire head, coming down off my tiptoes and huffing out a long breath. "Okay, okay, I'll use your driver. He doesn't...He isn't going to say anything about...you know, how I got here?"

"It's unlikely he'll say anything at all. He understands how much I prefer non-judgemental silence."

I sagged into myself, relieved. "Oh, good."

"How far is the studio, so I know when to expect you home?"

Westley raised his brows matter-of-factly, and I had to bite back my grin at the word "home."

"The silks studio I train at is on 5th and Maple, downtown. So maybe thirty minutes from here? I'd like to stay for a few hours, if that's all right since you'll be working."

Westley buttoned his cuffs, then reached for a tie and circled it around his neck. He began arranging the fabric into the typical Windsor knot, and I smoothed my hand down the silky red garment.

"Hmm..." He narrowed his eyes at me playfully, and I put on my best pout.

"Please...Daddy?"

Westley's eyes flared, and that quintessential sadistic grin spread across his face. "Oh, little pet. Now, you've gone and done it. I'm going to be running just a little late, it seems."

Cocking my head, I maintained my innocent expression. "Oh, why?"

"Because Daddy's good little kitten is going to get down on her knees and suck my cock as payment."

Immediately my pussy tingled, clenching, and then Westley shoved me to the floor. He'd yet to put on pants, so I pulled his hardening dick through his briefs and began my work. It didn't take long for Westley's erection to jump deliciously against my tongue and spurt his cum into my mouth.

There was nearly as much as last time, his cock

flexing twice as he shoved his cock down my throat to prolong things. His distinct taste flooded my senses, and I couldn't get over how much I loved watching him come. Seeing the white, sticky spend milked out of his cock was just shy of enough to make me orgasm right there.

"Such a good girl."

This time was much less messy than the last, and I swallowed down Westley's release, getting to my feet again. I was already dressed for the gym, and the light grey leotard I'd found was wet at the crotch, my nipples standing out obscenely against the thin fabric.

Westley ran his gaze over me, tilting his head to appraise my outfit. I knew instantly that he could tell I'd left a spot, and he licked his lips.

"Oh, pet. That pussy always gets you into so much trouble." He ate me up with his gaze, predatory and malicious. "If it weren't for this..."

Gripping me between the legs, Westley dug the heel of his hand into my folds, and I whimpered.

"I might have forgotten to remind you that you are not to pleasure yourself in *any* way while we're apart. Understood?"

With a final torturous circle, Westley pulled his hand back, and I sagged against his grip. "Un-under-stood, sir."

"Good. We need to get going now, so take care of whatever else you need, and I'll ring the driver to meet us downstairs."

Spinning around, Westley quickly left through the door, and I was left standing there so damn worked up it hurt. It took everything not to break his rule, but I held back, sucking in a breath and straining things, before I grabbed my thin wraparound sweater and went to join him.

I swear to God, the damn silks are going to get me off at this point.

———⚬———

Pulling up to the aerial gym, my spirits lifted in a way nothing could replicate. I adored being up there. I had since I started studying it, and I knew being alone with the silks, losing myself to the flow, was exactly what I needed. It would get me out of my head, ease my stiff muscles, and just like I'd told Westley, it would keep me nice and flexible.

"Thank you, Richard. I'll be a few hours, so if you'd like to go and get coffee or something?"

Westley's driver met my stare through the rearview mirror, cocking a brow as he smirked.

"Right, Westley, probably told you to stay. Well, if you get bored, you're more than welcome to come in and watch."

I shrugged, and Richard actually let out a little chuckle. He was more stoic than Westley in a lot of ways. He was also like sixty, and I couldn't imagine many others taking him in as their employee. *Oh, Wes. You're so much more of a sap than you let on.*

"I'll be just fine, miss. I assure you. I've a book, and I'm used to entertaining myself."

It was so stupid, getting my curiosity going like I was, but I just couldn't help myself. "Oh, whatcha reading?"

"Oh, it's a true crime book actually. Discussing recent unsolved serial killings over the last decade. I've gotten to one now that's quite intriguing. The Final Girl killings of San Domingo University."

My stomach dropped and I fucking blanched like a damn ghost.

"Fuuuck," I chuckled out, "remind me not to piss you off, Richard."

He immediately backpeddled, apologizing way too much, and I smiled as I slid forward on the seat and reached for the door.

"Don't worry, bud. I get it. It's fascinating. Just make sure you tell Westley in case we need any of that knowledge in the future."

"Of course, miss." He smiled. "Do enjoy your practice, Andi."

With a lively grin and practically a spring in my step, I stepped out of the limo. Leaning back into the open window, I waved at Richard.

"Will do! See you soon!"

Walking up to the shabby brick building in the arts district of Harmstead, I pulled open the creaky door, which weighed a damn ton, and proceeded to the small lobby. Jessica was working the desk right now, and since I was a long-time regular, I was allowed to use the space basically whenever I wanted.

"Hey, Andi. Long time, no see. Feel free to go on back. I think Katie is in there."

I immediately perked up. Katie was the closest thing I had to a best friend in the entire world, lone solitary lobster that I was. We'd started training at the same time, and we were always there for each other to help work on moves or give a critique of our form.

Best of all, we'd actually hang out and binge shitty TV on occasion, which was actually really nice. Katie completely understood that I got overloaded from being around people a lot, and she never judged me for it. She was happy to see me whenever I had the spoons.

In short, Katie rocked. She had amazing taste in smut, too.

"Thanks, Jess! I'll see myself right on back."

I hurried down the short hallway to the large aerial gym at the back, my soft slippers dusting over the hard-wood floor that creaked with every step. As I entered, Katie was up on the silks to the left, hauling her impressive six-foot frame up to the top for a drop.

Standing back and observing, I smiled to myself as she absolutely nailed it. When she finished with her routine, she turned around from facing the window and finally noticed me.

"Andi!" Her voice echoed off the high ceilings, and she ran over to give me a massive hug. "Oh, my God. You were supposed to call me, you bum. How'd it go?"

Katie had been the only person I'd told about going to the club.

"Well, actually," I smiled, shaking my head because even I couldn't believe what I was about to say, "I'm just coming from my...purchaser's penthouse."

"Penthouse?" Her brows shot to her hairline. "Umm, okay, well, I think you did well then."

I couldn't stop the laugh, feeling my cheeks heat as I considered just everything that I'd done with Westley. "I really did. I...like him."

"Oh, well." The corners of Katie's mouth turned down in an impressed smirk, and she waggled her shoulders. "I'd say sign me up, but I think Carl would have objections."

My face softened, and I awed at the easy glow that filled her cheeks when she talked about the hubby.

"Aww, how's he doing? I really hope he enjoyed that book recommendation."

"Andi. If you could have seen his face." Katie looked up and closed her eyes, miming a chef's kiss. "Perfection."

"Ha! Well, I'm always happy to help. We should schedule a real date, like a lunch or something."

"Yes, totally. Let me check ye old calendar, and I'll text you." She hugged me again, cocking her head as she smiled down at me. "You seem...well, hell, I'll just come out and say it. You look like you got laid."

I barked out a laugh, barely able to catch my breath. "Well, that's an accurate appraisal."

"Holy shit, girl. You actually popped that cherry. Congrats."

Cue more laughter and a searing burn in my cheeks that I knew Katie noticed. I coughed through my next few words, trying to school my shock.

"Okay, wow. Well, yeah. Thank you, I guess?" She nudged me with her elbow, and I let myself be rocked to the side. "Yeah, yeah. It finally happened. But you probably have a husband and a dog to get back to, soooo..."

"Oh, sure. Shove me off right when it got interesting." She giggled. "I do. You're right. But I'll text you, and we will hang out. And you will give me all the hot details so that I can tell Carl and he can step up his game. Yes? Good."

I hugged Katie close, humming in that grateful way when you were getting attention and snuggles from your bestie, and I nodded.

"Yes, all the deets. For now, I'm going to practice. Because I'm still as a board." I eyed her. "Don't say it."

"That's what he said."

We both burst out laughing, lost in it until neither

one of us could breathe properly. Then we said our actual goodbyes. I waved to her as she left and then walked to the far corner to drop off my bag.

I needed several rounds of stretching before I could hop up on those silks, so I pressed play on the stereo system that Katie had paused and let the tunes rock me into that dream-like place where all that mattered was the music and the movement.

"Renegade" played over the speakers, and I was immediately transported to the playroom in my mind. The commanding lyrics replaced Westley's voice for a time, and I completely let myself go.

My body swayed against the silks, and I spun myself around in lazy circles across the floor. The smooth black fabric drifted through the air along with me, and I made sure to hold any stretch or pull that felt like it needed it.

After a few minutes, I was good and warmed up. I lifted myself up using the two halves of the silk and then flipped backward to catch my hips in the well of the fabric. I swung, enjoying the light breeze as I traced through the sky like I was swimming in the air.

Everything fell away. It was just me and the rig, floating, twirling, and wrapping up tight. I felt Westley there with me even though a part of me thought it was ludicrous. Still, I tumbled through a freestyle routine that felt like each of the steps we'd taken so far.

A low, rumbling ride across the floor like the car, crawling up the silks like rising up the elevator, and a hard drop for the moment he took my virginity–freely given and hungrily demanded.

The motion, the music, it was sex and trust and experience, and suddenly I was all too ready to see what Westley had planned for the evening.

I teased myself with binds, tumbling down the silks

and letting them coast between my legs. It was nearly breaking Westley's rule, but I never allowed it to go too far. I had a feeling my Dom would be proud.

As the song ended, I let the music continue, just finding my way through the rhythm and the moves until Richard would come inside to fetch me.

It wasn't sex, but damn it was wonderful.

21
The Escalation

Him

Prancing around like she fucking owns the place. *Thinks she can just get what she wants. We don't get want we want, bitch. We don't get what we deserve or work for.*

I sighed, clenching my jaw so hard it hurt, cracking and grinding as the TMJ condition flared up.

No. You have to take it. You have to demand your due and make people pay. And you're going to help me do that. Won't you?

Watching Westley's little blonde whore twirl around in those silks, I could imagine them tangling around her neck. One little jerk and then...Pop. Little broken doll and then Westley all sad and ruined. Not now, though. There was still so much to set up.

It all needed to be perfect. Ready. Secured.

I wanted to take my time, after all. *Can't rush things. No, that won't do.*

Spins and lifts and drops, the bitch danced around in that nothing leotard. Glorified hooker, that's what she was. Just hooking Westley with her pussy and using her wiles to earn a quick buck. Well, bitch there were better ways to land yourself some dough.

Slut. Corrupted, little slut.

She'd basically sold her soul for that fucker's cock. It wasn't proper–not clean or good. She needed to be squashed beneath a righteous boot. *My* boot.

It is pretty, though. Ain't it, boss? Yeah, pretty enough to want to take it apart. Take it down to the pieces. Chew 'em up. Spit out the bones.

I pulled a drag on my cigarette, stamping down the spent fucker in the grime of the building's floor. This one wasn't used. Abandoned. Good view from the window, however, and that's what mattered.

The smell of smoke lingered in my fingers. I'd used the cigarette down to the filter. I needed another pack. I checked my wallet. Ten bucks and a coupon for a sandwich at the gas station. *That'll have to do.*

Roy's by the highway attracted truckers, too. Good targets for getting what I needed, they were. Good fucking targets.

I'd be eating fine, and it was best to go around sunset. Slower traffic, and people weren't on edge like they were at night. I'd got the coat on me from a real nice one. He'd been off in the head. The tall fucker had said sunsets looked like someone had stuck a stick in the sky and swirled it around like paint.

Stupid.

Talked nonsense about being a good man. Had pictures of his homo partner in his wallet. Shot him in the head.

I'd had to leave the gun, though. Shame. They were handy.

Still, I'd get another. Still had an account at Jim's.

He didn't check backgrounds or new reports—just cash payments and out the door. *Perfect.*

Movement inside the building made me look up. Andi slut was getting fancy with her moves now. Bitch. Her legs were stretched long in the splits. If she landed wrong—or if someone took a thick mallet to her—those kneecaps would shatter. *No moving around then, huh?*

Just a little smash-smash, and she'd be good for the fucking. I don't need 'em to move after all. Westley's damn sloppy seconds. *Ugh.* At least the cunt would be the same in her ass—not all stretched out from his fucking dick.

Want her titties, though. Want to rub on 'em. Cut 'em. Blood could be as good as mother's milk.

Andi girl dropped down, then dismounted those silks. She walked to the stereo. Had it already been a few hours? Hmm, times did fly. I had to finish setting up. I'd strike soon. I'd get her all to myself for a moment.

Fun. Good fun was right around the corner.

22
The Trust

Westley

The phone at my desk rang, and for a moment, I hesitated to answer. The odd prank from the other day was still sitting in my nerves like an itch. But that was ridiculous. I was at work, and this extension, as well as the number, weren't given out to just anyone, and they were listed, either.

"Mr. Stanton."

"Hello, sir. Mr. Capezio from the board is on line two."

I nodded to myself, sighing a bit as I heard Charlize's voice on the other end of the phone. "Oh, thank you. How'd he sound?"

"Good, actually. I don't think I've ever heard the man sound chipper, but this was damn close. Oops, sorry."

Chuckling lightly, I leaned back in my chair. "It's all right, Charlize. Go ahead and put him through."

The line clicked over, and I answered as soon as I heard the echo. "Hello, Mr. Capezio. How are you?"

"I'm doing just fine, Westley. I just got off the

conference call with the board regarding the new direction and funding for the chip project. They've really liked that you've appealed to Brunswick. He's a solid player. They're onboard to stick with your timeline and grow out the beta trials for later next year."

The neverending tension that sat in my shoulders eased, and I let out a long breath while still trying to stay quiet so that Capezio couldn't hear me. The man had a penchant for long-winded talks about managing my stress, and I was not listening to another Gerald Original right now.

"That's Excellent to hear. I have some good news as well. The production department, along with R&D, has managed to devise a new approach to counter the overheating. It looks promising. They're a third of the way through trials now."

"That is good news. Well, I'll leave you to it then. Please make sure to have the quarterly reports in by next week. I know you're CEO but we still need to see where the funding is going, yeah."

"Of course, Gerald. I don't foresee any issues. Talk soon."

"Yeah."

With that, the man hung up. I set the phone receiver back in the cradle with a much more audible sigh, crossing one leg over the other at the knee. This was fucking good. I needed a win. Well, when didn't I?

But the investors and the board were happy. They'd agreed to the more reasonable time frame, and the chip itself was moving along through production without nearly as many hiccups. Things were actually looking up on the business front, and with Andi waiting back home...

My cock twitched at just the thought of her. *Daaamn. I need...well...*

"I should do something nice for her. A little celebration for the both of us," I rambled to myself.

The heady feeling of excitement threaded through me, and I stood up out of my chair, ready to call it an early day and get back to the one place I'd never get sick of–namely, between Andi's legs.

"God, nothing could kill this mood."

Packing up my laptop into my briefcase, I punched the intercom to tell Charlize that I was heading out when my office door opened, and her voice came through the line.

"Umm, heads up, Mr. Stanton. I tried to stop him. Several times."

My stomach clenched as the suspicion about who'd barged into my office hit me. With my finger still on the intercom, I answered back in a hushed voice.

"Get security."

Finally finding the strength to look up, I was unsurprised to see my uncle standing just a foot or two past the door. His gray suit was ill-fitting, the patches on the elbows clearly there for purpose and not style. He'd been born significantly after my father, but you'd be pressed to tell that he was only sixty-three–haggard and unkempt as he was.

"Get out." I wasted no time on formalities. There was a standing order to keep this money-grubbing asshole from setting foot in this building, and security was going to be in deep shit for allowing him to get this far.

"Come on, Wes. I'm your uncle, for Christ's sake. We should be helping each other."

If i didn't know any better, which, of course, I did, I

would have thought the man was suffering from a stroke for how slurred his words were. It had nothing to do with latent health conditions, however. It had everything to do with the fact that the man was already drunk, and it was barely past noon.

Yes, I knew well enough that addiction and mental health weren't to be brushed off. Hell, I knew I was addicted to my relationships with my subs in a way, but Adam Stanton had scoffed at every attempt I'd made to help him, and I was just...done with it now.

"I'm not interested in trying to help you anymore. And I've locked the account, again, so you're not getting the money. I'm very clearly not in need of a custodial manager."

"Hey now," my uncle swayed on his feet, and I clenched my jaw, fighting against everything to toss him out myself, "I deserve a part of that money. That was my brother's. He put me in charge of that trust all the same."

Grumbling, I hiked my briefcase up on my shoulder, gripping the strap hard enough to turn my knuckles white.

"You were added as a manager because I wasn't eighteen. I'm not having this discussion with you again. Just leave. Security is on the way."

My uncle's expression pinched, his brows coming down over his eyes as he glared at me. He looked so much like my father when he did that, and the jolt of fear that zinged through my spine made me immediately nauseated.

"You're a little shit, you know that. I deserve my due!" His voice raised, and I was sure people down the hall could hear him. "I wouldn't put it past you to have been the one to cut their brakes. Ungrateful kid. Your father was doing things with the company before you came along and mucked it all up with your fucking 'ethnics.'"

Rolling my eyes, I swallowed hard, trying to ease the need to swing by roaming my eyes over the black bars that crisscrossed through the glass window behind my uncle.

"It's ethics, you moron. And excuse me for cutting off your embezzling ring. You should be in jail, and yet here you are. You should just be glad that there was no solid evidence against you."

Adam stepped forward, stabbing his finger through the air at me. "Fuck you, Westley. You fucking killed them, didn't you. Didn't you?!"

Before I could step in, my security team rushed up around Adam, pulling him under control into a bear hold. He fought against them, screaming obscenities for the entire office to hear. It was fucking humiliating to be associated with that fucking leech, and my fist shook as I squeezed them with everything I had.

"If I was responsible for their deaths," I mumbled, "it would have happened a lot sooner."

But I'd never had the strength to stand up to my father, and my mother had never been there to listen to my pleas. Coked up, high on prescription meds, recovering from plastic surgery, take your pick. Whatever she could do to focus on herself and avoid our little "family," she did.

It was a good five minutes before I could bring myself to unclench, relaxing—if only slightly. I shook my head, starting for my office door. As I flicked over the lights and locked the door, I passed by Charlize at her desk.

"I'm so sorry, Mr. Stanton. He shoved right past me. I–"

"It's all right." I looked over at her as I spoke, noticing the way she hugged her arm. "Did he hit you? I swear to God, if–"

She shook her head. "I stumbled into the doorframe over there when he pushed by. I'm fine."

"Absolutely not." I mirrored her head shake. "You're going home. Now."

"Mr. Stanton, I..." But her words drifted away as I walked over and pulled her out of her chair.

Handing Charlize her purse, I looked her dead in the eye. "Go home. I'm not staying. You won't be needed here more than you need to ice that shoulder."

Charlize's eyes welled up, and I had to swallow against the big display of emotions. She secured her purse over her head, a habit of hers thanks to "thieves," and nodded.

"Okay. Thank you. I'm...It actually really hurts. So, yeah. Ice pack."

She was a beautiful woman with dark, long locks that touched her lower back. She'd been gifted eyes the color of actual turquoise, and she had a charming little mole right above her lip. I'd toyed with the idea of asking her to be one of my subs, but aside from the career complications that would cause, she was just too...sweet.

I wanted her to meet someone real, someone who would be there to date her, not just fuck her. I wasn't sure if that was something I could ever give someone. My chest squeezed, and I thought about the woman waiting back home for me. *But Andi is...*

Shaking myself out of the thoughts, I smiled at Charlize and guided her toward the elevator.

"I'll ride down with you. Safe as houses."

She didn't like walking through the parking garage alone, and I could hardly blame her.

"Thank you, Mr. Stanton."

"Of course." I nodded. "Now, I definitely think it's time for both of us to be heading home."

23
The Rig

Westley

I tossed my keys down into the catch-all and wandered to the kitchen, grabbing a thick rocks glass and filling it up with ice. Walking to the bar I had in the corner of the living room, I poured a healthy amount of gin over the ice and a bit of tonic from the tiny fridge that sat beneath it. Swirling it around only briefly, I put the glass to my lips and took a long pull.

Christ, what the hell had today even been?

Walking to the patio doors, I opened them wide and stepped out into the warm spring air. I'd been so thrilled about the development with the board and the chip, and then my fucking uncle had to come in and ruin it all. Still...

I couldn't let myself be so swayed by just a single encounter with the man, right? Right. I needed to shove it down with everything else and re-find my bliss between the legs of the most beautiful woman on the planet.

Andi.

She was truly remarkable for the way she let me take

control. Beyond being a natural submissive, Andi was queued into my desires almost innately—like she was... made for me.

"Okay, sap. Come on."

I rolled my eyes at myself. However, I knew there was something to be said about how good we fit. She hadn't agreed to the permanent placement yet, but I held out no small amount of hope that she would. Andi was certainly acting like she'd say yes, not that I was excellent at reading the minutia of a woman's thoughts beyond the bedroom.

I'd never been interested before, after all. Now? Now, I was very keen on knowing what made Andi tick, how I could make her smile, make her squirt, and make her beg. I had a pretty good idea about those last few, but making her smile...

The silks.

Andi had been so desperate to practice, and that's how I'd found her, of course. She was a performer and an artist, and what artist doesn't love getting things that help them perfect their craft? My heart rate ticked up, and that thrill of excitement built in my gut. I rarely got this excited about something that wasn't fucking, but right now, I was damn near giddy to enact my plan.

Reaching into my pocket for my cell, I opened the internet browser and did a quick search. To my surprise, it didn't take much to find what I was looking for. At least after I'd waded through the instructions on how to do it myself, which would *not* be happening. I pulled up the business with the most and best reviews and gave them a call.

The line rang two times before a voice answered. "Starlight Silks Installation. How can I help you?"

With a grin, I began to pace around the penthouse as I spoke.

"Hello, I'm looking for an installation to be done in my home. I have a suitable area, and I need it done today. Right now, actually."

I could practically *hear* the man on the other end gape.

"Umm, well, I'm not sure if we can get there today, but if you don't mind leaving your infor–"

"Today. I'll pay whatever you want to get a crew here in thirty minutes. It shouldn't take that long to install. I'll have the space cleared for the next three hours. See that it's done."

There was a long pause, and I actually had to bite back the chuckle that wanted to squeak out. I knew this was *an ask*, but I wanted that smile, dammit, and I was going to do whatever it took to get it.

"I'll have to bring in a few guys who are off-duty right now. They'll get time and a half for working. Refueling the truck and expediting the loading time. That's going to rack up the charges quite a bit, Mr...."

"Stanton. And done. Money isn't an issue. Does ten thousand seem appropriate?"

"Holy shi–" The man cleared his throat. "Yes, that would suffice. Thank you for your business, Mr. Stanton. Now, if you'll provide me with the details of the space, I'll make sure that we have everything necessary to have your rig set up in three hours."

"Perfect."

———❦———

After an impressive two hours and thirty-five minutes, the rig was done. It sat beautifully in the column of space within the stairs spiraling upward, taking advantage of all that massive height. The huge windows also provided incredible lighting, and I stood there proud as could be for making it happen for Andi.

Sure, it was the workers who'd lifted the real weight, but I knew I was paying them well over what they needed and I hoped that provided them all with the funds to go enjoy themselves for a while. I knew I would be.

My phone buzzed in my pocket, and I pulled out the thing to check the message. It was a text from Andi.

> Hey, heading home now. Will you be there, or should I have Richard stop at McDonalds for me?

> Oh, and remind me to tell you about his book. Hilarious.

> I'm home, and I'm well aware of Richard's interesting reading habits. Lol

> Oh, and I have a surprise.

I glanced up happily at the swaths of bright crimson fabric, running my fingers down the soft edge. Andi deserved something nice. I'd been enjoying her "services," as it were, for days now, and this would be just for her. Though, I'd be lying if I said I didn't have a few plans for what types of routines I'd like to see her perform.

Another message.

A surprise? 🙂 Hmm...well, I'm very excited, and I've told Richard to step on it, so...

I'll see you soon, pet.

Sliding the phone away into my pocket, I finished the few inches of scotch I'd poured while the men were getting the rig set up and wandered up the stairs to the playroom. I wanted to grab just a few things in case the mood struck–namely a blindfold and the nipple clamps.

"Hurry home, kitten. I am so very ready to give you your gift."

24

The Performance

Andi

The drive across town back to Westley's took far too long, and I was more impatient than I'd ever been in my life. *Fuck, get me home, Richard. There's a surprise, and I don't care what it is as long as that man fucks me.*

I supposed that was a bit untrue. I did not care what it was. I was excited, but I also knew that whatever Westley had gotten me or done, it was going to be perfect. Sometimes, it really was the thought that counted, and that's entirely how I felt now. He'd explicitly done something or purchased something that was just for me.

That was more than enough.

Traffic let up as we got out of downtown, and Richard navigated the streets, taking side alleys and little-known shortcuts to get me back home as quickly as possible. I froze in my seat at that. I'd thought of Westley's as my home, and it didn't feel...wrong. If anything, imagining myself with Westley for the long term felt as natural as breathing.

He offered me a permanent contract. I haven't said anything, but...Hmm...

"We have arrived, Miss Andi. I'll pull up the car right to the elevators so that you can make your way up."

"You are a gem, Richard. I adore you, but like... don't murder me, k?"

He chuckled as I grabbed up my bag of stuff and slid close to the door to get out.

"Of course not! I wouldn't dream of hurting anyone who makes Westley so happy. I don't think I've seen him smile this much since...well since he launched his company."

A terrible burn set up shop in my eyes as I forced myself not to cry, and my chest squeezed. Shaking my head, I ignored the tremble in my fingers and put my hand on Richard's shoulder.

"Thank you."

I slid back to the door, opening it wide and stepping out. As I leaned over to yell another goodbye, I thought I saw movement by the security booth. But there were two guards working at present, so I shrugged it off.

"Next time Westley is feeling generous, I'll make sure he includes you too."

Richard blushed slightly, nodding. "You're too kind, miss."

"Nah, just used to being poor, and all this is super weird. Bye!"

I waved, and Richard just laughed as he pulled the car into its usual spot. I wondered for a moment where Richard lived—if he'd be having to make the trek across town again to his apartment. I hoped not. Harmstead wasn't massive, sure, but commuting back and forth every day would be exhausting. I made a mental note to ask Westley about it.

As I stepped up to the elevators and pressed the call button, the sound of a twig snapping made me spin around. There was a tiny person huddled over by the bush to the outer wall, and I noticed the dingy, unkempt air they carried.

I'd brought a bit of cash just in case I needed a snack from the vending machine, and I still had both said snack and five dollars left. I wasn't even really sure why I brought so much with me unless it was this.

Yes, I could be extremely sappy about fate, but with a shit string of luck most of my life, I liked to think of it as my rebellion against the world that had tried to crush me. The security booth was just a few feet from the bushes, so I felt safe enough to go over.

Walking up to the person, who, judging by his size, I believed was a man, I pulled out the five-dollar bill and the salt-and-vinegar potato chips, feeling silently bad for having chosen such a strong flavor.

"Hey there," I said softly, "are you all right? Would you like a bit of cash and some chips? It's all I have on me right now."

The beggar looked up, and I met his dark eyes, trying to offer a light smile. "I'm sure the security guys can help you find a ride too if you need."

"Just fine. Thank you. That's nice that you, uhh..." He stared down at the money and food I held out toward him. "Yeah."

He took it, and I gave a nod. Gesturing to the two gentlemen watching us from the security booth, I waved with another polite smile.

"They're not bad. I promise. They won't kick you out if you just ask for a bus ticket or something."

"Hmm, I'll consider that. You, uh," his tired eyes looked me up and down, and for some reason, I had to stifle a shiver, "live up there?"

My mouth opened, and I shook my head. "Oh, not really. I'm...I'm sort of dating someone who does. He's actually waiting for me right now, so I'm going to go, but I really do suggest the guys. They'll make sure you have somewhere to go for the night."

He scoffed, and I had to remind myself that a lot of drifters, people who just existed like this, didn't like to be patronized.

"Nah. I'll be fine." He stood up, circling around the short wall of the parking garage that shared half the space with the long rectangular bush and slung a backpack over his shoulder. A photograph, like a silly instant, take one, fell out of an open zipper at the front.

As I stooped down to pick it up for him, he snatched at it before I could get there. I'd upset him someone by going for it, and I held my hands up.

"Sorry. Just wanted to help."

He stared at me.

"Hmm, yeah. Help. I..." A smile spread over his lips, but it didn't reach his eyes. "I'm fine. Best me on my way. Got things to do."

I couldn't imagine what that meant, but I let him go and turned to go back to the elevator. As I walked there, I noticed that one of the security guys had stepped out from the booth and was hovering closer to me.

Holding up a hand, I smiled and nodded. "I'm good. Thanks."

The guard nodded back, and I hurried over to the elevator button and pressed it again. The thing was right there, so the doors slid right open. I stepped inside, and when the doors were closed again, I let out a heavy breath.

Something about the interaction had made me nervous, but I knew I was just being jumpy. He'd been totally nice, if a little off. But you couldn't blame people in his situation for forgetting their manners.

As the elevator reached the top of the building, I excitedly waited for the doors to open, my foot tapping Moris code into the floor. The ding sounded as the metal box came to a stop, and the two panels in front of me slid open. I smiled wide and practically lept out so that I could rush down the short hallway to Westley's door.

When I was just a few steps away, it opened, and he stepped out. The grin he wore was remarkable, and I could see the hint of pride and excitement thanks to his little surprise, whatever it was.

"Hi!" I ran up, wrapping my arms around his neck and pulling him in for a kiss.

He obliged, of course, and I got lost in the sensations, completely forgetting that there was something inside that I was supposed to be waiting for.

"Well, hello to you, too." He said into the skin of my neck when he trailed his kiss down. "I'm so glad you're back. Are you ready for your surprise?"

Giddy as a fucking school girl, I nodded, bouncing between either foot. "Yes. Why did you come out here, though? Were you just soooo excited to see me?"

Westley smirked, a twinkle in his eye that betrayed that outwardly steely composure.

"Maybe." He kissed me again. "You're also going to notice it the second you step inside, so..."

I laughed, my mind reeling at what could be behind that door. God, I hope he didn't get me another massage or something? I was still set after the last pampering, and those women needed a day off.

"After you, pet." Westley's voice was gentle and hushed as he looked down at me.

Then he swept open his arm and gestured to the penthouse door. I smiled–a little nervously–and went for the knob. As I pushed the thing open, I realized that Westley was right. I noticed this thing right away.

"Oh my God! Are you kidding me?"

I launched myself inside the penthouse, going straight for the gorgeous lengths of red silk hanging from an aerial rig in the center of his massive 20-foot-high ceiling near the stairs. My heart was soaring higher than even that, and I couldn't stop the downright school-girl giggle of joy that erupted from me as I stared up into the billowing silks around me.

Unsurprisingly to anyone who even remotely knew me, I teared up. I'd never received a gesture like this, and I truly couldn't fathom what to do to repay my gratitude. Or comprehend why he'd gone and done something so incredible for me. I really didn't desire this kind of extravagance.

"You put this in for me?" My voice wavered as I spoke, and I fought against the tightness residing there.

"Yes, pet." Westley's voice was silk as he reached into the fabric and pulled me close. "And I have a few ideas on how to put it to good use."

Every inch of me hummed, and I smiled up at him like he was the damn sun itself.

"I can't believe you did something like this..." I shook my head. "Just for me. I...Westley, you're...you're amazing."

"I just wanted to say thank you." He laid a gentle

kiss on my lips, holding my chin. "For everything you've done for me while you've been here."

"Me?" I gapped. "I haven't done much. I've just–"

"Hush." Westley put a finger to my lips. "If you're really feeling like you need to thank me in some way, how about you give me another show? It's been since the club, and I...I'd like to *see* more of you."

To be sure I got the point, Westley tugged on my loose sweater that covered the leotard. I felt my cheeks heat inferno strong as I nodded. He stepped away, and if it weren't for the halfie that I'd also felt–pressed against my thigh and so very welcoming–I would have been concerned. As it was, Westley just went over to his stereo system that was hidden behind a sleek cupboard in his entertainment center.

The thing chimed to life, and as if he'd had the song picked out in advance, "Never Tear Us Apart" by Bishop Briggs began playing.

It was perfect, and I immediately snapped into gear, warming up with the silks in a slow circle as Westley took a seak on a low club chair that he'd centered right in front of the rigs. As he sat, his eyes were a tangle of dark intent and wonder. Warmth pooled in my core as I met that hungry, primal gaze, and I let the music take me.

Easing into it, I reached for the silks, drawing them into their hoop so that I could wrap them around my back at the shoulders. Right on beat, I flung myself back against them, letting my sweater ride up high.

I kicked my leg up next, creating the momentum to get myself spinning. As I twirled, I was able to use that force to swing my legs up and around the silks, gripping them with one bent leg. My sweater had been perfectly positioned when the silks pinched against my back, and

I let it fall over my head and down my arms to the floor before beginning my climb up the silks.

I made my way up in a bind that I could use to make my first drop, posing strategically as I did. When the beat of the first chorus hit, I released my hold on the silks, spinning down them to land right as the music swelled. The silks were still beautifully spinning, and I wound myself into another good position for the next chorus, slipping an arm out of a strap on my leotard as I did.

The music filled me, a different new movement style that I'd never tried surging in me. I spun and spun, flinging myself through the silks as I wound and unwound myself through the loop. It felt like magic, and by halfway through the song, I'd gotten the top half of my leotard down around my waist.

Oh, God...I feel so...Alive.

My spin continued until I was unraveled from the silks. I gripped them around my wrists as I spun myself on my legs and sides around the smooth, cool floor. Somehow, after years of trying and failing, I found that inner sensuality that fueled a good strip tease. I hoisted myself up off the floor, whipping my hair back before acing a body roll like I never had.

I took a rare moment to make eye contact with Westley, and the raw lust, molten hot and endless, powering from his gaze made me feel like the most powerful person on the planet.

I could hear him growl even from where I stood.

Sliding down onto the floor, I used several well-placed arches and leg kicks to work my leotard free before standing up. I pumped my body up and down over the floor as I did, nailing that sexual push-up—with one leg up in the air even.

Goddamn, this is even more...everything. Being naked.

A wonderful, terribly filthy idea sprung forward in my mind, and I absolutely went for it. Spinning around on my knees so that my back was facing Westley, I threaded my hands through the silks, twirling them around just right. *Just like I did for my first performance.*

As I made to stand, I planted my feet wide, scooping my ass up as I rose, knowing full well that Westley could see *everything* when I did. Footsteps sounded on the tile floor, but he didn't stop me, just moving closer–oh so much closer.

Right at the crescendoing swirl of music, I turned to face him, my hands outstretched in the silks like they were tied up for him. Westley's composure was gone, and all I could see was that exquisite, sadistic smirk of my Master.

I played in the ropes just long enough in the bind before circling myself out of them to fling myself into a back bend again. Climbing up through the silks one last time, I wound up for a final drop. At the last beat drop, I let the silks unravel. Just as it was ending, I rewound my wrists in the silks, leaning on them and angling myself forward toward Westley with a grin.

He was just a few feet away, and he slowly began to clap as he approached me.

The tension hung over me, poised on a knife edge, and just as he reached, snatching my hair in his grip, Westley smiled down at me.

"Well done, pet. Now," he raised his brows, "get down on your knees."

25
The Silks

Westley

I was blown away. There was no better way to put it. The way Andi got to me, made my entire body come to life in a way I'd never experienced, was utterly mindblowing. The past few days we'd spent together, the bullshit from work, it was all spiraling together in my brain as I watched her, sensing how she seemed to instinctively know what I needed from her.

How did she see me like this? See *through* me like this? It was maddening. It was intoxicating. It was... fuck, I was getting very close to breaking the rules I'd come up with for myself.

And still, I couldn't find it in myself to care enough to stop.

Andi stared up at me, that beautiful submissive awe painted over her face, and she slid down onto her knees, her wrists still bound up in the silks.

"Such a good pet." I smoothed a hand down her blonde bob before threading my fingers through Andi's locks at the back of her neck and gripping. "Stick those hips in the air, kitten."

She angled forward, resting in the silks as she lifted her ass high in the air. I circled around her and dropped to my knee, gripping her hips and pulling her up toward my mouth. I dove my tongue between Andi's slick folds, the vibrant taste immediately powering through my tastebuds. She was already so fucking wet for me, and my cock dripped beneath my pants.

I lavished her tight little pussy with my tongue, sucking and flicking and toying with her clit until Andi was mewling for me. She was already on the edge, and I licked up her seam once more before moving back to stand.

"Westley! Please!"

"Oh, I'm not done with you, pet." I reached for the silks past her face, tugging lightly. "Get yourself good and wound up for me. Make sure I can get at that slippery cunt of yours."

Andi hopped to work, winding herself through the silks except for one leg. She let it dangle, her toes barely brushing the floor. It gave me perfect access to her pussy, and when I knew she was good and settled, I took the loose bit of slack in the silks and wrapped it around her wrists, securing them for me again.

"Please, please, please." Her words were a tumble of desperate whispers, and I beamed like the fucking sun.

"Goddamn, I love when you beg for me, pet. Music to my fucking ears."

I held her wrist pinned with one hand while I reached down for her slit with the other. Her soaking cunt was so warm and needy, and I thrust my fingers inside her with a hard shove. Andi cried out, clamping down around me as she bucked in the silks.

She swung nicely for me, and I appreciated how similar this was to having her suspended for me.

Pumping my fingers in slow, deliberate penetrations, I glided a third in alongside the others. Andi squeezed, her head kicking back as she moaned. I fucked her in swirling strokes until I hooked my fingers into her G-spot.

Even just doing that was enough to get her trickling, and I rubbed my thumb over her sensitive clit. Andi's pussy fluttered, and I could see her tremble even bound up in all that silk.

"Sir, fuck, oh, fuck. Fuck!"

I melted as she switched in sub-space so beautifully, and she tightened around my fingers as I upped the pace against that bundle of nerves that I knew would make her squirt for me. I stopped right in the middle of a hard thrust in, watching with glee as Andi's face screwed up in a frustrated cry.

"No! Please. Please, Sir."

"Do you need it *that* bad, my little pet?" I rolled my fingers across her G-spot again, achingly slow. "Does Daddy's little whore want to squirt all over the floor?"

She nodded, whimpering, and holy goddamn hell, my cock *hurt* it was so damned hard. The way she fell apart for me. God, I...loved it.

"Yes! Yes, Daddy, please!" She squirmed, but it was no use. Without her hands, she wasn't coming free of that silk binding.

Perfection.

"Say it. Say Daddy's little whore wants to squirt for him."

I slipped my fingers free, much to Andi's chagrin, and licked across the glistening cum coating my fingers. She nodded, frantic, jittery movements, and I held my fingers to her lips.

"Daddy's little whore wants to squirt for him." I shoved my fingers into her mouth, fucking her with them until I heard that delightful pattering sound.

"Oh, you really do, don't you." I pressed my lips to the shell of her ear. "As you wish, pet."

Tearing my hand free, I went straight back to Andi's needy pussy, shoving my fingers inside and thrusting against her G-spot roughly. Her cunt pulsed as she rocked right to the head of her orgasm and then tumbled over that edge in a great wail.

"Fuck!"

I gave it everything I had, and Andi did exactly as told. She gushed for me like a good little girl, and I fucking glowed, the sadist that I was, for how much I was milking from her. I knew she was still so embarrassed by how she did this, and damn, did I love making her just sit back and take it.

A puddle formed on the floor as I forced Andi to give me orgasm after orgasm. But I needed her on my cock, and I needed it *now*.

Releasing the hold on her wrists, I stepped back far enough to let her get free.

"Unwide yourself. Then back on your knees, kitten."

She took a moment to get herself worked free of the silks, and I couldn't be mad about that one. Andi was already so blissed out that I was sure unwinding herself was much more of a challenge than normal.

As she was at last free, Andi got down on her knees and looked up at me with lidded eyes. I loved seeing her so destroyed.

"Open up."

She was quick to do so, and I freed my erection

through the zipper of my pants. Shoving into Andi's mouth hard and fast, I bottomed out down her throat. Andi's eyes flared wide, the somewhat exhaustion stolen away by the brutal thrust.

"Mmm, so pretty." I patted her cheek, making her breathe around the cock in her mouth.

When I did pull back, I snatched up the length of silk next to her head and wrapped it around her neck, closing the loop just enough to pinch. I started up my vicious pumps again, fucking Andi's mouth with abandon. She took everything I dolled out, yielding everything she had to me.

Goddamn. So fucking gorgeous.

The lovely way she swallowed me down was beyond impressive, and I kept up the relentless pace until my shaft burned with need. I was right on the edge of an orgasm, and I yanked myself free, letting Andi catch her breath.

"Such a good kitten. Eating up Daddy's fat cock like a filthy slut." Slipping the silk over her head, I let it fall as I rubbed my dick across Andi's face. "Do you like that, pet? Do you want your Owner to fuck that soaked cunt?"

Andi moaned, her eyes closing as her breaths heaved. I smacked her harder with my shaft, and she jolted, yelping for me.

"Do you?" I ground out.

Swallowing hard, Andi nodded. "Yes. Please, Sir. I want you to fuck me so bad."

I could tell she was fatigued something fierce, but there was no lie there. Andi wanted it, but as I narrowed my eyes on her, I decided that she needed a bit of a "wake-up call" before I let her come again.

"Hmm," I circled around her, yanking her to her

feet and smacking a hand down over her ass in a hard spank, "I think you need to scream for me. So..."

Laying down another ferocious strike, I smiled as Andi jumped against my grip, reaching out for the silks to maintain her balance.

"Scream for me."

26
The Mirror

Andi

My entire body felt raw and exposed. I was sagging against the silks and not because I wanted Westley to stop or give me a break. I was just so damn tired behind everything. I'd trained for hours at the gym and then the strip tease. Oh, yeah, and the multiple orgasms.

I was beyond spent, but there was nothing I wouldn't give Westley to show my appreciation for the gift. Well...for everything.

Being with him had changed my life so much in such a short time. I'd never been treated like this, and I... I didn't want it it end. I wanted this to be my life. I did. I couldn't deny it anymore. And I couldn't deny how much I cared for him either. My soul reached and snagged a hold of him right away, and it wasn't letting go.

I wasn't letting go.

His hand slamming down on my cheek brought me out of my head again, and I screamed into the echoey expanse of the once-empty stairwell.

"Such a good, slutty little pet." Westley reached past me, grabbing a length of the silks. "Bend forward."

I did as told, gripping onto the other half of the silk hoop for balance. As I did, Westley wrapped the fabric around me. He'd widened it to the full width, and it cocooned me across my chest and legs, leaving my hips purposefully uncovered.

"Mmm, like a tasty little present."

A round of consecutive blows rained down on both ass cheeks, making me cry out in nearly ceaseless screams. When my skin burned so badly that I thought I might die, Westley's cock stroked through my slippery folds, teasing my entrance. The shallow in and out was nothing compared to the way he could shove inside me up to the hilt, hitting my cervix.

But then he pulled back, and I felt the blunt head of his dick pressing against my asshole.

"Oh, fuck. Fuck, fuck, fuck." The words spilled out of me, and my body slowly yielded to him, welcoming him inside me.

"That's right, pretty girl. Daddy's going to fuck this ass, push you to the brink like a good little whore."

He sunk inside me, and I clamped down all around him, my pussy dripping furiously. The telltale sound of his belt sliding through his pant loops sounded behind me, and in a quick jerk, he tugged the thing free. A whoosh of fabric signaled his pants falling to the floor.

"I want you to squeeze around Daddy's cock, precious." I felt the smooth leather caress my sore ass. "Let me feel how much of a pain slut you are."

A crisp smack rocked me as the belt came down hard. I cried out, clamping down around Westley's shaft just as asked. My pussy pulsed as the burn radiated through me, and I swelled at the feeling of him stretching out my tight hole. Cum slid down the inside of my thigh as I got closer to another orgasm.

Another cracking strike on the opposite cheek, and I did it again, gripping Westley tight, and this time I came, shoved recklessly over the edge as he thrust his cock deep in my ass as the blow landed. Warmth gushed from me as more of my slick rained out.

"Good fucking girl," Westley grunted.

Two more blows had me on the verge of passing out, but fucking hell, did I love every damn second. As Westley bottomed out inside me, more cum rushed out. I whimpered as an odd swell of embarrassment claimed me, and then Westley slipped free.

I whined for the loss. *No, I'm too empty. No.*

Looking over my shoulder, I watched, desperate and whiny, as he stepped out from his pants and briefs, kicking them to the side. His button-down was next, undone at the top and swiftly yanked over his head. The jut of Westley's erection from his hips was damn delectable, and he walked in front of me holding the belt.

As he approached the chair he'd sat in, he grabbed something small off the cushion, and I noticed that scar on his back again. The one he didn't want to talk about.

I wasn't sure how, but without any proof, I just knew it had been put there by one or both of his shitty parents. The way he talked about them, or didn't rather. The way he'd reacted to my own sob story. Someone had hurt him, and my heart broke, shattered into a million pieces.

Tears had already stained my face, and as he turned back to me and stalked over, the glorious look of sadistic glee was too much for me to take. The tumbled out all the harder, and as he pet my head,

Westley secured the nipple clamps to me over the fabric.

I yelped and whimpered, but there was no using that safeword. I was falling apart...but I fucking needed to.

Westley lifted my chin up with the folded loop of his belt, forcing me to look at him. "That's right, pet. Break for me."

My head dropped hard as he whipped the belt away and smacked it down across my back. The wracking sobs took control of my body even as my pussy hummed, begging for more. He wanted me to break for him? Well, I was—down to my core.

Time ceased to exist, my body pushed to the ultimate limit, and then a gentle whisper touched my ear, the featherlight sensation somehow screaming loud against the backdrop of steady, thundering aches.

"You look so damn gorgeous, pet. Destroyed, flayed wide open. Now," he nipped at my lobe, "let me put you back together. The only one."

The tears streamed harder, but not for the pain.

Circling back around me, Westley sheathed himself home in my ass again, and I howled—roaring into the air as I splintered. It was too much, not enough. It was perfection, and I...

"Wes—Sir! I...I..." Somehow, my voice was gone.

Westley's brutal thrusts assaulted me like a battering ram, and my nerve set ablaze. I was coming. Or was I dying? I couldn't tell.

"What, pet? Tell me."

My head spun, the truth ripped from my lips by his wicked pace and exquisite torture.

"I don't deserve this." It was almost a whisper, but I knew he heard me.

The vicious confession tore from my soul, from the depths of me where all the bullshit lived that I shoved down on a daily basis. And then I couldn't stop the words from exploding out of me.

"I'm nothing. A no-one. I'm worthless."

Westley jacked his hips forward so hard that I flew forward, my screams filling the entire penthouse, and I just came all the harder.

"Look at me," he growled low.

I could lift my head, the sobs taking me as much as the pleasure roiling through my entire being.

"Look at me!"

Jumping, I whimpered, but then I summoned my strength, looking over my shoulder at Westley and meeting his dazzling green eyes.

"You'll be punished for saying such things about what belongs to me." He thrust his cock deeper, making me shudder. "You hear me?"

I nodded, barely.

"Do you hear me, Andi?!"

My eyebrows shot up, my attention zeroing in on the way he looked at me, the way he felt inside me.

He said my name.

"Yes. I hear you," I managed to choke out.

"You belong to me. You're *mine*. And nothing of mine is worthless."

I just locked eyes with him, taking the furious assault of his hips as he fucked my ass relentlessly. We didn't look away, couldn't. I felt the truth of his words burn into my skin with each pulse of my aching skin, with each pound of his cock as it forced another orgasm to rush through me, and with every shimmer of his eyes as he focused on me.

It was like looking into a mirror. Everything I felt

and believed was reflected right back at me, and I knew right there and right then that I did. I belonged to Westley irrevocably.

And he belonged to me.

Raw, unbridled connection filled me so full I could scarcely stand it. Westley's animal, savage strikes drilled into my ass, my pussy fluttering and gushing for him. In moments, he thickened, shooting his cum into me with the power of a rocket. I warmed, my entire being humming.

For at least this one moment, Westley and I occupied the same space, and I knew I'd never be the same again.

27
The Breaking

Andi

The sun was here again, and I could move. Everything ached so profoundly that I thought I might never be able to walk again. Westley had carried me to the master bedroom after he'd unwound me. We slipped into the bed, clinging to each other silently until we fell asleep. I was still naked, covered in the evidence of our evening, and my jaw ached as my body forced me to yawn.

"Morning, pet."

Westley's voice was a bit hoarse, and I looked over at him, grinning sleepily as consciousness solidified more and more.

"Hi." I could hardly whisper, and I winced.

"Bath?" He cocked a brow at me.

I just nodded, and again without words, Westley helped me up and out of the bed to the bathroom. He ran the water, staying right next to me, and when the tub was full, we settled in together. We sat there for a long while in the quiet, just the dim light from the toilet area lighting the room.

After what could have been years for how I processed time, my stomach growled. Westley's chuckle jostled me as I lay against him, and he kissed the top of my head.

"Food, then?"

I nodded against his chest, reluctantly leaning up to let him reach for the plug.

Everything we were doing was backed by this odd silence that neither of us could stand to break with more than a handful of words. I knew I was still reeling, processing everything that had happened, but there was also this tenuous magic that was being woven between us.

Fragile strands of connection were hardening in the light of day, and if we moved too quickly, they would snap.

Eventually, we made our way down to the kitchen. Westley had wrapped me in a massive terrycloth robe, all-white, and I sunk into the warmth of it as I sat at his breakfast table, eating eggs.

And then it happened. I felt that tug on what we'd done last night, the questions that I'd been holding in, and I knew that it was now. I had to do this now, or I never would. *We* never would.

"So," I sighed, and Westley looked up from his plate, "how did you get the scar on your back? I've... noticed it. A few times."

There was silence, and I dropped my stare to the eggs again. But I couldn't stay there. I looked up from taking another bite, and my chest squeezed as I saw the expression on Westley's face. I'd hit that nerve again.

"Christ. I'm...I'm so sorry." I shook my head. "I just...I want to understand. I can tell it's something, but..."

He didn't move, hardly breathed.

"Maybe I just shouldn't talk."

As I stared at him, Westley's expression was beyond grim, and I instinctively sat farther back in my seat, trying to give him as much space as I could without actually getting up from the table.

The silence hung around us for eons. When it continued without any indication of letting up, I seriously considered sliding off the chair onto the floor, slinking away like a slug. Then, Westley finally cleared his throat. Our eyes met, and Westley...Westley was *crying*.

"Oh, no." I hurriedly put down my fork, waving my hands in front of me. "I...shit. This isn't what I wanted. Crap, I'm awful. I'll...go. I'm so sorry. I'll go."

I pushed up from the table and headed for the stairs to retrieve my things, not that they'd do much in the way of clothing at this point. Maybe he wouldn't mind if I stole the robe and a few items from the closet?

Goddamn, Andi. What were you thinking? You're not his girlfriend. The fuck is the matter with you?

Then Westley was behind me and spinning me around. He pushed me up against the glass wall that framed the stairs just behind the silks he'd installed. He gripped the two halves of the robe in his fists, which went white from the strain. His eyes bored into me, making my mouth fall open.

"Don't. Don't you dare leave. You..."

Westley's eyes were wild, and he shook his head before slicing right through me with his stare again.

"No one has ever done this to me. And you did it from the first moment I laid eyes on you. How are you doing this, Andi? How are you getting inside me and cracking the walls I've painstakingly built for years?"

"I-"

Westley tore the robe from me, throwing it across the room. I yelped, rogue tears spilling down my cheeks as I was bared to him. My body was littered with the evidence of how he'd claimed me. I was so vividly aware of them, even as I love each and every one.

He shook his head again, then let it hang, his hair brushing my bare chest.

"I knew finding you would destroy me."

Everything that had cracked open last night tore open again, the flimsy scab of a little sleep and a few hours yanked free. Our wounds bled, oozing out the infection that wormed through the both of us.

"You've tunneled into my heart, and I...I never wanted that, Andi. I wanted a permanent submissive. This...this is..."

I trembled, but there was a new strength behind me, my shattered pieces put back together and forged with gold veins.

"Different. I know."

Westley's head shot back up and eyes flared as he stared at me, a slow nod creeping forward. He knelt down, running his hands down my brutalized body and forcing my legs apart.

"I could worship you for hours, Andi. The perfection here...How is this real?" His voice was a slim thread that wound through the air between us.

Westley slung one of my thighs over his shoulder, opening my cunt up for him and making it weep. I pressed back against the wall, a potent exchange billowing between us as I looked down at Westley on his knees before me.

"Westley," everything was spiraling, and I needed to

understand, needed to hear it all, "how did you get the scar?"

His eyes shot up to mine, and he forced his fingers inside me. "Andi, I..."

I held that dagger stare, lowering my chin to focus entirely on Westley's emerald-green eyes. "You're going to tell me, Westley. How did you get the scar?"

Tears swelled in his eyes, and when he spoke, his voice was a rough whisper. "My parents...were cruel, my father in particular. I..I never was worth much to them. They didn't...see me."

A low growl rumbled out of him, building into a roar as he sunk deep inside me with that same desperate intensity as last night. I arched, pressing my shoulders into the wall as Westley pumped his fingers in and out of my pussy.

"You're worth something to me," my voice was shaky as I struggled to speak through the pleasure and sorrow and euphoria mixing through my veins like drugs.

"Because of this?" Westley licked up my wet slit and drove his tongue inside me, joining his fingers.

I cried out, nearly losing my balance. Westley's other hand gripped my hip, pinning me back to the cool glass surface. My own tears spilled out, the dam breaking.

"Because...because you saw me. Because you trusted me not to disappoint you."

I recognized Westley's pain reflected in my own, my body thrumming with visceral need as I felt bound to him. Gripping the roots of his hair, I looked down at him—my Westley.

"Because when everyone else viewed me as temporary and broken, you saw me as your...forever."

As I marveled at him, Westley met my eyes. His

tongue swirled inside me, and then he pulled back, sucking my clit into his mouth and biting lightly with his teeth. Westley's fingers curled up inside me, finding that magic spot, and I started tumbling over the edge.

He milked my orgasm with his fingers, sending me to new heights that caused me to flood with cum, squirting it into his mouth as he hungrily lapped it up.

When my shaking finally stopped, I met Westley's stare again. He was coated in my cum, his expression blown wide open, vulnerable. Sliding his fingers free, he stood back up and crashed his lips into mine. I tasted myself on his tongue, new heat coiling in my core.

His hard cock pressed into me through the thin material of the sweatpants he'd hastily pulled on this morning.

Westley pulled his lips from mine, "I...I see you, pet."

My throat tightened, and I fought against the string in my eyes. "I see you, too."

Westley's lips were back on mine as he pulled his pants down. Then, he spun me around, pressing my chest up against the wall so that my ass stuck out. His cock quickly found my pussy and thrust inside up to the hilt. The vulgar sounds of his skin slapping into my wet cunt echoed through the room. Westley pressed his thumb into my asshole, fucking me with it as he pumped into me.

"Say you're mine."

Westley smacked my ass with his thrusts, all the more sore and overly sensitive from what we'd done just hours ago. My breaths huffed out of me as he forced me into the glass. Westley's grip, his pummeling hips and tone, were fervent and desperate.

And I let it out, releasing anything left inside me that was holding me back.

"I'm yours, Westley."

"Say it again!" He growled, the vulnerability clear.

My voice hitched. "I'm yours."

Westley's pace was relentless, and my legs shook so bad I could barely stand. I didn't need to. I needed this. I needed *him*.

"How did you do this, Andi?" His voice was so small as he continued to pound into me, gripping me for dear life.

I struggled to speak through my thundering breaths, "Your broken...matches...mine."

"You're *mine*, Andi."

His hips rammed into mine, forcing his cock as deep as it would go like he needed to be a part of me–connected.

"You belong to me."

Looking over my shoulder at him, I tried to put everything I was feeling into my face.

A tear slid down his cheek as he held himself inside me, just breathing. "And I am *nothing* if not yours."

With that, our bodies exploded into action, clawing hungrily for each other and frantic to embolden that invisible string that was sewn between us. We crescendoed, shattering as we launched into the blissful unknown and fell apart together. Our cries filled the empty space around us like a depraved duet, and then we collapsed to the floor. Westley was still behind me, and he laid his head down on my hip.

"I...I love you, Andi. I shouldn't. I didn't think I *could*. But I do."

I turned, guiding Westley's head into my lap.

Smiling down at him, the burn still stinging in my eyes, I stroked my fingers through his hair. "I love you, too."

28
The Revelation

Westley

W e lay there on the floor until our breathing calmed and the air around us got too cold to stand. I scooped Andi up and took her to the master bedroom. Under the covers, she snuggled into me, her body warm and solid. Andi put my hand on my chest as my heart pounded against my ribs, and I ran my fingers lazily up and down her arm.

Holy shit.

I squeezed Andi tight to my side and exhaled hard. Taking her chin in my hand, I made her look up at me as I roamed her face with my eyes, memorizing every tiny detail.

"You..." My voice cracked, and I cleared my throat. "You are worthy of the world, Andi. I'll do whatever I can to give it to you, but..."

I swallowed, feeling it slide through my chest. What the fuck was I doing? *Oh, hell, just say it.*

"I understand if you want to...go back home. Our contract isn't legally binding. It's just paper. The club won't like it, but it's not like you were formally employed by them. You...you don't have to stay here. We can take things slow and–"

"Contract or not," Andi pushed up onto her elbow, looking down at me as my heart hammered against my ribs, "I'm staying. I want this. I want *you*."

Relief washed through me, and I let my eyes fall. It was Andi's turn to lift my head.

"But I want all of it—not just pleasure and pain. I want everything that comes along with being your submissive *and* partner. Deal?"

My eyes flared, my brows shooting to my hairline. All I could do was stare at her. Andi took my hand, squeezing as she held my eyes with her baby blues.

"I said I love you, dummy. That means I'm sticking around. I don't just toss that shit around like it's confetti. So?"

The world tilted on its axis. Up was down, left was right, black was fucking neon green. Andi wanted to stay. With me. After everything. I shook my head, my horrid eyes welling again. It was like now that I'd let the dam leak a little, it was easier for the bastards to slip out, and my heart pinched, battered against my ribs.

I knew I hadn't laid out much of a red carpet per se, and I *knew* what I was like. Ignorant and stupid weren't words I'd use to describe myself, after all. Although, even I had to wonder about that sometimes. I'd blanketed myself in that world of repressed rage and overuse of compartmentalization.

Therapy bills were likely the smarter investment over the club, but I'd never lasted more than two visits. That awful swirl in my guts was back, and my brain felt like it was melting. How was Andi saying yes? No was beyond the logical answer.

But she just...

I didn't understand how any of this was possible in the short time I met her. Life was not a fairy tale, it was not a romcom, and it was usually not fair. In the slightest.

And yet, something about the way Andi had been a completely open book–how she'd ridden the turbulent waves of my unspoken baggage and weathered it all in stride–not only tore my walls down, it crumbled them to dust.

She'd just walked into that club and let herself be auctioned–to me, of all people–with no prior knowledge or understanding of the community. It was foolish and incredibly brave. What's more, she just walked into my life and saw me, saw past the money and circumstance. Andi zeroed in on that hurt, the pain that haunted my every waking minute and didn't turn and run.

Hell, she'd made me face it more than I ever had.

After years of never trying to create something real because of a fucked delusion of worthless and, well, let's face it, fear, what I'd apparently truly wanted–what I *needed*–was right fucking here.

"Andi," I shook my head, aware that I'd been silent for too long, "I just...Jesus, pet. You're just..."

I pulled her closer to me, breathing in everything she was and wanting to cement it to my bones so that I could wear it as armor. And then the words came tumbling out.

"When I decided to give this a shot, having a permanent submissive, I fully expected it to never work. I assumed that the woman I finally brought back here would choose to leave after she saw the mess I really was, and that would be it. The years of self-sabotaging would be proven right, and I'd be able to say I gave it a good old college try and drop it. I'd just continue to visit the club and fuck on a completely casual basis."

Andi didn't say a word, letting me have this space I needed to work out everything that was going on in my head. She was so much wiser than her years gave her credit for, and my chest pinched at the internal reminder that we'd both been forced to grow up too fast.

"That did *not* happen." My eyes burned and for once, I didn't fight it. "From the moment I saw you, I knew there was something special about you, and it went way beyond your exquisite dancing. The way you move in the silks, the way you give yourself to the rope, to me. It broke me, and I really thought I'd be the only one doing the breaking."

A familiar sense of dread had crawled over me as Andi presented her terms, her own contract, so to speak. She wanted all of it; she wanted real, and I was beyond terrified to get there with someone. Behind the layers of money and schooling, there was darkness and pain. Opening that up to someone felt like an invitation for more of the same.

But...

"I agree. If you want to try this with me, which I can't guarantee that I'll always be fun to be around, I want to try too. You're breaking open some walls that I've had locked around me for decades, Andi. But being with you, seeing you become more and more of your-self, it feels well worth it to me."

Andi's mouth was on me in seconds, and I smiled against the kiss, the feeling of her lips on my splitting me open just as sure as they were sewing me back together.

When she pulled back, Andi wore a falsely serious

expression, gripping my hands in hers and meeting mine with the perfect portrayal of gravity.

"You should know," she spoke, her voice grim, "I'm very broke. I have no prospects, and worse, I have absolutely *no* desire to go out and find some. I love to dance, and that's all I want to do—aside from you, of course."

The warmest, most genuine laugh of my life erupted from me in the tune of submission. I was submitting myself to this, wholly and down to my bones.

"Hmm...I think I'm amenable to those terms." I held her tight to my chest, her breasts pressed up against me.

"Oh!" She sat up with a start, her eyes flaring wide, "I think I just had a great idea."

Andi's grin was mischief incarnate, and I positively swooned.

"Yes?"

She held out her hand. "I want the contract. When it's been a week, and then a month, and then a year, and whatever, I want to sign it. I want to *keep* signing it, over and over, so that you know I'm always here. That I've always chosen...this."

Damn, this incredible woman for making me fucking tear up again. My heart was gone, in the fucking stratosphere at this point, and I never wanted to come down from this high.

"All right." I nodded, a bubbling excitement kicking up my pulse. "I'm sure I can ask the club for it since... you'll be staying a while."

I stroked the side of her face, continually marveling at how I could never seem to get enough of it. Of her.

"Good." Andi snuggled under my chin, and dammit, I love it. I love her. This...this life that I'd been dredging myself up from each morning felt light and sunny and full of things I never dared dream of.

Cocking a brow, I smirked down at her, feeling warmth melt into me as we sat together. "Is there anything else I should know on my end? Since I'll be signing that contract, too, of course."

She furrowed her brow, considering. With a decidedly strong nod, she counted off on her fingers. "I hate olives, I prefer dark beer, and I absolutely adore holiday romance movies."

I stifled a laugh at that last one, rolling my lips between my teeth. "Noted."

"Anything else you'd like to tell me?" She angled her face up at me, eyebrows raised and her lips hovering over my own.

"I'm obsessed with hockey, though that hasn't really come up. I can fly a plane, I've shared a bed with someone a whopping one time now, and," I adjusted to better look at her, losing myself to those baby blues, "If you ask it of me out here when we're like this without contracts or Sirs or rules, I'll probably do anything for you. Except for shave."

"Well, it's a good thing I like the beard, then. So, Westley," Andi's voice raised as she set up her words, "How do you feel about watching 'My Valens-date?'"

Grimacing only slightly, I nodded, a disbelieving chuckle filtering out of me. I had a feeling I'd be doing that a lot.

"Sounds great," I said, grabbing the remote from inside my nightstand and handing it to her. "But you'll definitely pay for it later."

I winked, and her amused smirk was too good for words. I did not deserve this woman. It was all too perfect. *Damn, I'm...I'm the luckiest man alive.*

Andi reached for my hand and shook it, "Deal."

Settling in to watch the movie, whatever the hell it was, I actually relaxed. Not from exhaustion or some attempt to just do the thing I was supposed to. I relaxed, my entire body a type of calm that I thought only monks were capable of.

Nothing could go wrong now. This was the end all and be all of my existence. I was on cloud fucking nine, and I was never coming down. Nothing and and no one could touch us.

This right here? This was our happily ever after. Book closed.

29
The Drop

Westley

T he sun was shining. The birds were singing. It was like a fucking Disney movie. I'd insisted that Andi let me take her out to celebrate, visiting her favorite indie vendors in the arts district. We were right by the shore, the ocean slapping against the beach just down the hill from this upper sidewalk. Dozens of people were flocking to the nice day and interesting wares.

"Ooh, Westley, look!"

Turning my attention away from the gentle roar of waves below, I looked over at Andi who was pointing eagerly at a stall full of paints and sculptures–likely created by the woman manning the booth. There were colorful pieces aplenty, and most of them appeared to be renditions of flowers.

Upon closer inspection, the flower and plant-like designs were also interspersed with depictions of skele-tons or bones. There were insects of various shapes and sizes hidden amongst the petals as well. While most of the prints were flat, two-dimenions versions of the scenes, the large canvases were the original 3D versions that used actual flora and fauna in the designing.

There was a gorgeous luna moth specimen surrounded by dried and preserved flowers and fruits sealed in by resin in a massive gilded gold frame.

"That's beautiful," I said, smiling at her.

Andi looked up at me cheerfully, and not for the first time since we came down here, I raked my eyes across the outfit she'd chosen. It was unseasonably warm for May on the Upper East Coast, and she was taking full advantage of that fact.

She wore slim-fitting black jeans, those strategic holes right at the knees, and had paired them with a blousy, very low-backed black tank top. The thin straps were barely anything, and the front dipped low enough to show off the slight curves of her breasts without giving away the entire farm, as it were.

A light denim jacket had been on the scene when we first arrived as well, but it had been quickly replaced by another one that Andi purchased from an edgy shop just five minutes after arriving.

The denim on this one was black, but there were massive panels cut out of the front at the shoulders and the entire back. They'd been replaced with a thin, lace-like material that was embellished with slithering black snakes that crisscrossed in every direction. A fair bit of skin was still visible behind the fabric, and it created an impressive allure, Andi's blonde bob dusting just over the collar.

"These are incredible. Did you make them all by hand?"

The woman running the stall smiled and nodded,

her warm brown skin glowing in the sun. "I did. And may I just say that your jacket is fabulous."

Andi beamed. "Why, thank you. My boyfriend just got it for me. Pray for him while I'm here because I just love everything."

The woman laughed, grinning at me, and I rolled my eyes playfully, stepping up to Andi and pulling her under my arm.

"It's true. My wallet is a bit confused because it hasn't seen this much air in a long time. But we're both happy about it."

"Ooh, keep him." The seller praised, and even I was blushing a little at this point.

Walking along the front of her displays, I admired the specimen pieces most of all, and I could tell Andi liked them too.

"Do you have any in red?" I pointed down to another butterfly piece in a gilded frame.

"I do, actually. Just finished this one the other day."

The woman held up a large black-framed piece featuring a striking black-and-red butterfly, the lower wings of which looked like they'd been dipped in the bright color. Behind it were white-and-red flowers as well as a preserved spiderweb stretched across the black background.

Even more intriguing, the white bones of a snake curved into a circle behind the butterfly as well, separating the black of its wings from the black background. It was slightly chilling but remarkably beautiful and intriguing.

I smoothed my hand up and down Andi's lower back. "What do you think, pet?"

She smiled with wide eyes. "It's amazing. God, it's

sort of creepy but in the best way, and the spiderweb strings make me think of the silks."

"Me too." I grinned, not breaking eye contact with her. "We'll take it."

"Westley are you sure?!" Andi shook her head, her eyes flaring even wider.

"Of course, I am." I faced the artist. "We'll take it."

The woman smiled and was quick to wrap it up and pack it in a protective box before it then went into a paper bag. I paid her, leaving a tip as well, and she beamed. My chest lightened for how thrilled she looked, and I laid Andi off to the next stall happily ooze money like it was going out of style.

I never went crazy with the spending, but this felt special. Still, since it was so different for me, I paused while Andi went inside a clothing booth to call my bank. I wasn't about to have them think my card was stolen.

She waved over at me as I stood just outside the fabric stall walls.

"I'm going to try these on, okay?"

Andi held up a pair of leather pants, and I nodded, the corners of my lips turned down in an intrigued smirk. I was very much looking forward to seeing her in those.

"Go on. I'll be right there. I just need to settle this."

With a happy little bounce, Andi slipped inside and walked to one of the people working the booth to try on the pants. The sun got warmer and warmer the longer I stood in it, on hold to ensure that the bank wasn't about to freak out over today's shopping spree.

As I waited for them to confirm that the card was good, I closed my eyes, boredom and heat getting the best of me. I turned, trying to put my back to the sun, and my shoulder knocked into someone entering the clothing place.

"Oh, my apologies. The heat seems to be making me clumsy. I'm sorry again."

The man looked a bit haggard, like he'd been out in the sun for much longer than I had and had spent most of the time drinking. He certainly smelled like it. Holding up his hands, the guy grunted something at me and then went into the booth.

I watched him stumble around for a minute, something prickling at the back of my spine. He didn't seem like the type to be able to afford this place, and while I hated to judge like that, it felt odd to see him go in and so clearly faking being interested in the clothes.

"Mr. Stanton?"

My attention snapped back to the phone, and I turned away from the loud chatter of a few patron gathered near this front corner to better hear my call.

"Yes. I'm here."

"Apologies for the delay, Mr. Stanton, but it was quite good that you called. The bank had just placed a lock on the card and I've had it removed. You should be good to go for the rest of the day."

"Oh, excellent. Good instincts then. Thank you." I heaved out a sigh, glad that I caught that before it was worse. "Tomorrow will be a regular day, however, so if something changes then, be sure to employ that lock."

"Of course, Mr. Stanton. Is there anything else I can help you with?" The woman was polite, with a clear tone that made her especially easy to understand.

"No, that'll be all. Thanks again."

"It's our pleasure. Have a wonderful day, Mr. Stanton."

"You, too." I smiled to no one in particular and then

hung up, facing the shop again and looking for Andi to come out in those amazing pants.

I didn't see her right away, and while that was hardly anything alarming, that strange tingle in my spine didn't back off. Scanning the area again, I didn't see any sign of that drunken man either. My stomach clenched, my heart rate ticking up. God, I was probably being ridiculous, except...

Good instincts. Dammit. I...don't like this.

Proceeding inside the clothing shop, I went to the same attendant that Andi had spoken to. I asked them where he'd pointed her, and following his instructions, I beelined for the back of the tent, looking for the sliding blue fabric of the makeshift changing room.

I flugh the drape to the side. It was empty. No Andi. Nothing.

But then as I turned to go back out front, something glinted on a small black chair that had been provided and I hurried over. On top of a pile of fabric was the framed butterfly we bought, the gold tag shining in a random strip of sunlight that cut through the tent's walls. Beneath it was Andi's new jacket, the black snake pattern unmistakeable.

She was in there, but...she was gone now. My pulse skyrocketed, my stomach dropping clean through the earth. I snatched up her things, and ran back out to the front of the shop. I stopped the attendant again, asking if he had seen her. I asked the other workers. I asked the shoppers, the random guy I saw walking by with his family.

Nothing.

The world spiraled, everything flipping as I tore apart that damn shop to find her. The employees wanted to be upset, I could tell, but they saw the panic in my eyes too. Andi was missing. I couldn't find her in the shop or either of the ones next door.

I ran across the walkway. Nothing. I sprinted to the public bathroom. Nothing. I ran to the artist with her insects again. Nothing.

My phone buzzed in my pocket, the ring muffled by the fabric. Who the fuck would be calling me right now. But as I pulled it out, I saw the unknown name listed instead of the number. It buzzed and buzzed in my hand as I just stared, my heart in my throat.

After three rings, I answered.

"Hello?"

There was nothing but silence, and I immediately thought of the prank calls. *No, no, no. This can't be-*

"You don't deserve nice things, Mr. Stanton. You've taken everything from me, after all. So, now..." a ragged breath cut through the line and then...

A scream.

"I'm taking everything from you."

"No." I reeled, trying to process reality because... because it couldn't be this. "You can't-"

Another horrible scream, and I recognized it.

"Andi!"

"Oh, quit your hollering. Face it, boss." The sound of wind or a fan rumbled thorugh the phone. "You've lost."

"Don't you touch her! I swear to God, if you lay one fucking finger on her, I'll fucking kill you!"

"Talk soon, boss."

The line went dead.

Andi was gone. No, Andi had been taken, and I was fucking standing there like a goddamn moron doing nothing. I...I had to get her back. Whoever this piece of shit was, he took her from me and there wasn't a single thing on this planet that I wouldn't do to get her back.

God, where did I even start.

"The police. I have to call them…I have to…" My eyes burned, bile crawling up the back of my throat. "I won't stand for this, Andi. I'm getting you home. No matter what."

30
The Spin

Andi

The achy throb in my skull reverberated down my spine, flooding my entire being. I'd been sore before. Hell, I'd been *extremely* sore before, but this was something else. I could barely lift my head, and it was like I was coming off a bender or something. I was dizzy, the world spinning, and I was helpless to stop it as I flinched against the cuffs holding my hands above my head. For as wonderful as being tangled up in my silks during a spin was, this was just as...terrifying.

I was standing. That was...different. At least, I was trying to be standing. Apparently, I'd hung by my shoulders for some time, and they hurt more than even my head. My feet slipped against smooth, damp ground as I tried to find my balance and not just crash into the wall again.

There are walls? Fucking hell, where am I?

"Westley, this..." My voice was scarcely loud enough for even me to hear, a weak croak that hurt to perform.

I stopped myself, trying to swallow down the nothing in my mouth. It was so damned dry. The pound behind my eyes doubled down, and I felt a wave of nausea crawl over me as I tried to open my eyes a crack. The light was too much, there was a dripping sound somewhere, and the cold creeping over my skin became abruptly clear.

This felt *wrong*.

"Wes, too much. I don't–"

"He's not fucking here, you slut."

My stomach dropped. The voice, the message, was very much not the Dom I was expecting, and a horrible sensation raked its claws down my spine. I couldn't even think to explain the level of terror that sliced through me–hot and raw. This wasn't home. This wasn't Wes. And this wasn't fucking good.

From seemingly nowhere, the man's voice rang again in my head.

He's not here....I'm fine. Best me on my way. Got things to do....

I knew that voice.

My head pounded all the harder, and the dread itching its way through my blood surged, making me flail against the cuffs on my wrists as I finally opened my eyes.

I was in a bathroom, dingy and disgusting. My wrists had been cuffed around a shower curtain rod above my head, and I was fucking dangling from it like a goddamn slab of meat on a rack. As I took in the too-bright light, the shadows forming in stark contrast against the once-white walls, I realized that a light was being directed right at me, a spotlight in an otherwise dark room.

Looking down, the cold air made that much more sense as well. *Fucking Christ.*

I wore only my think black tank. My pants were

missing, I had no shoes, and the slick, cool sensation beneath my feet in the tub wormed through me like a disease. My jacket was long gone, too, and I couldn't even remember if I'd put it back on after the changing room.

The changing room!

This man, the man that I'd seen at Westley's penthouse, had taken me right from the fairgrounds. Westley had been right there—just outside the shop on the phone. How the fuck had this happened so easily. Whoever this asshole was, he'd just, just snatched me up and dragged me back to wherever the fuck this was.

And for whatever the fuck reason.

"L-let me...go." My words were slurred, a scramble of consonants that I couldn't wrap my tongue around.

My steps faltered as I tried to stand straighter and take the weight off my wrists. But the tub was wet at the bottom, and my legs were Jell-O. When I tried to steady myself, another wave of vertigo tore through me, and I groaned.

I'd done drugs a handful of times thanks to the Burlesque circuit, but this? This was so much worse. I had to imagine that I'd been hit with GHB or, hell, chloroform if I knew anything about how creepy kidnappers worked. Which, of course, I did not. Why on earth had this guy come for me anyway.

"That's," the man laughed in a sharp bark, "yeah, no, no, no. Not going to *fucking* happen. He...he needs to pay."

In another twist of my guts, my stomach clenched, and I heaved nothing. Whatever he'd given me wasn't sitting right. *And fuck, the guy said he. He can't mean...*

"Westley?" I tried to peer around the light blinding

me, but all I could see was the rail-thin shape of what I had to assume was the man.

That horrid laugh started up again, and I pushed harder against the floor to stand. My vision swam, my blurry sights between blinks revealing a rather nondescript bathroom. It was white, or used to be, from head to toe, and the curtain rod I hung from obviously held no curtain. The thing must have been reinforced, too, if it were holding my weight successfully.

"Ugh, shut it! I'm sick of hearing your stupid voice saying his name!" Something flew out of the darkness and hit me in the stomach, making me cough. "It's all the two of you fucking do! Talk and fuck and then talk some more. Going out and spending money like it has no goddamn real cost! You fucking think a bag of chips is gonna save me!"

As much as I already knew that his guy was the same from the parking garage, hearing him say it out loud forced a shiver down my spine. And it was obvious the asshole had been watching for a while, watching us... watching *me*...have sex.

My skin crawled, a dark humiliation tainting the joy that I'd found with Westley. How had this man done all this without being noticed? *Why* had he done all this? Saying it seemed personal was a vast understatement, and it seemed much more directed at Westley than me. Though, apparently, I was in for a penny in for a pound.

Of likely very real, very cut-off flesh.

Stop, Andi. Don't do this to yourself. You've managed to...distract yourself even a little with memorizing the bathroom. Don't...

But I'd let a crack of the fear spread, widening up along the fault line. My forced composure was slipping, and I felt the terrible sting behind my eyes. I didn't want to cry. I couldn't. This piece of shit didn't deserve my tears, and still, I knew I wouldn't be able to stop them for long.

Westley was out there somewhere, hopefully looking for me, but then what? And how long would this guy let me dangle here like bait? Goddamn it. He couldn't; Westley couldn't come here. This man, this monster, had set a trap for him, and he was going to kill him with it.

At once, the light that shined directly on me shifted, making the dizziness clinging to me flare. The lamp or whatever it was moved over to the sink, the lip of the counter just lit up underneath it. My kidnapper stepped forward, his scraggly hair coming into view as my head lulled back without warning.

The hair was mousy, dishwater–not blonde and not brown. His thin fingers reached out in my direction, one pointing and jabbing at me. *Look, Andi. Look at him. Get a description.*

I tried. I tried with everything I could, and against the drugs still swimming through my veins, I could pick out dirty fingernails as he gripped an invisible throat and rung it. I could pick out cuts and scrapes along the man's arms and several days-old stubble.

"Ugh! I should just end you now and be done with it! It's not like I can't still play once you're gone."

I gagged, forcing myself to keep things down for fear of how he'd react. But it just got worse, the bile giving me immediate heartburn as I watched this person walk up to me. He wore a stained white tee, black and brown and red bits splattered and smeared across the fabric. He wasn't as tall as Westley, but he was still much taller than me at my whopping five foot two, and I couldn't stop myself from cowering as he stepped into the tub.

His pockets and pants bulged, a terror-induced imagination assuming that he was carrying a gun as well as that disgusting semi.

"How'd you get that job of yours, whore?" He reached into his pocket, pulling out a thin knife that flicked open, making me jump as it did. "Hmm? Think I could have bought you if I had the funds to be a part of your fancy club, of course. Don't get nothing in his world for free! Oh no."

"Please," a strangled noise came out with my words, horror making my eyes sting all the harder, "I beg you. I have nothing to do with this. Please. Let me go. I won't...I won't say any-anything."

The man shook his head, a ghost of a laugh sneaking out as he pointed the tip of the blade at my side.

"Nothing, huh? Not a thing, then? Sucking his cock ain't nothing to do with it?"

His weasely hand snaked out and snatched the hem of my loose tank. As he held it away from my stomach, he jabbed the knife up through the thin material and dragged it up, creating a large slice.

"Think this'll go through skin that smooth. I've sharpened it plenty. Hmm..."

A tear slid down my cheek. I couldn't stop them now, and I shivered more, the cuffs clinking against the pole. I was so cold, and it was such a stupid thing to be upset about. But my legs were frozen, and my toes were well on their way to numbness just like my fingers.

"Shaking, hmm? Not cold enough though, huh? Need 'em out. Better for seeing what I'm doing. Still gonna take my time, though."

The guy reached around me, and I instinctively flinched away. He just chuckled and went for the knob to the shower. He turned the water on high, leaving the temperature icy. In seconds, I was coated from head to foot in the frigid spray. That's when the true shaking set in. That's when the panic choked me.

If he didn't kill me with the blade, I'd freeze to death soon enough in these conditions. But then the water was shut off, and he came back around to stand in front of me again. I had to do something. I couldn't just hang there.

Kicking out at him, I knocked my foot into his shin, and he cursed. Unfortunately, there wasn't much more I could accomplish and I was rewarded with a firm slap for my efforts. The burn in my cheek was almost welcome for how cold I was, and I knew that sensation well enough to not scream or cry harder.

"Fucking cunt bitch. No! None of that."

The man stepped out of the tub and reached for something on the counter. When he came back, I noticed the thick roll of duct tape. I flailed and flailed, trying to kick him or knock this curtain rod down. But it did fuck all to help me.

Another slap distracted me long enough for the guy to grab my ankles. He was surprisingly strong, and he wound the silver tape around my legs so I couldn't move. It pressed into my bare flesh, and I knew from taping days gone wrong that it would pull horrendously on my skin when it came off.

If it came off.

Worse, of course, was that I was now basically motionless. Another blast of cold water hit me before he turned it off again, and the man's knife was back at my shirt. He held the fabric poised against the bottom hem, right in the center.

"Go away! Stop!" It was pointless, but some part of me felt like I had to at least yell, try to make him stop, or

I was basically giving him permission to do this. And only Westley had permission to touch me.

"Shut it!"

This time the attack was a firm backhand from the fist that gripped his knife. My head was knocked back as I saw fucking stars, and then the knife slit a clean line through the front of my shirt. It split the thing into two halves that flopped to my sides, exposing me.

"No!"

My body was rigid as I struggled to angle myself away from him. *This is wrong. This is wrong.*

Cold metal touched the skin right above my aerola, and I froze. A sob tore from me as I glanced down to see the knife pressed to my flesh. The sharp edge dragged across the ridge of my nipple, biting into me at cut ever so slightly.

"There they are. I could take these off and put them in a book to look at."

I screamed, despite the futile effort to maintain some type of resolve, I screamed and screamed. The fucker sidled up against me, his filth rubbing along my chest and legs. I could feel the erection behind his tan courderoy pants, and I nearly threw up. I may have if there was anything left in me. But as it was I hadn't eaten since before the shopping, and I didn't know how long it had been.

"Stupid, pretty whore." The knife smoothed up and down my chest, pricking my skin only a hair when he turned it to a new direction. "What's the difference? You sold yourself to Westley. I heard the talk about the contract."

He laughed to himself, etching a long line down the center of my sternum with his knife. I hollered into the room, knowing in the back of my mind that it clearly didn't matter how loud I screamed. This person had planned for this. He'd taken me to wherever this was on purpose. *His* playroom.

I sobbed, sagging against the cuffs as he pulled the knife away.

"You saying you really wouldn't do your job if I was the one that bought you?"

I glared through the tears, seeing his swamp green eyes cleary for the first time. They were nothing like the emerald of Westley's, the way my Wes's gleamed where this man's were a dull, stagnant puddle.

"Fuck you!"

It was reckless. I knew that, but I wouldn't give this fucker what he wanted. I wouldn't beg or lie. If I was dying, I was doing it as Andi. As myself. As the woman I'd become thanks to my time with Westley, and this piece of shit wouldn't take that away.

Another smack, but this one was more of a punch, and my head jacked to the side, hitting the wall next to me. Warmth trickled down my face as blood oozed from the site of impact. The blurry vision just got worse, and focusing became damn near impossible.

"Doesn't fucking matter, anyway. I don't need you moving or warm. I just need you screaming long enough to bring your boy running."

Cold pressed to my hip, and I guessed that he was sliding the knife under the waistband of my panties. A quick jerk, and my suspicions were confirmed, the fabric of my underwear falling away from me on that side.

"I was damn good, you know. Investor relations. Commission structure. Which was fucking jacked. Skewed to his damn favorites. So I snapped at one of 'em."

The other side of my panties was next, and in a

quick slice the garment were cut through and yanked away between my legs.

"He hurts you all the damn time? Why ain't you wet, slut?"

I yelped, trying to hold back a flinch as the flat of the blade pressed on one of my labia. I heaved again, feeling invisible beetles crawling beneath my flesh. The knife moved, the point scratching up my skin. When he hit my side, it dug in harder, and I screamed as he dragged it over my ribs.

"Doesn't really matter, does it?" I struggled to glare, to do anything, against the throbbing pain in my head and the burns that scattered over my body. "I'm gonna take what I want anyway."

The point found the underside of my breast, poking in until I screamed at the pressure and pain.

"Tiny little tits. No meat covering them bones, either. All that dance, dance, dance. Spinning around like a damned piñata at a kid's party. Ha! I could see it! Stringing you up and waking you good until all the shinies fall out."

It was impossible to imagine this man as a normal employee, but I was sure he hadn't lied about that. He was just a normal guy—a normal person who just snapped when life dealt rough cards. Given the right amount of pressure, this could be anyone, and that thought didn't help.

I wanted him to be memorable and noticeable so that Westley could identify him to the police. I *needed* the police to come, and I had no clue how that would ever be possible.

At last, he pulled the knife away, and I sagged against the wall as best as I could. Shock and waning adrenaline and exhaustion pulled at my edges. I was going to pass out soon. I didn't know if that was a good thing.

My kidnapper leaned in again, sniffing my hair as he held the knife idly inches away from my face. Just past the glint of the blade, I could see the pink of my blood mixing with the water at the bottom of the tub as it ran past my toes.

"He doesn't deserve you. He doesn't deserve love or money or success. But here the fuck we are!" My head throbbed as he shouted so close to my ear. "So, I'm going to ruin everything he cares about. Starting with you."

31
The Hunt

Westley

"**Y**ou have to fucking do something about this! She was fucking taken right from the damn shop!"

I was livid, fury raging through my veins, and it had been hours since Andi was taken. *Kidnapped*. I hadn't slept or eaten, and when I heard that the police department was still just "investigating," I'd stormed down here and burst straight into Captain Geofferies' office.

"Westley, please. I can assure you that—"

"So help me God, if you fucking say we're doing everything we can, I'm going to scream. Andi was taken right out from under my nose. By fucking *someone*. I can't let this stand. She...she means the world to me, and she has no one to look for her but me."

Geofferies nodded once, his expression softening as he shut the file on his desk. The one he'd opened for Andi's kidnapping.

"Westley," he gestured to the thin chair in front of his desk, and I reluctantly took a seat, "we are. I need more to go on. So, if you're here, work. Tell me anything that you can think of to give me an idea about what's happening."

An exacerbated sigh bled out of me, my entire body sagging into the chair as exhaustion tried to pull me under. I was barely keeping my head above water at this point, and as much as I hated it, I knew the captain was right.

"Goddamn it. I don't know. It just happened so fast. One minute, I was on the phone with my credit card company; the next, she was gone."

Another nod from Geofferies had me almost screaming again, and then he tented his fingers beneath his chin.

"Did anything strike you as off. You have good instincts, Westley. I've known you for a while now, son. What struck you?"

Memories swirled through my brain as I tried to think around the recollection of terror that coated me from the inside out. *Come on, Wes. What were you seeing? What made you look for her?*

"I'd gone outside the tent to make that call. The woman on the line said the same thing. Good instincts. They'd just locked by card because of the spending." Focusing around the haze that clouded my mind was nearly impossible. "It, umm, it made me stop."

And then it hit me.

"There was a guy. He seemed drunk. He was wearing baggy clothes, dirty. I bumped into him, and then he went inside the shop. Near the back."

The captain sat up straighter in his chair, his eyes widening as he leaned forward. "Description, Westley. What did he look like?"

I closed my eyes, trying to picture him. "Sunburned skin. Stubble. His hair was mostly covered by a hoodie, but it looked like very light brown or dark blonde, right on the threshold. Umm, he was stumbling. He smelled like alcohol."

Something else clicked in the back of my mind, and my eyes flared open as I looked down at the floor, my pulse racing.

"Right after she was taken, I got a phone call. The line was just dead air for a while, and I'd gotten calls like that before. But when he spoke...he called me boss."

My stomach was a roiling mess of too empty and too heavy. I wanted to vomit, but there was nothing to throw up. Pieces were falling into place, pieces that I'd been too fucking blind to notice.

"Boss?"

As Geofferies spoke, I shook my head, leaning forward onto my elbows until the weight of the truth was too much to hold in. I sat up, slamming my fist down on the desk in front of me.

"Adkins."

When I looked up, Geofferies was furrowing his brow at me, the cogs slowly turning faster. "Owen Adkins? The man you filed a restraining order against?"

"It has to be him. We fired him for poor customer service and taking home classified documents—essentially theft. He was furious. I've...I've never seen someone go off like that. He threatened me and my entire staff. I had to have security drag him out."

The captain pulled up his laptop, typing away on the screen. After a moment, he tipped the screen in my direction with the employee ID badge image of Adkins on the screen.

"This the guy you saw? Can you be sure?"

I leaned closer to the screen, trying to imagine the

man with stubble and severe weight loss. It was difficult, but the eyes...the eyes were the same.

Nodding, I fought down the bile rising up my throat. This was my fault. *I* did this to Andi.

"Yes, I'm sure."

"Well, that's something, then." The captain reached for his phone, pressing the intercom button. "Calloway, get in here. We have a lead."

The world picked up speed at that, suddenly everything was moving faster than light, and I could scarcely process what went down. Calloway entered, and as she took the seat next to me, all I could do was watch and her and the captain chatted away at each other.

"I need an APB out on this man. He's he primary suspect in the Andi Carlisle case."

Calloway took the folder as Geofferies handed it to her, eyeing the screen. "Owen Adkins. He was fired from your company, Mr. Stanton?"

"Mr. Stanton?" The captain asked.

Fuck, they were talking to me.

"Yes, sorry. Adkins was my employee for about two years. He was fine when he worked for us, but we found out he was being rude to investors and stole company data."

Calloway nodded. "I'll have the bulletin posted. Can you tell me anything else about him?"

Swallowing, trying desperately to stay in my seat and not run off and try to find him myself, I nodded.

"Well," I looked down at the floor again, racking my brain, "he was quiet, but a normal guy. He was always a bit pushy about speaking up, though. He hadn't earned a place on the R&D team, which I knew frustrated him, but he wasn't really a team player. He wanted glory.

That's not what my company is about. I want to help people."

"When he didn't get the job," Calloway offered, "is that when he started taking company ideas?"

"I'm not sure, but I assume so. It took us a while to figure it out. I'll give him that. When we fired him, well, that day, he was dragged out yelling that I'd pay for this. 'Rich fucking scumbag,' I think were his exact words."

"Do we have your permission to review the security footage at your company and home? If he was that upset and saw you go to the fairgrounds, I have a feeling he was watching you."

My mouth fell open slightly as Calloway held my eyes. It made complete sense, of course, but that nausea was just getting worse at the thought of Adkins spying on me–on Andi.

"Of course." I nodded, and Calloway mirrored the gesture.

"Great, I'll contact the company now to send over the footage. Can you stay at the precinct to identify him through the video footage?"

Glaring, I balled my hands into fists, my jaw nearly cracking under the pressure of my bite. When I met the detective's eyes, I made sure to keep my voice even.

"I'm not going anywhere until I know where Andi is."

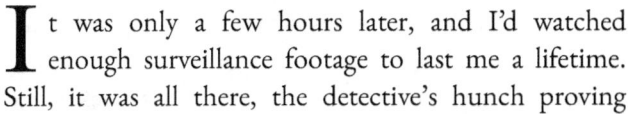

It was only a few hours later, and I'd watched enough surveillance footage to last me a lifetime. Still, it was all there, the detective's hunch proving correct. Adkins had snuck into the building that day I'd left Andi alone in the penthouse. He was there walking to a junker car when we left and went to the club that night I needed Andi badly. He was there just the other day, and Andi...

She'd given him something, waving at the security guards who were right there, right near by.

We hadn't noticed a thing. I hadn't, and now...

"It's him. He was there over and over. He followed us."

I wasn't sure who I was talking to, and then I heard Calloway say something to one of the uniformed officers nearby.

"Run these plates. I want to see if we can find that car."

My stomach was in worse knots that ever before, and I stood up from my chair, the legs scrapping across the floor and making a terrible, high-pitched groan. Pacing in front of Calloway's desk, the gnawing panic that I'd been holding off with fury began to win.

"He fucking took her and all this." I flung my hand toward the screen. "Days. Weeks! He'd been fucking watching us. All this time."

"Mr. Stanton, I–"

"It's right there, detective. And we saw nothing! He..." I stopped abruptly, my hands going to my hips as I let my head fall. "He's doing all this just to hurt me. Why doesn't he just hit me head-on? To go for Andi..."

Detective Calloway stood up from her desk, stepping toward me and putting a hand on my shoulder. I looked over with a glare, and she swiftly pulled it back.

"We'll catch him This is what I do. I'm good at my job."

Nodding absently, I felt a buzz in my pocket and

reached for my phone. Distracting myself with some inane bullshit seemed as good an idea as any. Swiping open the screen, I noticed the notification for an email to my work address. It wasn't unheard of by any means, but I'd sent a mass email blast that I was dealing with a personal emergency and not to be disturbed.

That prickling on the back of my neck started up. *Good instincts.*

I clicked on the notification, pulling up the email from a strange address. *9876**0@live.com.* There was no subject. Even my email provider flagged the message as suspicious and warned me not to open any links. Tapping my finger on the empty subject line, the email opened, and my idle pacing stopped.

(no subject)
Hey there, boss man.
Got something you might want. And you have what I want. Bring 50 mil in untraceable bills to 4769 Sycamore. Funny business gets your girl's guts on the floor. You have two hours.

My breaths shuddered out of me as I tumbled down into the chair that was luckily behind me. Detective Calloway noticed immediately, and she was taking my phone as I stared into the middle distance.

"Captain! He's made a move!"

Geofferies was there at Calloway's desk in a flash. They were talking, but I didn't process the words. Adkins wanted money. A ransom. Of course, he did. And I had no problem giving it to him. That was way more than a chunk of change, but to get Andi back? Done. Still, I wanted him to pay for this, not the other way around.

That fucker had the gall to take Andi from me, and I wasn't about to roll over and play his game. Absolutely fucking not.

Visions of my father's drunken rages bloomed in my mind. The familiar sting of his words in my head made me clench my teeth together. *Andi. You...made me better. I...I'm not letting him hurt you. I don't care what it costs me.*

"I'll go. I'll bring the money."

My words cut between the captain and Calloway. They stopped speaking, their heads whipping in my direction as they gaped at me. It felt as if the entire precinct stopped what they were doing and focused in my direction.

I glared at them. I didn't have time for this shit. "I said, I'll go."

"Mr. Stanton, it's not in the department's policies to let a civilian into–"

"Don't fucking give me that." I interrupted, and Calloway narrowed her eyes on me, putting her hands on her hips. "I bring him the money, you be there for *after* I get inside. It's done."

"Westley." Geofferies put a hand on my shoulder, his expression sympathetic and grating.

"I said it's done."

They both sighed, and I was glad that neither of them appeared to be willing to fight me on this. It was a good plan objectively, and Geofferies, at least, was smart enough to know that arguing with me wasn't going to do any good.

"We can't just let you in there without a plan, son." Geofferies sat down at Calloway's desk as she leaned over it. "How long will it take you to get the money? That a feasible timeframe?"

I nodded. "Less than thirty minutes. I'm priority at the bank."

"Okay, then let's take those two hours to set up. We'll have a team station themselves around the house. If we have that time, we can infiltrate slowly. It's more discreet that a rush. And we'll have time to plan an entry, get the blueprints from Property Records."

"Fine. I'll need a vest."

Calloway's eyes flared, but she was quick to roll her eyes and nod. "You're really sure about this? Do you have any self-defense training?"

Glaring, I shoved my phone back into my pocket. Nodding in the captain's direction, I started thinking about the best course of action for once I was inside the house.

"I'll let the captain speak to those skills for me."

Adkins was unhinged at this point, and I had to assume he was going to hide somewhere, lure me into a corner to shoot me or something. I knew he wouldn't be happy with just the money. This was far too personal. Adkins meant to kill me in that house, and likely Andi as well. I wouldn't let that happen.

At least not to her.

Geofferies nodded, his expression still dour as his movements blended into a head shake. "Yeah, yeah. He's got training. For some time now, I think."

Normally, I would smirk at the allusion to the years of boxing and martial arts that I'd invested in after my father. Not now. I'd never had a call to use the skills I'd learned, and I couldn't be sure if training was going to matter in the slightest against Adkins. It was a live wire situation.

But as long as I could get Andi to safety, I didn't care what happened to me.

"He's still at a huge risk. You're really going to okay this, Captain?" Calloway looked at her superior, her brows up to her hairline.

"There's no use arguing with him. He'll go even if we say not to. Isn't that right?"

"Yes." I didn't even blink as I answered.

Geofferies had pulled me out of several scrapes as a kid and being in over my head had beome my MO.

"Fucking hell. Okay," Calloway grumbled. "We're getting you suited up, *and* you're wearing a wire."

Looking between the two of them, I stood up from the chair. "Great. What are we waiting for?"

32
The Reunion

Andi

At some point, I'd blacked out. Freezing cold and pain didn't lend themselves well to consciousness, and as I jolted awake, I was frankly shocked that I was still alive. Though, I supposed the asshole who'd tortured me needed his bait.

I wasn't in the bathroom anymore. Instead, I was cuffed to the leg of a bed in what I guessed was likely a bedroom. The wallpaper was peeling, graffiti covering the once floral pattern. It stunk of urine and sweat, and as I looked down at the floor, the grime covering the surface was shiny and clumped.

Stifling a gag, I tried to adjust, my wrists aching along with my shoulders as I half-leaned against the bed. The mattress was sheetless from what I could see, and whatever coated the floor made my legs stick to it, a horrible sound echoing slightly as I pulled my calf free from the disgusting mess.

Jesus fuck. What the hell is this place? A crack house?

It probably wasn't far off in terms of guesses. I knew that squatters and dumb teens alike used abandoned houses for their illicit activities. In fact, I could make out at least two used condoms a few feet away from me on the floor.

A loud pop sounded as I rotated away from the bed, my shoulder cracking. Searching at first for a window, I noticed the boarded-up square to my left, weak streams of light slipping in through the gaps. I couldn't see anything through them, though, so I looked for the door out of the room. It was just to my right, a few steps away from the foot of this bed.

And it wasn't locked.

Of course, the handcuffs did enough to stop me from reaching it, I supposed. I turned my attention to the restraints. They didn't look professional, and the metal wasn't especially thick. I assumed they were from a sex shop. It was an easy place to get cuffs and rope without anyone asking questions.

My stomach pinched as I remembered the existence of such places, which naturally led me to wonder what happened when I'd passed out. I didn't want to consider it, *couldn't*. What I could tell was that there were only a few more slashes over my skin than before I'd gone unconscious. I wasn't sure how long ago that had been, however, and my guts twisted all the harder as I thought about how long I'd been missing from Westley's.

I sagged against the foot of the bed as worry gripped me. I was so damned tired, a combination of exhaustion and trauma and hunger that created a potent mix perfected to keep me weak. Westley was out there somewhere, though, and I had to hope that he was coming for me.

Or I wasn't going to last much longer.

"Look who's up, and not a scrap of bacon to be found."

I stiffened, my brain confused as to whether food sounded wonderful or horrid. As the sound of footsteps moved closer behind me, I fought the urge to turn around and look in his direction. It was the modicum of control I had over the situation, and I was going to hold onto it until I literally couldn't.

"You was out cold for a long while. Not even the water enough to wake you." The man came around in front of me, kneeling down. "Still got some good shots, though."

A stack of squares hit the floor in front of me, and as much as I knew I shouldn't look at whatever this fuck was showing me, I couldn't help it. My eyes tracked down, and there on the floor was an array of imitation Polaroids—all of me hanging from the shower rod.

Bile pulsed in my gut, traveling up my throat and burning my esophagus as it went.

"I like them pictures. Hipster nonsense for the camera, but it works." I watched his hand scoop up the photos, tears stinging in my eyes. "Your boy toy should be here soon."

I sat up straight, the edge of the cuffs immediately digging into my wrists. My mind couldn't settle on whether it was glad or horrified. Every bit of me wanted to see Wes, but at what cost? This guy's plan was so clearly about more than money, and the thought of Wes getting hurt because of some fool's attempt to bargain with him...was razor blades to my heart.

"Please," I croaked, "don't hurt him. I promise it won't do anything to make you feel better."

The smack of his hand across my cheek landed right on the already sore bone. I yelped—a dog kicked while it was down—and the sobs tore free of me. I didn't have the strength to hold them in anymore. The pit of my stomach was too hollow, and the rage in my blood was diluted by exhaustion and fear.

"It's gonna make me feel a lot better, bitch. Been thinking about it so *damn* long." He glared down at me, cocking his head like he was studying a specimen in a jar. "Need you quiet, though. Can't go ruining everything with that dumb loud mouth."

He stooped down, and I was helpless to keep him from securing a thick length of rope between my teeth. I tried, of course, thrashing back and forth, but all it earned me was a punch to the gut. I coughed, gagging as I tried to suck in air, and then the foul taste of chemicals and sweat spread over my tongue.

The man stood back up, and he went for the knife in his pocket. I watched as he flicked it open, shining it in the dim lighting, this way and that. Suddenly, the point was just in front of my eye, and my kidnapper dragged it along my cheek until he hit my hairline. His other hand gripped a chunk of my hair, and with a quick slice, he cut off a lock of my hair.

"Collection starter. I'll add these," he jabbed the point of the blade toward my breasts, scratching me just enough for me to whimper, "later."

As he stood, a loud creak sounded near what I assumed was the front of the house. He snapped his attention that way, gripping the knife as his eyes went manic. He was as happy as a kid in a fucking candy shop, and I tried to scream against the rope in my mouth. It was muffled and shitty, and another slap had the noise dying altogether.

"Quiet!" he screamed through a whisper. "He's here."

The singsong tone of his voice was rusted barbed wire on my nerves, and I tried and tried to pull my cuffs free of the bed leg. It was made of metal, and the pieces rubbing across each other made a terrible grinding sound.

This time, however, the guy didn't bother with yelling at me to be quiet or kicking at me; he just rushed for the door, closing it behind him. Trapped in the room alone, I fought against the cuffs. I couldn't hear anything else from the hall or the rest of the house, for that matter. So, I just yanked harder and harder. The skin on my wrist tore, blood smearing across my skin.

I couldn't get out.

Westley. Oh God. What's happening?!

Westley

T he weight of the briefcase was heavy in my hand. I'd truly filled it with 50 million dollars. In case the fucker decided to count the bills. It wouldn't do him any good, of course. I wasn't letting him leave this shit hole of a house alive. He'd hurt Andi, after all, tried to take her from me, and he was going to pay with his fucking life.

"One way or the other."

Stepping up onto the porch outside the front door, the wood creaked in a loud groan, and I was sure that whoever was inside heard it. I waited only a second before I reached for the doorknob.

"Check for any wires or heat near that door. It could be rigged to blow." Calloway's voice sounded in my ear.

Examining the hinges, the wood, and the knob itself, I didn't see anything out of the ordinary. I gently pushed the thing forward, stepping back several paces as it swung open with another loud creak. Nothing.

"Now check the floor at the threshold."

I hated this fucking guide-me nonsense, but Calloway was at least proving useful. She'd lose visuals as soon as I got inside, too.

There was nothing on the floor, so I gripped the briefcase tighter, stepping inside and looking around me for Adkins. The house was a typical ranch-style for this area, remnants of beachy decor utterly destroyed by what I could only guess was years spent being used as a squatter's den, a drug hangout, and a porn set going by the plethora of used condoms lying around. At least some of the assholes had thought to use them.

"Adkins! You want your money or not?!"

My voice ricocheted off the grimy, graffiti-laden walls. There windows were boarded up, too, blocking the light. There was no furniture to speak of, unless you counted the pile of cardboard boxes in the corner or the single bit of foam from a couch cushion.

The groaning of more floorboards directed my attention slightly to the right and in front me. Coming down from a seemingly short hall was a tallish, lithe figure.

"So, you figured out it was me. So damn long, it took you *so* damn long."

"Here." I tossed the briefcase at his feet, and it landed with a heavy thud. "Now, where's Andi?"

Adkins looked even worse, if possible, though that may have been the environment rubbing off on him. He shook his head as he leaned down to grab the money, his eyes never leaving me. When he stood back up, he reached for his pocket, and I had to assume he was pulling a weapon.

Sure enough, the glint of a blade caught the little bit of light coming from the setting sun and street lamps outside.

"That's it? No foreplay? You're just gonna fuck me and be on your way?" He chuckled to himself, and I clenched my jaw so hard it cracked. "Oh, wait. That's what you do. Isn't it? You just go around like you own the place..."

His eyes flared wide, and he jabbed the knife in my direction. "And fuck me!"

"You got what you want, Adkins. Take your money, and tell me where Andi is."

He clucked his tongue, shaking his head as his thin, chapped lips turned down.

"We can't see you, Stanton. Don't push it with this guy. Use that signal if he's got a weapon."

I didn't respond to Calloway, saving my police-mandated "safe word" for later.

Adkins met my eyes, his unsteady wobble turning into a slow gate as he circled around the room. I kept as much space between us as possible, and soon, I stood with my back to the same hallway he'd come down. Andi was down this hall. There was no other place for her to be. The blueprint had shown there was no basement to the place, and no other floor.

She was right fucking there behind me.

"I want more than your fucking money, Westley." Adkins waved the knife around, letting the briefcase drop to that couch cushion. "You left me with nothing. Destitute. Alone. I wasn't this! I was a good ol' worker bee! And then you..."

He was shaking his head again, his steps moving

311

closer instead of just sideways. This was it. He was going to strike out at me.

"You know what you did?" He shook the blade as he spoke, then tapped the point against his head. "Broke it. Broke it all up. But it wasn't totally right then in the first place, I guess. I just told myself not to gut people like you cuz jail and consequences."

I sunk into my heels, poising my thighs to take the weight of his lunge when he came at me.

"I'm not fucking crazy, though." He *pfted* at me. "I know what I'm doing. I know it's wrong and all that bullshit. I just...Don't. Fucking. Care."

With that, he shot forward across the room, his blade hand sticking out to stab me. I captured his wrist, flipping him down to the ground as I isolated the weapon. Adkins landed on his side with an echoey smack. Sound bounced too damn well in here, and the cops would be coming soon.

Twisting around to the other side of Adkins's hand, I put the palm of mine against his elbow. With a hard shove forward, I cracked the joint out of place, and he screamed into the empty house. *Dammit. Too loud. Ugh. Andi first, then...Adkins.*

I took off down the hall, which, of course, was just a few feet. There was a cracked door at the end of the hall and then two on either side of it. I didn't bother with the slight ajar one. Adkins would have wanted it closed up all the way. Turning to the left, I kicked the door in, but I revealed just a bathroom.

So, the other door it was. Smashing my foot into that one, the thing flew open, and my eyes landed on an empty mattress–stained and sheetless.

"Westley!"

I looked down to the foot of the bed and around near the side closest to the other wall. There she was.

"Andi!"

Rushing forward, I got to her side. She was cuffed to a bed leg, her wrists raw from pulling against them. I gripped the cuffs, yanking against the metal leg to try and pry the links at the center of the handcuffs open. They didn't budge, and my heart sank. This wasn't going to work.

"Key? I need a key, love."

Andi shook her head, her eyes wide and tearful. At that point, I finally looked over her, and I nearly broke down right there because of her state. Dirty, injured, bags under her eyes that were large enough to notice from across the room, it was all horrendous, and she deserved so much better.

"What the fuck did he do to you?"

She shook her head again, sagging against me until her head hit my chest. "Please tell me you're not alone."

"No. The cops are outside." I pulled Andi's chin up to look at her, needing to see those baby-blue eyes for myself. "I think it's time to c–"

"No!"

Her scream tore through the room, and I spun away from her fearful, wide-eyed shock to face the door where I'd come. *Well, fuck.*

Andi

The kidnapper burst in through the door behind Westley, babying his right arm. But his eyes were mad with rage, bloodshot and wild. He rushed forward toward Wes, clutching that damn knife. I tried to shove Wes out of the way, and he rolled naturally to dodge the attack. Still, the asshole collided with him, taking Westley down to the ground.

"Westley!" My call rang out, and I tried again to pull myself free from the cuffs.

They were too strong though, even for fucking sex toys, and the edges of the metal just dug into my skin as I fought uselessly. Westley and his opponent tangled together in mass of limbs as they battled for the place on top of the dog pile.

"Leave him alone!"

I couldn't stay chained to the fucking bed. *Do something, Andi!* My pulse was a frenzy, and adrenaline pumped through my veins harder than ever before. I was a flailing mess as I struggled against the leg of the bed frame.

Get up, lift it, something!

Tears streamed down my face as everything felt more and more hopeless. Westley was shoved down to the ground with a painful sounding thump, and the man slashed down at him with the blade. Splatters of blood colored my peripheral vision as Westley held up his arms to block the attacks. *No, no, no. I can't lose him.*

Something snapped inside me, and I twisted up onto my knees toward the bed. Using my shoulder, I shoved up the mattress hoping to knock the thing to the ground. It was a shitty model, and the few inches of foam slumped off the bedframe to the side. Without the weight of the mattress on it, I tried to lift up the metal bedframe, using that same shoulder and hauling upward using the cuffs to support the weight.

The pain that burned into my wrists was immense, and I looked back over my shoulder at Westley. Just as I got the frame up about an inch, he bucked hard, tossing my kidnapper to the ground. Wes was quick to get to his feet, a better position than on his back on the floor.

"Scumbag fucker! I'll feed you your own cock!" The man cried out, and as he dove for Westley again, Wes jabbed a fist forward and clocked him right in the head.

"Fuck you, Adkins," Westley growled low.

A scream blared from me as I pushed with all my might to stand up, my thighs burning from the strain and lack of calories to fuel it.

"Ahh!"

The cry was backed by a terrible grinding noise, and then a massive clang as the weight of the bed slammed down onto the floor, the link chain link in the middle of the cuffs snapped in half. I stumbled back, landing on my ass. But I had no time to worry over the bit of pain, the blood seeping from my wrists.

Zipping around toward Westley, I watched as the asshole Wes had called Adkins launch himself at the love of my life again. The knife darted forward as Adkins struck out wildly–uncoordinated and reckless.

But Westley froze with a deep grunt, and Adkins's eyes flared with a sick joy.

"No!"

Adkins was going to go for another strike. He was going to kill Westley. I had to do something. Scanning the room in a frantic search for some type of weapon, I noticed the small lamp toppled over on a teeny night-stand. It had no shade or bulb, but the base was made of metal. I darted to the side, snagging it for before heading directly toward Adkins, whose back was toward me.

It took two seconds to get there, and I brought the lamp down over his head with every bit of strength I could muster.

With a horrible shriek he went down to one knee, the knife clattering to the ground. Westley was quick to snatch it up from the filthy floorboards, and in a hard jab up and forward, drove the point between Adkins's ribs.

A gout of blood blurted from Adkins's lips as he coughed, his eyes widening even more as Westley sunk the blade in up to the hilt. Adkins gurgled, terrible and wet, and I dropped the lamp to the floor, tumbling to my knees.

Westley's eyes shot to mine. "Andi!"

He rushed to my side, wrapping me in his arms and squeezing me so damn tight. But I didn't care that it hurt, that my bruises and strained joints ached from the pressure. I needed him. I *needed* Westley right the fuck there, proving to me that this was reality, that...Adkins was dead.

The sobs poured from me as I heard boots pound down the hall. I jumped in Westley's arms as the room flooded with officers and swat. They shouted orders, screaming for us to put our hands up, and it was all too much.

My mind blanked, and then Westley was letting go of me. I cried all the harder.

"Fuck off! He tried to kill me, kill Andi!"

Wes was screaming back at the armed men in the room. Everything spun, and I worried I was going to pass out again.

"Don't move!" a stranger called.

The more footsteps, and there were people in strange button-down shirts flocking around me like crows. They spoke but I couldn't concentrate on the words. I needed Westley.

"Wes! I..." I reached blindly for him as the sobs racked me.

"Let me go to her, please!"

I heard him call out, and I swatted at the hands trying to touch me. No one else. I wanted no one else touching me.

"Let him go," a new voice ordered, the tone deep and low, "Westley did what he needed to. We heard everything on the wire."

Warmth enveloped me in moments, and I calmed as the familiar smell of Westley's cologne filled my nose. Minutes stretched on as I clung to him, and eventually, the tears died down. As I looked up into Westley's face, I traveled my stare down over him, proving to myself that he was really there.

But his shirt was torn on his side. Wait–

"You were stabbed!" I reached for his side with one hand as I gestured for who I realized were EMTs to come look at him.

"Andi. Andi, calm down, love. I'm fine." I shook my head, but Westley lifted his shirt. "See. I had a vest on. Just grazed me. I'm okay."

I met those wonderful green eyes of his again, and Wes just nodded for me. We stared like that for how long I couldn't say. All I knew, all I needed to know, was that he was there. We were together, and we were safe.

"You're here." I nodded, tears stinging again. "He's...he won't hurt us anymore?"

Westley stroked down the side of my face, his eyes softening as he pulled me even closer. "No, love. He won't. And I *promise*, I'll never let anyone harm you again."

"Home, Wes. Take me home."

"Anything, pet. I will do anything for you."

And I knew he would. He'd just proven as much. "I love you, Wes. I love you, I love you, I love you."

"I love you, too, Andi. Forever."

33
The Catharsis

Andi

I was oddly nervous when Westley had texted and said that he was coming home early from the office. The investment meeting had apparently gone well and in the weeks following the incident with the not-so-dearly-departed Adkins, Westley and I had taken every available second to reconnect. I'd signed the contract to stay with him permanently, which was, of course, just a formality at this point, and he'd taken me out on several "real" dates.

Sure, there was nothing particularly innocent or PG about those encounters, but that's what I needed— what I still needed. I didn't want Westley to handle me with kid gloves. When I'd recovered enough, I went back to the silks he'd bought for me and let myself fall apart in them quietly.

But the thing was, I'd already broken once, and I was better at it now.

Yes, there were more cracks in the Ming Vase that was me, and Westley and I both agreed to sit down and talk with someone about our issues, but I was forged from fire and the molten gold that filled in those fissures was stronger than the porcelain had ever been.

And in a surprisingly nice turn of events, I was invited back to perform at the Scarlett Oleander on a regular basis. Something I was pretty sure Westley had a hand in.

Apparently, that's where he was taking me tonight, and my heart thrummed, a low current of electricity humming through my body stronger with each minute I waited for him to get home. I'd been instructed to dress appropriately, and I'd purchased a new version of the leotard I'd worn when I first met Westley for just such a special occasion.

I'd also shaved, gotten a haircut, and waxed every-thing to perfection. *It's still weird how warm that shit is on your bits.*

As I tapped my foot on the floor, my toe to the tile creating a monotonous rhythm, the front door swung open. I spun on my heel in that direction, and when I met Westley's mischievous green stare, I sprinted across the room and lept into his arms.

"Well, hello." He smiled, kissing me as he leaned to the side to set down his briefcase. "I'll never get tired of these greetings."

I fucking beamed, running my hands through his thick, dark hair as I marveled at the streaks of silver that were just so effortlessly sexy.

"Good. Do you think that you could, I don't know," I rolled my eyes playfully, "tell me what we're doing then?"

The sinful darkness I knew so well filled his stare, and Westley's fingers toyed with the hem of my leotard where it stretched over my ass.

"No." He cocked a brow as he looked down at me. "But this? This was the perfect choice. So lovely, pet."

Any disappointment I might have felt about him not telling me what was on the agenda was quickly swept aways as the proximity of his fingers made my entire body warm. I rubbed myself against him where my core was flush against his waist, and I groaned low as he nuzzled into my neck.

"We should go, though. We don't want to be late."

"Late for what?" I wined, and he swiftly smacked my ass.

I let out a high-pitched squeak, the crack of his palm against my skin making my pussy fucking *drip* for him.

"The only thing I'll tell you is that like always, you can say no. But fuck, I don't want you to."

I nodded aginst him, burying my face in his chest, and Westley just turned on his heel, taking me through the door and down to the car. Richard was there at the door, ready to open things up for us, and I smiled easily at him.

"Hi, Rich!"

"Hello, Ms. Andi." He bowed his head. "I hope you enjoy yourself."

"I'm quite sure I will. Thank you."

I gave him a quick hug as Westley set me down and the stepped into the long car, amusing myself with the champagne that was already poured.

"You are such a wonderful boyfriend. You even got my favorite kind."

Westley grinned as he ducked inside the car. "I listen. It's not *that* hard. And honestly, I'm a little more than just your 'boyfriend,' don't you think?"

Chuckling lightly, I shrugged with a grin, knowing I was getting under his skin just the way I wanted to.

"There's not a great term for permanent Dominant, you know?"

"Hmm, fair enough." He nodded at the little bar where the bottle of champagne sat. "What's that?"

I looked over, and there was a long, thin case sitting next to the glasses, and a envelope in plain white that wasn't sealed. Furrowing my brow at him, I grabbed the case first, opening the red velvet box. The hinge squeaked slightly, and inside was the most beautiful necklace I'd ever laid my eyes on.

And more than that, I knew what this was–a collar.

"Oh, my God, Wes!" I smoothed my fingers over the delicate white gold filigree that stretched like veins to a center circular o-ring, which featured a tiny bell that would hang right at the hollow of my throat. "It's gorgeous!"

"I'll take that as a yes to wearing it then." He shuffled across the seat toward me reaching for the necklace.

I spun around offering him my neck as he wrapped the thin collar around my neck.

"It locks at the back. See the key?" Westley left it in the box until the necklace was secure, and then he took it, holding it tightly in his palm. "I'll be the only one able to unlock it. A reminder that you belong to me."

"I adore it. It's so...subtle, but anyone who knows will *know*."

His smirk was adorable, and Westley tucked my hair behind my ear as I turned to face him.

"Exactly. It's called a day collar. Designed to be discreet."

"It's perfect." I looked back over my shoulder. "But what's with the, umm..."

Gesturing toward the envelope, I narrowed my eyes at

him. Westley grinned all the harder, playfully shrugging so that I had to just take the thing and open it. Inside the simple white paper was a thicker piece of what looked like a form. It was bordered in an embossed blue pattern of lines, and at the top was a large heading in script font.

"Certificate of..."

My mouth fell open as I realized what it said. The surge inside me, that excitement over tonight and the collar, it all doubled, tripled, and I felt the sting of tears prickle behind my eyes.

"We just need to sign it, and then it's done. I'll file a copy at city hall, and we're done."

"You want..." My voice cracked. "You want to marry me?"

"I want you to be mine. I want everyone–inside and outside of the community–to know that we belong to each other. So, yes. I want to marry you."

"This is probably the weirdest proposal in the history of proposals, but," I took his face in my hands, locking my eyes on his, "yes. Of course. Do you have a pen?"

Westley grinned from ear to fucking ear, reaching into the breast pocket of his jacket and retrieving the utensil. I scribbled my name over the line where my name had been printed, using Westley's chest as a writing surface. He just smiled down at me until I was finished, taking the pen and signing his own John Handcock on the line.

As he tucked the document away in the folder, Westley placed it back on the bar, and stroked the side of my face.

"Well, *wife*," his smirk was sinfully seductive, and I fucking melted at hearing the word, "I have one more surprise for you at the club. And now, I give you permission to call me either Sir, Owner, Daddy, or..."

With a speed I'd come to love, Westley yanked me toward him by the hair, slipping his hand between us and finding my already slippery slit beneath my leotard. I moaned against his fingers, and it did not bode well for any edging that I was already this worked up.

"Husband. But if you do," he circled the pad of his finger over my clit, and I bucked against him, "you better be coming."

We'd slipped inside the club and into another private booth, though this one was much more akin to a room and the area inside wasn't lined with thick velvet cushions but leather and latex seating as well as a small rolling tray made of mental that sat off to the side and was covered by a thick, fabric-like piece of black paper.

Westley had dragged me inside, demanding that I be patient, and I was failing miserably as he fucked me with his fingers until I was a sobbing mess, desperate to come.

"Sir, I can't! Please!" He found my G-pot, hooking his fingers into the sensitive nerves, and I had not choice but to leak all over the shiny black surfaces for him. The patter of cum hitting the floor was familiar and still I reeled with delicious embarrassement.

"Did you just come without permission?" Westley yanked his fingers free, smacking my clit until I screamed.

"No, I swear," I whimpered, my strength and resolve gone as I fought against the amazing sensations. "I really didn't. I just couldn't stop...umm..."

Shoving my legs further apart, the bottom of my leotard cut once more and hiked up around my waist, Westley rocked his hips, and his erection dug into my ass. God, I wanted him to fuck me. To fuck me there because I was becoming such a fan of the delirious joy that filled me when he tortured my pussy with is cock in my ass.

"Oh, pet," he dragged out, his other hand going between us and working the buckle of his pants. "You're such a filthy little kitten for Daddy. Just wait, precious."

As his rhythm slowed, Westley freed his cock from his pants, forcing me to stand up off him before I was quickly shoved back down. His thick shaft stretched me and I rolled my hips to get comfortable as he reached up inside me, right up to the hilt.

A gentle knock sounded on the curved wall that separated us from view of the club. I knew better than to cower or hide, so I just focused on the wonderful feeling of Westley's erection shoved deep in my tightest hole.

"Oh, good. She's here."

I looked up, and the woman whom I'd seen at the penthouse, the Domme, stood before me. My pussy clamped down as I raked my stare over her glimmering latex attire. She smirked, a devilish expression like Westley's, and I watched fascinated and edged beyond belief as she walked straight to the rolling tray.

"You're in for a treat, little one." She was taller than most, so I wasn't surprised she saw me as something tiny, and my submissive heart actually ate it up.

Westley bucked his hips forward, and I yelped as his

cock sunk deeper in a hard thrust. As I looked back over my shoulder, Westley grabbed my chin, holding me there as he met my stare.

"I want her to pierce you." My stomach dropped as Westley spoke, his tone deadly serious. "I want you to wear that."

He nodded toward the Domme, and I returned my attention to her seeing her slip on a pair of black gloves that had been waiting for her on the tray and continue to set up her equipment like a professional. She held up a small bit of jewelry last, and I studied the small but thick ring that appeared to have no end or beginning.

"I don't..."

Westley leaned into my ear, whispering as he pumped into my ass. "It's a locking barbell. You won't be able to take it out. No one will. It'll be permanent. Really, truly permanent."

Realization struck. Everything that Westley had given me tonight was, in theory, removable or breakable. He wanted something that neither of us could undo or back out of. Commitment. Trust. Dedication.

I reeled, but the idea of having something so personal to me, claimed like this for Westley's pleasure, was undeniably arousing. It hit me straight in the heart, and I nodded.

"Yes. Yes, Sir, please."

Westley fucked into my ass—slow, purposeful strokes. "God, you're fucking perfect, pet."

The Domme finished her setup and then knelt before me. I'd watched her retrieve the sterile equipment, and when I looked down at her, the apprehension clear in my expression, she smiled. It was genuine and warm, and the thread of nervousness that hummed behind the constant arousal eased.

"It's nothing, sweetie. In fact," she looked back at Westley as he held me down onto his cock, unable to move, "if what he says is true, I think you'll love it."

Reality blurred at the edges as the Domme cleaned me up for the piercing, and Westley's cock pulsed inside me, ramping up the desperate need to climax.

"All right, hold her still. And you," I looked into her fierce eyes, "come for your Master like a good pain slut."

I blew out a deep breath, my entire body humming. I was right on the edge. Westley's incredible torture of my ass, the way he'd fingered me before, it all burned into me, making me mad with the hunger for release. As I sucked in another breath, Westley clamped his grip around me and offered another hard pound into my ass. The Domme took hold of my clit, and the fire in my nerves roared higher. That was nearly enough to make me come right there.

And then the needle slipped through my skin like it was nothing.

The sharp sting made my entire body clamp down, and I squeezed around Westley's cock, coming and coming as a steady stream of slick dripped out of me. I didn't even feel the jewelry go in or the woman clean me up. I was too far gone.

"That's my good girl."

Westley waited just a moment for the piercer to move her hands, and then he fucked into me in several rough strokes. I just kept coming.

"Can you handle one more?" His voice was a seductive whisper, and I knew that the adrenaline rush was going strong enough, my sinful love of pain flaring, that yes. Yes, I could.

I nodded.

Again too fast for me to really comprehend, another

piercing was situated just above the last, threaded through the skin at the very top of my slit. I orgasmed again, more of my cum gushign out of me as I clenched around Westley's cock.

"So very good, pet."

"She's good. All clear."

I had no idea what the woman was referring to, but then Westley readjusted his grip, squeezing my hips, and then he fucked my asshole with abandon. I was gone, destroyed, and loving it. He owned every inch of my skin, my soul, and I orgasmed all the hard until I felt his cock twist inside me, pumping his cum into my ass in warm torrents.

It overflowed down my cheeks, and the wonderful feeling of being so fucking filled up with his spend drew out another shuddeing release.

I was just aware enough to look back over my shoulder. I found Westley's green eyes, smiling. "Thank you... Husband."

Westley twitched inside me, another gout of warm cum shooting into me, and he grinned like a fool.

"You are so damn welcome, wife." He sighed, lowering his head to my shoulder. "Let's go home."

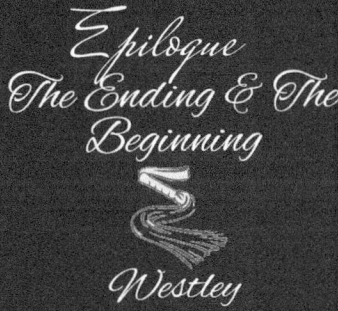

Epilogue
The Ending & The Beginning

Westley

A year later...
As Andi went to sign her name for the fifty-second time on the contract, I watched how she had to raise herself up on her tiptoes to reach. I'd purposefully hung it a little too high because I loved watching her struggle for it.

"Need help?"

"Absolutely not. Shoo!" She waved her hands at me, and I laughed.

I'd started doing that a lot more over the past year, and it was all thanks to Andi.

"There. Your turn." She swung around and handed me the pen.

As I walked to the contract where it hung on the wall in our bedroom, I felt that delightful twinge in my chest whenever I thought about everything we'd done and gone through, from the meeting each other and bringing our walls down to surviving after that man had nearly taken her from me for good.

Signing the paper for the fifty-second time felt as

wonderful as the first, and pride be damned, I could admit that Andi had softened me up quite a bit–at least outside of the bedroom.

"So, it's our anniversary! What do you have planned?" Andi's eyes twinkled with expectation. I enjoyed the way she looked when she got excited, but I *loved* the look she gave me when she was completely undone. And oh, the plans I had indeed.

"Now, now, pet. You know it's a surprise. But," I walked her to the large table in our room, "I do have some new accessories for you to wear."

I removed the thin silk that covered the items I'd picked out weeks ago, and Andi gasped.

"Westley! You listened! Oh, I shouldn't be surprised, you crafty devil. Should I wear them now?"

"Only if you want a treat for being my good girl," I smirked at her, dark glee lighting me up from the inside as I thought of my plans.

Andi smiled up at me, laying a brief kiss on my lips before lowering back down. "Oh, sir. Yes, please."

She stripped down to nothing and started dressing herself in the gifts: a set of wrist cuffs with hooks attached, an upgrade to the leather cat mask that came with a matching gag, and long back-seamed stockings. She would need my assistance with the last two.

"Would you please help, sir?"

"Of course."

I spun Andi around, leaning her over the table and reaching for the collar. It was thick black leather with a small heart-shaped charm that dangled from the front. It read "Master's Little Kitten." Andi positively purred as I wrapped it around her throat, making it just tight enough to squeeze a bit. I'd take care of truly choking herself myself, after all, and I hardened at just the thought of it.

"Oh, babe. I love it so much." Her eyes twinkled, and I stroked my thumb over the charm. "Your collar."

"One of them anyway. I may have something for late. Something that'll be easier to wear in public."

Her eyes flared again, and my heart was so damn full it could burst.

"Ooh! Sir, you spoil me."

I smirked. "Don't get used to it, pet."

Leaning closer to her, my chest pressed against Andi's back. I lowered my lips to the sensitive shell of her ear. "I have *plans*, after all."

Andi whimpers, and I reached around to toy with her hardening nipples. She let her head fall back on my shoulder, immediately giving herself over to the sensations. God, it was gorgeous.

The last toy remaining would need a little more... maneuvering, and I kissed her neck, playfully biting.

"Put your knee up on the table and stroke that sweet little pussy, pet," I growled in her ear.

She did as told, moaning as her fingers found her already dripping cunt and the sinful little beads that danced around her clit. I watched for a few moments, glorious hunger pooling in my gut, and then shoved her hand aside to slip the silver metal plug inside her, wetting it for her tight ass.

Her cum coated the shiny chrome, and I drew it back before pressing it slowly into her asshole. Andi squeezed down around it, clenching her thighs and a low growl billowed out of her.

"There we are. My perfect little kitten."

I swished the tail attached to the plug with a sadistic smile. Andi looked over her shoulder at it with a massive grin, her hand returning to stroke herself but only until I glared at her, silently commanding her to desist.

"Kneel."

Her wide doe eyes glowing in the dim light of our bedroom, Andi got down on her knees in front of me and slid her hands up my legs.

"Now, be a good little kitten and drink your cream."

Acknowledgments

Thank you to everyone who made this book possible, not the
least of which is my wonderful friend, Tori, who encouraged
me to go after a contemporary pen name—even if it was just
so she could write books with me. I adore you.

To the patrons who got the first look at this little tale when it
was just nine parts and loved it. I'm so glad that Westley and
Andi spoke to you so that I could take the dive and
make their story a fully-fledged book. This has been an
absolute blast, and I thank you. A special shout-out goes
to my Patrons—Kayla, Brittany, Cheyanne, Mandy, and
Denis. You all rock and keep my creativity and passion
flowing like never before.

As always, this book wouldn't have come to fruition without
the support of some truly amazing people: my author
friends for sharing their resources with me, my first-look
readers, and, of course, my PA, Kaitlyn, who kept me
pumped to write this from beginning to end. You are a
gem and thank you for telling me that the spice wasn't,
in fact, too much but just enough.

To my ride-or-dies, Ally and Rachel, I thank you for every
book you continue to read from me. Your support is incredible. To family and buddies who have helped me form a support system I know I can count on.

And to the one and only Ryan. You've been my rock when
life gets lifing, and I am so grateful. You've been there to help entertain the kiddos when I've needed to get the writing
done, and you never once told me to stop pursuing my dreams. I love you more than anything.

In the world of Liz Highland, you are encouraged to embrace
the dark side of romance.

Author of dark contemporary romance novels and novellas,
Liz Highland tells tales that revolve around intimacy, lust,
love, and every way that a heart can both break and grow.
Focusing on characters who all flaunt their red flags proudly,
you'll find stories fit for fans of the darkest of the dark and
the spiciest of the spicy.

During their off time, Liz can be found enjoying a cold cup
of coffee that's been microwaved at least six times at this
point because their tiny goblins keep interrupting them and
reading all the delicious dark romance they can get their
hands on.

Check out everything Liz has to offer by following them on

social media and be on the lookout for more stories coming

from the world of the Scarlett Oleander.

If you enjoyed Bought & Bound, please feel free to leave a review. Indie authors live for them and they can be make or break for their careers. Liz encourages fans to tag them in edits, fan art, and appreciation posts for the book across socials.

Also by Liz Highland

Fallow Trilogy

Hunted - Fallow Trilogy Book One

Wanted - Fallow Trilogy Book Two

Trapped - Fallow Trilogy Book Three (May 2024)

The Scarlett Oleander Series

Bought & Bound - Scarlett Oleander Series Book One

Traded & Teased - Scarlett Oleander Series Book Two (TBA)

Edged & Ensnared - Scarlett Oleander Series Book
Three (TBA)

Masked & Manipulated - Scarlett Oleander Series Book
Four (TBA)

Stalked & Saved - Scarlett Oleander Series Book Five (TBA)

Anthologies

Royal Debts - Drama Queen Anthology (September 2024)

Stalk Me

For the latest updates from Liz Highland, be sure to follow them all on their social media

Follow them on Facebook
https://facebook.com/lizhighlandauthor

Follow them on Instagram

https://www.instagram.com/lizhighlandauthor

Follow them on TikTok

https://www.tiktok.com/@lizhighlandauthor

Follow them on Threads

https://www.threads.net/@lizhighlandauthor

Join the Demon Club on Facebook
https://www.facebook.com/groups/rejohnsonsdemonclub